Praise for Elizabeth Goddard

"Elizabeth Goddard has done it again. She's a brilliant romantic suspense writer with fast-paced stories that keep you hooked from start to finish. Amnesia, a hero with dangerous ties, and a deadly storm all combine to create a thrilling ride, perfect for devouring in one sitting. Looking forward to the next one."

Lynette Eason on *Storm Warning*

"Elizabeth Goddard's *Storm Warning* is perfectly named. This book takes readers by storm. Highly recommended."

Nancy Mehl

"Fans of romantic suspense will be truly and rightfully impressed."

Interviews and Reviews on *Shadows at Dusk*

"Goddard weaves a gripping mystery."

Publishers Weekly on *Cold Light of Day*

"Elizabeth Goddard has once again proved she is the queen of romantic suspense thrillers."

Urban Lit Magazine on *Cold Light of Day*

DEADLY
CURRENTS

Books by Elizabeth Goddard

UNCOMMON JUSTICE

Never Let Go

Always Look Twice

Don't Keep Silent

ROCKY MOUNTAIN COURAGE

Present Danger

Deadly Target

Critical Alliance

MISSING IN ALASKA

Cold Light of Day

Shadows at Dusk

Hidden in the Night

HIDDEN BAY

Storm Warning

Perilous Tides

Deadly Currents

DEADLY CURRENTS

ELIZABETH GODDARD

Revell

a division of Baker Publishing Group
Grand Rapids, Michigan

© 2026 by Elizabeth Goddard

Published by Revell
a division of Baker Publishing Group
Grand Rapids, Michigan
RevellBooks.com

Printed in the United States of America

Library of Congress Cataloging-in-Publication Data
Names: Goddard, Elizabeth author
Title: Deadly currents / Elizabeth Goddard.
Description: Grand Rapids, Michigan : Revell, a division of Baker Publishing
    Group, 2026. | Series: Hidden Bay ; 3
Identifiers: LCCN 2025033846 | ISBN 9780800746162 paperback | ISBN
    9780800747893 casebound | ISBN 9781493452729 ebook
Subjects: LCGFT: Christian fiction | Romance fiction | Thrillers (Fiction) | Novels
    | Fiction
Classification: LCC PS3607.O324 D42 2026
LC record available at https://lccn.loc.gov/2025033846

Scripture used in this book, whether quoted or paraphrased by the characters, is from The Holy Bible, English Standard Version® (ESV®). Copyright © 2001 by Crossway, a publishing ministry of Good News Publishers. Used by permission. All rights reserved. ESV Text Edition: 2016

Cover design by Mumtaz Mustafa

Baker Publishing Group publications use paper produced from sustainable forestry practices and postconsumer waste whenever possible.

26 27 28 29 30 31 32   7 6 5 4 3 2 1

To my husband, Dan,
who brought me to the Pacific Northwest
so I could fall in love with the wild,
breathtaking beauty of the rugged coastline,
misty forests, and snowcapped peaks.

It is not down on any map; true places never are.

Herman Melville, *Moby-Dick*

1

*T*he sea never gives back what it claims . . ."

Her father's voice echoed through her thoughts, gritty and sharp—like the wind whipping around her and the salt cutting into her cheeks early on this Monday morning. Cressida Valentine stepped back inside the wheelhouse where Captain Everett "Salty" Malloy stood at the helm of the *Mariner's Gambit*—an older-than-time fishing trawler.

Next to Malloy, she curled her fingers around the binoculars and peered at the dense marine fog chasing them along the Washington coast. Uneasiness pressed down on her as she scanned the mist-veiled horizon. Her father had spent his life chasing secrets buried in waters too deep and too dark to trust.

And here I am, chasing them too.

Out of the white rolling cloud, a speedboat emerged, and it headed straight for the *Mariner's Gambit*, startling her. "Looks like someone's coming toward us," she said.

"Let me see those." Malloy took the binoculars she offered—they were his, after all—and peered through.

Then he swore under his breath. Gave her an apologetic look. "Sorry."

His reaction wasn't a good sign. "Who is it? What's going on?"

Captain Malloy handed the binoculars back, then stepped to the helm. Despite the early morning cold, sweat beaded his temples, his knuckles white on the wheel. A man on a mission to escape?

"Doesn't matter." The tension in his jaw said otherwise.

"What do they want?"

He didn't answer.

Not good enough. Cressida grabbed his arm. "Captain—"

"Not now." He shrugged out of her grip and shoved the throttle forward, and the *Mariner's Gambit* groaned as it accelerated, slicing through the swells. "I need to get away from them."

"In this?" She bit her lip, regretting the question. They'd traveled between five and ten knots around the Olympic Peninsula from Port Angeles because fishing trawlers were built for endurance, not speed, Malloy had informed her.

Granted, the old trawler had been updated, boasting modern electronics and "smart" instruments on the dashboard. A necessity, he'd said, since he and his thirty-something son, Dax, were the only ones to crew the sixty-five-foot fishing and sightseeing charter vessel.

He didn't respond to her comment.

"Why is that boat headed straight for us?" She peered through the binoculars again, hoping to see if Malloy had put more distance between them.

"I don't want to find out." He suddenly turned the wheel, and the boat veered hard to port, into a fifteen-foot swell, throwing her sideways against the wall. She lost sight of the pursuers.

"This can't be happening," she whispered.

But it was.

She wanted to trust Malloy, to believe him, but he wasn't making it easy.

Her mind raced through the possible scenarios and outcomes—the good and the bad. When the trawler suddenly decelerated and the rumble of motors dimmed, Cressida looked out at the fast-moving fog. "We're slowing down?"

"They gave up the chase."

"I'm impressed. I didn't think the trawler had enough speed to escape."

"I only had to beat them to Hidden Bay. They wouldn't have followed me in. But that's not what happened."

The roar of another engine sliced through the chaos. Cressida turned toward the horizon—and froze. A massive Coast Guard cutter loomed in the distance, its white hull cutting through the waves. Relief washed over her, so sudden it left her knees weak.

Malloy exhaled sharply. "The *Kraken*."

"I'm sorry . . . what?" Visions of a mythical creature rising out of the ocean depths, long tentacles flailing, emerged in her mind.

"That's what they call her—the *Kraken*." The ghost of a grin tugged at the corner of Malloy's mouth. "And she's on our side."

Cressida clutched the railing on the wall as the cutter closed in, chasing their pursuers into the eerie fog. Over the last year, she'd traveled the world to research and finish her deceased father's book about shipwrecks, ghost ships, and the maritime folklore surrounding them.

Dad had been on the *Mariner's Gambit* too, with Captain Malloy at the helm giving him a tour of the Washington coast. That's why Cressida had been willing to pay Malloy the ridiculous amount to charter her out of Port Angeles, through the Strait of Juan de Fuca, then down the stunning rocky coast to Hidden Bay. She'd wanted to take the same path Dad had taken before he suddenly cut his research trip short. He'd traveled to DC for an alleged emergency, the details of which he conveniently left out of his journal notes. He hadn't returned to finish his research.

Or his book.

With thoughts of her father's untimely death, her heart edged into a dark place, which she couldn't afford if she was going to finish Dad's manuscript.

"Captain Malloy. I paid you well for this service. I need to know what is really going on. Your pursuers were obviously known by the authorities or else they wouldn't have chased them."

He grunted in reply. A nonanswer. Fine. She got up and took in the scene with his binoculars again, searching for the Coast Guard cutter, but both vessels had disappeared into the fog, which was now rapidly gaining on the *Mariner's Gambit*.

By tomorrow, she'd be in Hidden Bay. Her maritime historian father had already completed most of the research, but Cressida had to go to each place and look for herself because she couldn't write the book that he'd wanted to write without personally experiencing the atmosphere of each location where various sunken shipwrecks remained. Of the three million sunken ships, her father had chosen a select few. In his manuscript, he'd focused, too, on ghost ships—those vessels that had floated aimlessly on the ocean, the crew mysteriously lost.

All the vessels had one thing in common—maritime legend that fascinated her father.

This last vessel was a more recent abandoned, crewless boat—*Specter's Bounty*. Dad had come to Hidden Bay for his research.

For this charter, she'd requested that Captain Malloy take

her to Cape Disappointment at the mouth of the Columbia River—which was around a hundred nautical miles south of Hidden Bay—then return to Hidden Bay, where she would release the charter. Her trip on the *Mariner's Gambit* was almost over. On one hand, she would be relieved to finally be at her last destination. On the other hand, she hadn't gotten much out of this man who had spent time with her father.

The threat of the chase over, she relaxed, though maybe she shouldn't have. "Now that's out of the way, we can get back to the tour."

Another grunt. "I'm cutting the trip short."

"What? Why?" She looked out the window and realized they were approaching the bay, not just traveling past on their way south.

"It's not safe. Told you I didn't want to take more than two days from the start. I agreed to this for your father's sake. I was sorry to learn that he died." His ominous tone left her confused.

Suddenly, the atmosphere in the wheelhouse had shifted.

"And I had hoped you could tell me more."

"I told you all I could."

What did that mean? That he knew more and was holding back? Or that he'd told her everything? She'd learned that too many questions shut him down.

He continued navigating toward the marina but stopped and dropped anchor out in the bay. "The pier isn't going to work. We'll take the skiff."

"So that's it?" she asked. "You're dropping me off here?"

"This is Hidden Bay. Your destination." He squinted. "I'm not leaving you empty-handed."

"How's that?"

"See that bunch of boats out in the middle of the bay? They call themselves pirates."

He couldn't be serious. "And why would I want to talk to pirates?"

He snorted a laugh. "They're not *real* pirates. That's just what they call themselves. They're liveaboards." Again, he gestured at a group of vessels sprawled in the bay, far from the actual marina and dock. "You'll want to talk to Diggins, specifically."

Diggins?

"Just a heads-up in case you were expecting to see fancy yachts instead of derelict boats. This particular group can't afford to live on land, so they live in the water. They were anchored in Puget Sound, but some of them got run off and moved to Hidden Bay, where they're welcome to stay."

"Why are you referring me to this Diggins?"

"You asked about the *Specter's Bounty*."

"And you didn't know anything."

"Didn't say I didn't know anything. I said I hadn't seen it. And if I had, the Coast Guard would have, too, and ended the story."

"What *do* you know, then?"

"I know you should talk to Diggins."

"Did you send my father to Diggins?"

"He didn't ask about the *Specter's Bounty*. He didn't ask anything. Mostly let me talk."

"And you don't talk much."

He lifted a shoulder, his face blank. Yeah, he was holding back.

Dad had worked in a museum for a reason. He wasn't an investigative reporter like Cressida before she'd been blacklisted from working as such, thanks to her mother. How had Dad learned so much for his book?

"Can you tell me—was it real or not? Or is it just a ghost story?" Her job was to get as many answers from the locals as possible. She wasn't letting Malloy go without asking.

"I sound like a broken record. Talk to Diggins."

His son, Dax, was sweeping the deck and gave a brief glance up at the wheelhouse. He'd avoided her, and now his father was being short with her. Rude, even. That boat racing toward them had clearly left him unsettled.

Cressida didn't like the idea of taking the skiff—the water looked pretty rough, even in the bay. Regardless, in her cabin, she gathered her things—a duffel, laptop case, and her shoulder bag—then met Malloy and Dax above deck. She descended the ladder and settled in the much smaller vessel. Dax lowered her items, handing them down into the skiff. From the deck, he crossed his arms and watched her.

Settled in the boat, Malloy turned on the motor. With his deep frown, he looked nothing like the smiling fifty-something man who'd been only too happy to take her money. Once at the pier, he tied off the small boat. "I'll walk you to the dock. This is where I dropped your father," he said.

"Any last words that he said to you?" She had to give it one last try.

His only response was the familiar grunt as he assisted her off the boat and onto the pier then handed off her things. Next to her, he lumbered across the rickety boards, passing between a few other fishing vessels and a couple of older cruisers. The wooden slats clanked as she and Malloy walked side by side up what looked like a recently rebuilt dock. Off to the right, she took in the Bayfront Chandlery, which looked like it also offered groceries, and next to that was a dilapidated warehouse. Weirdly, no town had built up around the marina like one would expect. On the other side of the chandlery stood a partially collapsed dock and a burned-out structure.

The fog had caught up with them and hovered around the older dock, wrapping around the building destroyed by fire and turning it into an eerie setting worthy of a chilling horror flick. Foreboding goose bumps crept over her skin. This was her last stop on her research trip. She wouldn't be chased away by today's earlier scare or tales of a ghost ship and its missing crew.

At the end of the pier, she stopped and faced Malloy. "How do I contact Diggins when he lives out on the water?"

"Mavis at the chandlery can help you." He leaned in. "I wasn't joking when I said it's not safe."

Before Cressida could process his words or ask him a question that he probably wouldn't answer, he turned and walked away. Still, he called over his shoulder, "Watch your back."

Creepy much? She watched him hurry back to his boat, then head out to the bigger trawler anchored in the bay. Good riddance. Adjusting her duffel, laptop case, and sling bag, she glanced at her surroundings.

So this is Hidden Bay.

About a hundred yards of sand-pebbled beach met high cliffs that spread a few miles in either direction, carving out a crescent-shaped bay of several miles. She made her way to the Bayfront Chandlery, concerned it wouldn't be open yet. It was just before seven in the morning. Cressida's cell got no bars, and she wasn't even sure if a rideshare was available here. She entered the chandlery, and a young female clerk named Kit assisted her. Mavis wasn't there. Kit called for a ride to pick Cressida up and take her to the Cedar Trails Lodge, where she wasn't due until tomorrow night. She could sleep in the lobby if she had to. Cressida asked the clerk to store her duffel and computer case so she could walk the beach while she waited for her ride. She kept her shoulder bag containing her wallet with her.

On the beach in the early morning hours, she took in what promised to be an indescribable setting, but with the fog growing thick and suffocating, she couldn't see much—

only a few people strolling the beach. While the bay water was relatively calm, beyond the crescent edges the ocean violently bashed the rocks on the shore.

She didn't want to get too far from the marina, so she perched on a rock to relax and listen to the waves. Maybe she couldn't see everything, but the sounds were calming.

It was too quiet.

Her father's voice echoed once again in her head. *"It's not the storms that sink sailors, it's the calm before them."* A reminder that she shouldn't let her guard down.

Footfalls sounded behind her, approaching too fast and close. She jerked around. "What are you—"

A man gripped her wrist and twisted her arm behind her. He covered her mouth before she could scream. She tried the maneuvers she'd learned, techniques to free herself if she was ever attacked, but against the thick, ropy muscles on this man twice her size and weight, her defensive skills did nothing.

Pain ignited in her head when he grabbed her hair and dragged her out into the ocean, then dunked her. Could no one on the beach see what was happening? Had the fog interfered?

Her heart pounded violently, consuming what little oxygen she'd gulped into her lungs before going into the salty, cold ocean. She tried to punch his vulnerable parts, but his arms were so long, he prevented her from reaching.

Play dead.

Just . . . be dead. She fought until she thought she might actually suck in seawater. Her lungs burned, then she gave up as if dead.

And floated.

Letting the ocean take her, she drifted along with the waves washing in, then back out, then in again. Salt burned her eyes as she peered underwater, searching . . .

His boots kicked up sand. He was still there. A few more heartbeats and she would die if she didn't breathe.

She had no choice.

And he finally disappeared, so she lifted her head to the side, sucked in oxygen, then once again let the ocean carry her. Her body drifted with the current, back and forth, slowly toward the shore, until she washed up onto the beach.

Like a lifeless body.

Play dead. Let him think she'd drowned. Had this ever worked before? If he wanted her dead, he could have shot her, but why do that when she could just drown and that would be the end of her story? No investigation required.

Limbs numb with cold, pebbles cutting into her palms and arms, she crawled forward on the wet sand. Gut and lungs heaving, Cressida coughed up brackish seawater, then she let herself remain in the sand, unmoving.

Tears leaked from her eyes to mingle with the grit and salt water clinging to her face. Grateful that the ocean had spit her onto the beach, she couldn't fight back the pure terror still racing through her.

Let him believe she was gone. Let the danger be gone.

2

Straddling his Ducati Supersport S, Detective Braden Sanders leaned into the curve as he ascended the steep hill, the motorcycle roaring beneath him. The rainforest was a blur of green streaks as he raced along the two-lane highway. At the crest, he throttled forward, feeling the machine's power vibrating through him. Descending the other side, edging over the legal limit, he thrust his knee out to maneuver the switchback that carved into the foothill.

Just the rush of adrenaline he needed to hammer out the indignation coiling around his chest. At this speed, nothing else mattered except the snaking road before him.

Until he was forced to slow behind a line of vehicles. It was summer and tourist season, after all, and those thoughts he'd wanted to avoid found their way in, bombarding him.

Keep her secret, she'd said.

For the sake of the country, she'd said.

Right.

While Braden was working as a special agent with Diplomatic Security Services, he'd had the fortune, or misfortune, depending on how you looked at it, to work with a very elite and powerful figure in the State Department.

Octavia Dane had offered him a chance at life, and he'd

taken it. In return, all he had to do was move to the Olympic Peninsula and work as a detective in a small county. He'd gotten the job quickly enough and suspected she'd made those arrangements.

Once again, he tried to ignore thoughts of Octavia and focus on nature. He steadied his breathing and concentrated on the asphalt, the lines, the curves, the trees to his right, the glimpses of ocean to the left. That hundred-foot drop about thirty yards ahead where the marine fog hovered, not quite rising to the highest elevations yet.

He never dreamed he would be sent to the middle of nowhere USA. This peninsula at the edge of the United States might as well have been the edge of the earth—mountains, a rainforest, one road in and out. A coastline he could not believe. And the vast Pacific Ocean. In fact, Cape Flattery, part of the Olympic Peninsula, was the most western location of the contiguous United States. And one of the most stunning places he'd seen.

At first, he'd thought he'd been sentenced to a kind of prison in such an isolated place with large swaths of zero cell service. Eventually, he'd come to appreciate it. Loved the region so much he didn't want to leave. But too many factors outside this dream world would eventually pull him far from here. Besides, he wasn't here for his personal enjoyment.

He had a purpose. A mission for which he was here to wait for instructions. Hence, he was working as a detective.

As his cover.

For months now.

To complicate matters, Octavia warned him that he should watch for something unexpected. How was he supposed to do that while he worked as an actual detective? She offered no additional information, so Braden was beyond suspicious of what this could mean.

Coming from behind, a siren alerted him to move over.

Lights in his mirror signaled a disturbance. He moved to the right and let the county cruiser pass him along with the line of cars in front of him.

If County Deputy Trent Riker realized Braden was the guy on the motorcycle he'd passed, he didn't acknowledge him. Braden should have turned around and headed in the other direction—he had the day off—but curiosity got the best of him, so he followed the cruiser, taking a side road that descended quickly down the cliffside to the Hidden Bay Marina. At the bottom of the hill, Braden navigated the Ducati up to the cruiser and parked right next to it, then hopped off. After removing his helmet, he set it on the bike. Trent was already rushing north on the beach, away from the marina. Braden followed, weaving, hopping, and climbing between and over large chunks of driftwood. The morning fog was waning, burning off earlier than usual.

Trent turned to look at who'd followed. The deputy nodded to Braden, then continued hiking forward. An ambulance swerved into the marina parking lot behind them.

"What's going on?" Braden called after Trent.

"A woman washed up on the beach," Trent said.

Washed up? "A woman . . . dead or alive?" He hated how crass the words sounded.

"Alive as far as I know," Trent said.

Beyond the cluster of driftwood logs, Braden continued to follow Trent, watching his footing on the precarious rocky, pebbled beach. The EMTs were going to love carrying someone across this rough terrain.

Trent called over his shoulder. "It's your day off. I'll handle it." The older deputy believed he had deserved the detective position, but Braden had taken it.

"I'm here. I might as well assist." Did investigators ever truly get days off?

When Braden had worked for the State Department, he

was always on call. And then always called upon. In this sparsely populated county, the complex investigations weren't common. Most of the peninsula was home to reservations where tribal police oversaw their jurisdictions with dedication, working closely with county law enforcement to ensure justice for all. Braden's burden here was light, and nothing at all like the high-stakes drama he'd experienced working as a DSS special agent.

No matter where he worked, justice for all felt like a lofty, unreachable goal at times.

A wave rushed up the beach, crawling forward and nearly saturating his now sandy motorcycle boots as he continued following Trent.

Without a dedicated law enforcement marine unit in Hidden Bay, the county sheriff's office handled any water-related incident as it came up and if necessary. No official harbormaster either, which could explain much of the neglect. Decisions were made by Mavis and her crew at the Bayfront Chandlery, and for any major incidents, of course the Coast Guard was called in.

After weaving between the piles of massive white tree trunks—driftwood brought in by the Pacific and left to bleach in the sun—up ahead, he finally saw the woman.

Wrapped in a blanket, she huddled on one such driftwood log, along with a couple in their late sixties, early seventies. Beachcombers? Friends or family? The man sitting with the survivor stood when he spotted officers from Timberbrook County approaching.

"We were starting to wonder if we should just take her someplace warm," the guy said.

That would have been a good idea, but Braden kept that thought to himself.

"An ambulance is here." Trent gestured over his shoulder. "EMTs will be here soon."

Surprising Braden, the woman rose, the blanket falling from her shoulders. Her long hair looked dark since it was wet, but he could still make out the bright-red tones against a freckled face. She looked familiar to him, unsettling his thoughts.

The woman lifted her chin. "I don't need an ambulance. I just need to report"—she forced the words out through strangled tears—"I was attacked and left to drown. My stuff was stolen."

Trent went right to work. "I'm Deputy Trent Riker, and this is Detective Braden Sanders. What's your name, ma'am?"

"Cressida. Cressida . . . Valentine." She looked at Braden— not Trent—and her striking light-green eyes flashed.

For a moment, Braden couldn't breathe.

How about Cressida Valentine *Dane*?

"If you don't mind," she said, "Deputy Riker, I'd prefer to talk to the detective."

Cressida stepped up to Braden, determination set in her beautiful eyes, but in them he saw an abysmal sadness. He might have fallen for her—just a little—the first time he'd seen her photo in her mother's office. She stared, waiting for his reaction. He'd better start acting like the professional he was. But Braden wanted to tell her everything.

I know your mother. She sent me here to investigate.

He didn't know what, but now . . . He still didn't know anything except Cressida was the unexpected surprise he'd been looking for. Of that he had no doubt.

And here you are.

He couldn't tell her a thing because he was bound to keep her VIP mother's secret.

Octavia Dane held all the power, had all the connections, had the impossible means to secure the experimental drug he required . . .

If he wanted his niece to live.

3

Detective Sanders wore a black leather bomber jacket over his broad shoulders and had the most intense steel-blue eyes she'd seen. And those eyes peered at her too long. His scruffy jaw worked back and forth. She shivered from the cold and not because she grew uncomfortable under his stare. Her arms and shoulders had ached under the weight of the thick blanket—compliments of the couple who'd been sitting on it on the beach—so she'd let it drop. They hadn't seen what happened. Just found her lying there.

Her head throbbed from where the attacker had yanked her hair and dragged her to the ocean. She tried not to think about how his massive hand had gripped her head and forced her under. She hugged herself and let her gaze travel to the cliffs overlooking this beach.

Her attacker could be up top somewhere watching her now, aware she had survived.

Carrying a gurney, two men stumbled along the beach, weaving around rocks, faltering over stones half buried in the gray sand. She didn't need their help. Did she?

"Ms. Valentine?"

The detective's voice pulled her back and, after another look at him, she was surprised her attention had drifted to the cliffside—but fear was driving her thoughts at the moment.

I could have died. That thought must have reflected in her expression.

"You're cold." He suddenly shrugged out of his jacket and wrapped it around her.

The too-big jacket was nice and warm. The musky scent of leather clung to it and filled her senses.

Her response was delayed. "Oh, I don't—"

"You do. You're shivering."

She couldn't bring herself to remove it. The man's action or his jacket, something, enveloped her and made her feel safe and protected and warm.

I'm okay now. Cressida had always been a fighter. A survivor. But never had she been so violently attacked. Still, when the EMTs finally completed their laborious jaunt to care for her, she shook her head.

The detective gently touched her shoulder. "You could be hurt, physically, and in shock. Let them make sure you're okay."

Shock? "Of course I'm in shock." But he hadn't meant it that way. "They can check me out right here. I need to talk to you."

"That's why I'm here. Tell me what happened."

"I will, but first . . ." She glanced around the beach. The fog had dissipated but still hung thick and gloomy out over the water. "My bag. He took my bag with my ID. Or someone took it. Please, it's important. Can you find it?"

"We'll do our best. Can you describe who attacked you?"

Cressida suddenly remembered the rest. "The chandlery. I want the rest of my things now, please." So she could hold them close.

Cressida took off on shaky legs.

"Hold on, Ms. Valentine!"

Behind her, his words faded as the wind roared in her ears. She was breathless by the time she finally approached the chandlery, where she'd left her stuff with Kit, then she slowed to catch her breath.

The detective was on her heels, but the EMTs and the deputy remained behind on the beach, taking their time.

"I need to make sure he didn't take anything else." She opened the door.

"What makes you think he would—"

"I'm so glad you're okay." Kit had obviously missed the detective's words as he and Cressida entered the establishment, and she cut him off as she came from behind the counter.

Confused, Cressida asked, "How did you know?"

Kit's cheeks turned pink. "Oh, a fisherman was in here."

"Did he witness it?" Maybe then she could learn who had attacked her and the man would be caught, her bag returned, and she would feel safe again.

"No. He listens to the police scanner."

"And you knew it was me?" Cressida approached the counter, edging closer to where she'd seen Kit store her things.

"I do now."

Whatever. "My duffel and laptop case. I left them here earlier."

"Everything's here." Kit showed Cressida her large duffel, wedged into a narrow closet.

Cressida lifted it.

"Wait—" Cressida's chest tightened. "Where's my laptop case?"

Kit's brown eyes grew wide. She whirled around to check the shelves with boxes behind her, and then she bent down to look under the counter. "Here it is!"

Relief welled inside as Cressida grabbed onto it. She opened it to look inside. Empty. "My laptop. Where is it?" Kit frowned. "I'm sorry, but I don't know."

Cressida forced her knees to lock or she might have collapsed. At least her cell phone had survived tucked away inside her pocket, wrapped in the rugged waterproof phone case. She'd already lost a phone earlier on this sea-faring adventure when she'd stumbled, and her cell had plopped onto the sand and a wave rushed forward and washed it away. She'd retrieved it but she wasn't able to revive it, so she'd learned her lesson.

A commanding older woman stepped through a door behind Kit and lifted her shoulders. She took Cressida in with a quick glance, then focused on the law officer.

"Detective, please find whoever did this. I don't mean to sound insensitive, but we're getting ready for the Hidden Bay Pirates' Bash this weekend. It brings in the tourists, and that's how we keep this place running. News of an assault . . ." She pursed her lips as she looked at Cressida, then lowered her gaze as if ashamed. "Could do us in. I'm sorry, Ms. . . ."

"Valentine. Cressida Valentine," she said. "Um, Pirates' Bash?" The name gave her the gist of it.

In fact, the poster to her right caught her attention, proclaiming an adventure-filled day with landlubbers and salty dogs dressed in their best pirate attire offering up swashbuckling fun and maritime mischief. *Whether ye be a salty sea dog or a landlubber, there's treasure to be found for all!* The post included the details, and on any other day she would be excited to attend. This was just the kind of thing to help her sink into the local culture and gather information.

But today she felt violated, and Mavis cared more about the bash. Cressida wasn't sure how she should react, but she couldn't afford to make enemies.

The doorbell signaled another customer, and a stocky middle-aged man stepped inside. "I hear someone needs a ride. What's the . . . Oh." He stared at the group. "What did I miss?"

"Hayes," Mavis said, "can you give Ms. Valentine a ride up to the Cedar Trails Lodge after we settle things? It seems that someone stole her stuff right out from under our noses."

They'd done more than that.

"So you're the one. I'm sorry for what happened to you." Hayes approached, his compassionate expression sincere.

"You have security cameras, I assume," Cressida said.

"Outside." Mavis placed her hands on her hips.

"We can see who comes and goes and watch the boats, but it's not the best quality." Kit shrugged.

The detective's gaze flicked to Cressida. Oh, was she stepping on his toes?

"I'll need that footage," he said to Mavis, then zeroed in on Cressida. "Before we can find your property, I need information. I'd like to get a full statement from you before anything else. I'll take you to the lodge myself." Then he looked at Hayes and handed off a folded bill. "This is for your trouble."

Cressida should have thought of that, but she wasn't exactly thinking clearly.

Detective Sanders gestured toward the back of the shop. "Let's sit down and you tell me everything."

He grabbed her duffel and empty laptop case and carried them for her as she headed toward the tables. At the back she spotted a blackboard with a few items scratched on it in white chalk—today's soup, clam chowder. Well, one item. And that was it. Nobody was in the back. Were they closed? Now that she thought about it, she was famished. But who could eat at a time like this? Maybe they just weren't officially open yet. After all, it was barely nine in the morning.

Cressida found a table and took a seat, even though she was sticky and salty from her dunk in the ocean. The pounding in her head increased. Elbows on the table, she rubbed her eyes.

The detective stood at the glass doors of a refrigerator. "What's your preference? Water, or would you like a soda?"

She shook her head. *I can't believe this day.* "Coffee would be nice. Is there coffee?"

"Sure there is! It's on the house," Kit called. "Whatever you want."

"I'll take a cup too," the detective said. "Happy to pay."

"On the house, Detective Sanders."

She wanted to like and trust Kit and Mavis, but Cressida couldn't be sure the women weren't complicit in what happened to her. After all, she'd left her things with them. Kit promised they wouldn't be disturbed. Her duffel was intact, but her laptop was gone. Cressida had made the mistake of trusting this down-to-earth establishment. Trusting Kit, with her warm and friendly smile.

How much did she tell this detective, also a stranger? Dad's notes about the place were sparse, comparatively speaking, and at the moment, she felt alone and like she couldn't trust a single person. This wasn't at all like Cressida. And this new feeling left her hollowed out. Deflated.

Not how she wanted to start this last leg of her research to complete Dad's manuscript.

Kit rushed forward with two coffee mugs, and Detective Sanders took them, handing one off to Cressida. He sat across from her, then took his time doctoring his coffee with sugar packets left on the table. Finally, he took a long swig from the steaming mug. She drank hers black, savoring the warmth.

Detective Sanders's hair was brown with a few wheat-colored streaks and looked windblown, which made sense. Nobody could escape the coast without that hair, but somehow, it looked like it was deliberate on this man, and like he'd been wearing a helmet. And he had a slight scar from his ear to his jawline, hidden beneath the dark shadow of a closely trimmed beard.

She found him both warm and intimidating. She guessed him to be in his mid- to late thirties, and his confidence said he was experienced in his job.

"Did you happen to come here on a motorcycle?" she asked.

He cocked his head. "What gave you that impression?"

"Your hair." She took another sip of warmth. Yeah, this was good and hit the spot.

A taste of normalcy.

"Can I have your name, address, and phone number? That'll work for now since your identification was stolen."

She gave him her full name, including the last name Dane. He'd find out anyway, and chances were that last name wouldn't mean anything to him. "I use my middle name in my work."

"Your work?"

"I'm a journalist, and I prefer to keep my legal name private."

"Makes sense." He scribbled the information down.

"You're writing this information on a *napkin*?"

"Full disclosure," he said. "This was my day off. I was out for a ride when I decided to follow my fellow county law enforcement officer down to the beach. That's my story, now what's yours?"

He set his smartphone on the table.

"Are you recording this?"

"Yes. Are you good with that?"

What if she said no? "Of course."

He clasped his hands and leaned forward with an intense expression to let her know he was listening and might even hear what she *didn't* say. She'd chosen to give her statement to *him*, after all, rather than Deputy Riker.

"This is Detective Braden Sanders interviewing Cressida Valentine Dane at the Bayfront Chandlery." He added the date and time. "Please tell me what happened."

What was her story, indeed? Where did she start? In her previous job as an investigative journalist—that is, before her mother ruined everything with her master plan—she was great at asking all the questions and offering all the answers. The turned tables threw her off-balance, and her thoughts were scrambled.

"I was sitting on the beach and a man approached from behind. I fought him, but he got the better of me and tried to drown me."

"How did you escape?"

"I didn't escape."

"You're alive. He didn't drown you. How did you get out of that?"

The detective was a blunt-force interrogator—right to the heart of things. No coddling for him, except to share his jacket.

She focused on the still-steaming coffee. What did it matter? Why was he asking that question? She tried to shove the drama, the emotion of that moment, behind her. Her breathing hitched.

She glanced up to his eyes. The steel had overtaken the blue and turned dark.

"I pretended to be dead."

His lids barely narrowed. He definitely knew how to control his expression and body language. "And that saved your life. You fought the guy, so you must have gotten a good look at him."

"I did, which might put me in danger if he learns I'm alive."

"It could. Can you describe him?"

She gave him her detailed description, gathered during the fight for her life, so it was probably emotionally distorted.

"We'll get you with a forensic artist."

"You have an artist out here?"

His brows shot up, and she suspected he fought a smile. "We can get the resources we need."

"I understand." Forensic artists weren't necessarily easy to come by.

He shoved his mug aside and leaned closer, his eyes piercing, studying, analyzing. She wanted to look away. To shift in her seat, but she held her own. This would be over soon, and then in private, she could lose it. Sob into a pillow. Whatever it took to get over this day.

"Any clue why the man attacked you and stole your bag and possibly your laptop?"

She recognized the trick question. "No. I mean . . ." Oh shoot. If she was going to let him ask the questions, she just blew it.

He stared at her, waiting, as if he might make her feel like she was the guilty party here instead of the victim.

The doorbell rang again, and boots clomped. Deputy Trent Riker stood over them at the table. The two male EMTs joined them too.

Detective Sanders stopped the recording. "I'm in the middle of her statement, Trent."

"I've talked to the few that were on the beach to learn if we have any other witnesses." His gaze flicked to Cressida, then back to the detective. "No one saw anything."

Detective Sanders didn't react to his words. "Get the CCTV recording on all these buildings, every one of them at the marina."

The deputy gave a slight frown, then nodded.

One of the EMTs stepped forward. "Ma'am, if you don't think you need medical attention, then we can be of use someplace else."

"I appreciate all you've done," Cressida said. "Thank you. If I start to feel funny, I'll get help."

The two EMTs and Deputy Riker shared a look as if they were friends and left her alone with the detective.

"Don't think that interruption distracted me." He switched the recording back on, adding an explanation about the pause. "You were about to explain to me why someone attacked you. Why someone stole your bag on the beach and your laptop from this chandlery shop."

"I wasn't going to tell you any such thing because I don't know."

"Look, anything you can tell me that would help me find your attacker will help to keep you safe, and also possibly retrieve what he took."

"I'm here for research so I can finish my father's book. He was a maritime historian. I chartered a boat, and the captain dropped me off here." *Cutting our trip short. He told me to watch my back. But why?* "I took a walk on the beach while waiting on my ride." She shrugged, fighting the swell of unshed tears.

"You mentioned that you're a journalist."

"I was an investigative journalist." *Until my own mother sunk my career.* He'd learn soon enough anyway, if he pulled additional background information. "I spent the last many months researching and traveling the world, making notes of my own. If I'm going to write his book, I need to experience what he experienced. And then I arrived here, and this

35

is the first trouble I've—" She stopped herself. "Now I just sound plain bitter."

Well, she was.

Bitter that all her hard work could have been destroyed.

"Ms. Valentine. Please. Take a deep breath. You've been through something terrible. Is there anyone I can call for you?"

"No . . . I . . ." She sagged. She hadn't meant to offer up more than the required information, but she was exhausted and just needed to say the words. "My father died. I'm finishing his book." She was repeating herself.

"You need to talk to someone. A therapist, someone to help you through these traumatic events. In the meantime, I'm here to help in any way I can."

"Like find who did this? Get my things back?"

"Yes, of course. Who dropped you off here?"

"Captain Everett Malloy, goes by the name Salty. His trawler is called the *Mariner's Gambit*. He cut our excursion short after a near run-in with a possible speedboat just off Hidden Bay, but the *Kraken* chased them away. He told me it wasn't safe here and to watch my back."

At the look he gave her she added, "I know it sounds nonsensical."

"Watch your back."

Footsteps behind her. Her face in the cold, salty water. Death so close.

Cressida squeezed her eyes shut and shuddered.

She had to escape!

4

Braden had meant to be completely hands-off. Instead, he was all-hands-on-deck, holding Cressida tightly. She'd jumped from the chair as if to run, and he caught her. He hadn't even hesitated when she'd started shaking through the memory. Her shudders left him unsettled.

He regretted having to ask her to relive those moments. But getting answers would always be part of his job—at least this county detective job. His position with DSS had included threat-assessment analysis, protective detail, and . . . keeping secrets.

While he hadn't known what to expect when he'd come to Washington, with the arrival of Octavia's daughter, he now understood—Octavia wanted protection for Cressida. But from what? From whom? He didn't know. And why here? Why now? Why hadn't Cressida needed protection before she got to Hidden Bay?

Octavia had some explaining to do.

Cressida calmed and slid out of his arms. "I apologize for letting my emotions get the best of me. I don't know what to say."

As if frozen in place, he kept his arms out. This wasn't awkward at all. "No need to say anything or apologize."

He turned off the recorder. There was more to her story. He could see it in her eyes, but he also knew that she wouldn't share until she was ready. He wouldn't press her, at least not now.

"You're not asking more questions?" Tears hung in her eyelashes as she blinked up at him.

"You've had a rough day. I'll take you to the lodge now, if you're ready to go." He raked a hand through his hair and looked out the window and remembered his ride. This wasn't going to work.

"You're on a motorcycle, aren't you?" she asked.

"I'll make other arrangements." He called Trent and confirmed the ride for her.

Was that disappointment flitting across her gaze? Not likely, given what happened today, but if she did ever want a ride on his bike, he was more than willing to oblige.

"Deputy Riker is waiting at his vehicle in the parking lot. I'll carry your duffel and computer bag." He opened the door of the chandlery for her and walked her out.

At his county cruiser, Trent gave a soft smile and opened the door for her, and Braden stowed her things in the back. He followed Trent's vehicle on his Ducati, his thoughts racing as he focused on the road and the cruiser ahead of him.

On the surface, "Salty" Malloy's warning that it wasn't safe could've been a general comment about Hidden Bay or the marina itself. Given the attempted murder and the fact that her mother had sent Braden here for a reason, it seemed clear that someone had deliberately targeted Cressida.

Though he wanted to be up-front with her, the moment she found out he had any connection to her mother would be the last moment he would have to protect her and keep her close. She and her mother were estranged.

At the lodge, Trent assisted Cressida into the main lobby and Braden walked behind them. He thanked Trent while he waited for Cressida to check in.

Trent leaned in close to Braden and spoke so no one else could hear him. "Do we need to warn the public a potential killer is on the loose?"

"I think that Cressida—"

"Cressida?"

"Ms. Valentine was targeted. The local news will report the attack, and people can come to their own reasonable conclusions—lock the door. Watch out for strangers. I plan to get Jo with her, and then we can put his picture on the usual outlets as we search for him. I'll talk to you soon."

Braden moved toward Cressida, effectively dismissing the deputy. Octavia wanted Braden on this, and he would protect her. He had to keep her close and couldn't risk Trent worming his way in and learning something he shouldn't.

What if Cressida held a secret Octavia wanted to learn more about or keep under wraps? He couldn't fully know what this was about and would call Octavia soon.

Once Cressida had completed her check-in, he snatched her duffel and computer bag before she could.

"I got lucky," she said. "I wasn't due to check in until tomorrow night, but my cabin is available now."

"Good. I'll walk you there." He threw the duffel over his shoulder.

"You don't have to do this," she said. "Remember, it's your day off, and even if it wasn't, you're a cop. Not my personal valet."

"I'm a nice guy even on my day off." Since he took on this investigation, he'd get paid and was working now, but he saw no reason to point that out. Let her see him as the nice guy. He'd chosen to follow Trent to the beach, after all.

What if he hadn't? Then he couldn't have as easily worked

his way into Cressida's situation, to be both investigator and protector she needed. Trent would have been that guy. Braden knew enough about him to believe that.

Braden wanted to throw that question in Octavia's face. She should have been up-front with him about the reason he was here instead of twisting his arm behind his back to do her will like it was some kind of game to her.

Cressida hiked to her cabin, and he followed, carrying the duffel and case. It was actually pretty heavy, and he saw now why she hadn't wanted to carry it on her walk on the beach. And he appreciated a woman who could allow a man to be a gentleman.

At the cabin, she unlocked the door, entered, and he followed, gently dropping the duffel and case next to the table. She glanced around the cozy space.

"How long will you be staying?" he asked.

She rubbed her forehead, looking frazzled and yet strong and in control at the same time. How did she do that? Must have her mother's genes. "I stay as long as it takes to learn what I need to learn. But I've only booked this cabin for three weeks."

That was expensive. "Why here?"

She stepped forward and studied him. Getting suspicious?

"Look," he said. "I'm trying to find out who attacked you and why. I like to ask questions."

"And I like a detective who's serious about his job." She stepped closer.

And his heart pounded harder.

Not good.

"Maybe you can help me more than you think. I'm here looking into the *Specter's Bounty*. I mentioned my father was a maritime historian and was writing a book. The bag that was stolen today had his journal in it, to which I added my personal thoughts on everything, including and especially

my notes on my experiences for the book. The entire reason for my travels. I need that back. It's not something I've
made copies of. Do you understand?" Her shaken demeanor
quickly gave way to the confidence of someone used to
being in control.

He arched a brow. "I understand."

"As for why I'm here at Cedar Trails Lodge in Hidden Bay,
specifically, it seems as good a place as any to meet with
people and talk. Find out what they know. What they've
heard. In my father's notes, he had a name with a question
mark beside it. Evelyn Monroe. I contacted her weeks ago
to ask for an interview while I'm here, but so far, she has
avoided my calls. Or rather, her gatekeeper has."

Interesting. "Why Mrs. Monroe?"

"Do you know her?"

He lifted his palms. "Not personally, no."

"What can you tell me about her?"

"Not much, I'm afraid. Why do you think your father
wrote down her name?"

"I don't know. But the reason he traveled to Hidden Bay
was to learn about the truth behind the *Specter's Bounty*. So
I assume Mrs. Monroe might have information."

He could help her on that front. And just like that he
might have found a solid way in to remain connected to her
instead of protecting her from afar, which was the worst
way to go about it. *Thanks for nothing, Octavia.* "You'll want
to check out the museum in Forestview. It's what goes for
a small town around here. It's just across the highway and
in the rainforest."

"What kind of museum?"

"The kind that might have the information you want."

"Seems it would be located at the Hidden Bay Marina
instead of the forest. Usually anything that includes maritime history is close to the water."

"Forestview is close enough and a few miles from the bay. The original museum was in the smattering of buildings you saw at the marina. It burned down. Now it's in town, away from the water."

"Oh." Her deep frown reflected her pain. "Artifacts, history, and archives might have been lost. That's awful."

"If you go to the museum, I'd like to join you." Now he might be crossing the invisible line between professional and personal.

At the look she gave him, he added, "I'm concerned about you, that's all."

She took him in as if trying to read if he was telling her the truth or a lie.

He'd stayed too long. Braden moved to the door, standing in the frame so she couldn't shut the door in his face. "Be aware that your attempted killer could try again because you're now a witness—you mentioned as much. I suggest that you try to move into the main lodge for more security."

She pressed forward as if he wasn't blocking her way. He had two choices. Stand his ground, which would put him entirely too close, or step outside. Usually, he stood his ground, but he gave way, stepping outside. What was she up to? In the little time he'd spent with her, he couldn't deny she had a lot of her mother in her.

Terrifying.

"Thanks for the advice," she said. "I'll keep that in mind."

"One more thing, how are you going to get around without a rental car?"

That proverbial deer-in-the-headlights look before her face relaxed. "I rented a car out of Forestview, and the rental company is bringing it to me in a couple of days. I wasn't supposed to be here until tomorrow night, so Wednesday morning they will deliver it." She bit her lip, then pressed them together. "I'll call the rental company and see if I can get it earlier."

"Not with your cell, you won't. No good service. You're lucky if you get half a bar. But the lodge has a landline you could use."

"Thanks for the tip and for carrying my stuff." Arms crossed, she leaned against the doorjamb.

Her hair had finally dried, revealing the same bright red as in her photograph in Octavia's office. With her striking eyes, the cabin at her back, and those wild curls, she looked like he imagined a forest sprite would appear.

"If they can't accommodate the change"—and he doubted they would—"I'm happy to give you a tour for the next two days. Take you around for your research."

Instead of taking him up on the offer, she narrowed her gaze again. He might have pushed her too far too fast.

"I'll let you know, Detective. Thanks for the offer."

"I'll contact you soon about the forensic artist. She's local," he said, "so this should happen soon, before you forget the details."

"Oh, I won't forget."

He dipped his chin and backed off. "Thank you, Ms. Valentine."

"Cressida."

He stared.

"You can call me Cressida. Nobody calls me Ms. Valentine, like we live in the nineteenth century."

"Just doing my job. It's a professional courtesy. But Cressida it is."

She blinked, then widened her eyes, almost accusing. Oh. He hadn't offered her the same use of his first name. He cleared his throat. "Please, feel free to call me Braden." He didn't require that she address him as "detective" to do his job.

But she gave him a funny look.

He allowed a half grin. "You got a problem with my name?"

"Not at all. You don't look like a Braden. I thought that the first time I heard your name."

He stifled an incredulous laugh. "I'm not entirely sure I want to ask what name you'd give me."

She was the one to laugh, but it was a good laugh, and all the awkward tension dissipated. She chewed her lip while she squinted. "I don't know. Maybe an Aiden or a Bradley. No, I take that back. You *are* a Braden, after all."

"Whatever you say, Cressida." Honestly, he'd never met anyone with *her* name. "You should get some rest. If you need anything at all, here's my number." He handed her a card he tugged from his jeans pocket. "If, that is, you can get a signal. I'm going to see what I can learn on your case and hopefully get your things returned to you."

Her face brightened with that news. "I hope to hear from you soon."

He turned and walked toward the lodge. At least this cabin was close and not one of those more isolated, deeper in the woods. His thoughts turned to Octavia Dane. He needed more information, especially now that her daughter had been attacked.

Braden dreaded making that call. It was better to keep that generous but conniving woman as far away as possible.

5

After the door shut, Cressida stared at the space where Detective Braden Sanders had stood—empty now of his presence. But she could still see him—his steel-blue eyes. Wide shoulders and protective demeanor. She let her mind dwell on him because that was better than reliving the cold shock of ocean in her face.

The gasp for breath.

Her aching, screaming lungs.

She tried to shake off the terror of those moments early this morning, and let the warm leather cocoon her. Wait. She glanced down to see that she still wore his leather jacket.

"What? Oh no!"

Cressida quickly shrugged out of it. The leather was worn and soft under her fingers. She couldn't let him leave without it. Opening the door, she glanced up the trail, could see the parking lot and the lodge, but no Braden. Well, that was just great. She shouldn't have let him go without his jacket, especially since he was on his motorcycle, but she'd put up a strong front for him too long and now she was ready to collapse.

Her entire body ached. Nothing an emergency room doctor could do for it that a hot shower and rest wouldn't fix. Her psychological state was another matter. Bottom line, she didn't have the energy to chase after Braden. If he wanted his jacket, he'd come back for it. And if he didn't, she'd make sure to hand it over the next time she saw him.

Now that Detective Bradley Cooper—Braden Sanders—was out of the way, Cressida could do what she really wanted to do three hours ago. She moved to the bed and collapsed. Sobbed into the pillow. Because a woman had to shed the tears sometimes, and she'd been attacked. She might know a therapist or two she could call—a friend of a friend of a friend back in DC. She hadn't been back in just over a year, and yet DC seemed like a lifetime ago.

And today's events seemed like her entire life had passed before her eyes—like she'd heard happens. Fortunately, she lived to talk about it, which only put her in more danger.

Good. Bring it. She was all for living to fight another day.

As for Bradley Cooper . . . No, she definitely shouldn't start thinking about him as Bradley Cooper, though he bore some resemblance. Maybe Detective Braden Sanders was kind of a rogue womanizer too, for all she knew. He had that quality about him—dimples and that scar on the right side, hidden by a thin layer of whiskers. And those sharp eyes.

Oh, Cressida. What is happening to you? She closed her eyes. She'd been attacked. Felt the physical and psychological scars to her bones. She had a mission to focus on. A reason to be here. And this man. This detective—out of the blue—had distracted her, and that distraction had nothing at all to do with the actual investigation he would conduct. But maybe it was a good distraction given the day she'd had.

She hadn't exactly chartered the cruise and traveled to

Hidden Bay with concerns about her safety. But today had left her completely unsettled. Captain Malloy's words came back to her.

"It's not safe . . . Watch your back."

Two separate warnings, and she couldn't have taken him seriously? Her experience on the foggy beach brought a whole new meaning to those words.

A knock came at the door. She sat up, sniffled, and swiped at her eyes.

She must look a mess. Probably the detective wanting his jacket back. Too bad she hadn't showered and freshened up. She opened the door to find an auburn-haired woman in her thirties holding a package.

"Hi, I'm Remi Beckett, the Cedar Trails Lodge manager. You must be Cressida. I'm so glad to meet you." Remi smiled, her eyes holding concern.

She must know about the attack.

"It's nice to meet you too." Cressida thrust out her hand. Remi shook and released it. "What can I do for you?"

Remi offered the package to Cressida. "Someone brought this to the lodge. I thought I would hand-deliver it so I could speak with you in person. My friend Detective Sanders also requested that you be moved out of this cabin and into the lodge. I have a guest leaving tomorrow morning, and the room is yours if you'd like."

Cressida couldn't hide her relief as she held the package. *Could this be . . . ?*

Before answering Remi about moving to the lodge, Cressida ripped the parcel open. A note was clipped to Dad's journal, and she quickly read it to herself.

You left this behind. Remember what I told you.

C. M.

Captain Malloy. She held the journal to her chest and closed her eyes. "Thank goodness."

Aware that Remi was watching, Cressida opened her eyes again. "I love my privacy and this cabin, but given the incident today, at least until the guy is caught, I should probably take that room. I mean, unless you think I would be putting anyone in danger."

"You won't. If you're concerned about your safety tonight, I have a sleeper sofa in my office that you're welcome to take."

Cressida gave a tenuous smile. "That's sweet, and thank you for the offer. I should be fine. If I change my mind later, I'll show up at the lodge."

"Sounds good. If you need anything at all, just find me. Cell phones rarely work out here, but just head to the lodge and someone can help you."

"The rooms don't have landlines?"

Remi lifted her shoulders and shook her head in a way that said she didn't get it either.

Okay, then. "Well, thank you." Cressida lifted the journal and shook it. "This is a lifeline." To her research. Her connection with Dad.

"I hope the rest of your day goes well." Remi turned and walked up the trail.

Cressida shut the door and opened the journal—Dad's notes along with her own thoughts mingled together on the pages. The last eight months of research she'd done to finish the book her father had started. She wasn't sure if his working title was quite right, though.

Echoes Beneath the Waves was a compilation of the mysteries and maritime legends surrounding a select group of shipwrecks, as well as the historical truth. Legends were stories people believed were true but had never been authenticated. Dad's work didn't center around authenticating but rather raised questions, because in the end, the stories surrounding these specific wrecks could not be proven true or false.

She flipped through the pages, looking at her handwriting. The tactile action had given rise to memories she might not have retained if she'd simply typed everything into a computer. Dad had already done so much work, and maybe she hadn't truly needed to travel to all the locations herself, but part of her had wanted to experience what he'd experienced, and that would make for better writing.

A deeper part of her wanted to put her heart and soul into his last work and make it shine, as if she could add anything more to what he'd already done.

Lying on the bed, she held the journal against her heart and closed her eyes.

Oh, Dad.

She still struggled to believe he was gone. Hit by a taxi while crossing the street. Such a ridiculous, tragic accident. This trip to the Washington coast and the research she intended to complete here would mark the last spot, the last unexplained crewless vessel, and in that way being here was bittersweet. She didn't want it to end, and maybe she would drag it out longer than necessary so she could squeeze out all the memories and emotions possible that would connect her to her late father.

As for his journal, she couldn't imagine that she had left it behind. That had been a huge mistake. On the other hand, leaving the journal behind on the *Mariner's Gambit* might have been the best mistake she'd ever made, otherwise whoever had taken her bag would also now have the journal.

In addition to the journal, fortunately, much of her research and notes were also on her laptop, and even if someone could figure out how to open it without her biometrics, she shut it down remotely. In fact, she could still access everything stored on the cloud—the bigger pieces. Not the nuances that she'd written in her journal.

After her sob, relief shuddered out of her in a long breath, like she had emptied out all the pent-up distress. Forgetting that she had been violently abused today, letting go, would take time.

She could hold on to the fact that it was going to be okay. Cressida would focus on her work for the rest of the time, and Detective Sanders would investigate what happened and return her things.

As the adrenaline faded, her aches and pains from the battle with the attacker reminded her that she'd planned to take a shower and wash away the grime of salty ocean and sand. *Then* she could read through her notes again. She set the journal on the desk, then thought better of it and instead stuck it under her pillow. She'd never felt the need to hide it before.

The long, hot shower turned into a short shower. She couldn't shake off the captain's warning—twice now—and then the attack. She towel-dried her hair and moved back into the main room, which included the bedroom and a kitchenette. A big window to view the ocean and a wood stove.

She'd love to stay here at another time without the weirdness of today weighing on her. On the floor, she found the note from Malloy had fallen out of the journal, and she picked it up to look at it again. *Remember what I told you . . .*

"Watch your back."

And she hadn't taken him seriously. Hadn't known he meant it in the way he'd said it.

Since that warning, someone had taken the bag she'd carried with her *and* her laptop from another location. Oh yeah, and she couldn't forget, drowned her—or so they thought.

What did Malloy know about this?

Could someone have been after her journal in the bag, or was she reading too much into it? Jumping to unfounded conclusions. But if that was true and the attacker had been after her journal, did that also mean once he discovered he didn't have it, that he would come back for it?

And kill me again, only this time make sure I stay dead?

6

At his small Forestview apartment, Braden exchanged his Ducati for his county-issued cruiser and drove back to the sheriff's office—though it would take him a good forty-five minutes away from Cressida—but he needed to speak with Sheriff Thatcher about the precarious investigation that now included a protective detail. But Thatcher wasn't in, so Braden settled into his small corner cubicle. His day off was officially over the moment he'd turned to follow Trent onto that beach.

In the county offices, a few deputies and personnel focused on their tasks and left him to his. Reports and paperwork were unfortunately the bulk of his job.

He needed to contact Octavia at some point today. If only he could cut all ties with her and live his life. If only he didn't owe her anything. Owe her everything. As if to emphasize that truth, his cell dinged.

Caller ID revealed the call was from his sister.

His neck tensed as he answered. "Lauren. Is everything okay?"

An incredulous chuckle met his ears. "Relax. I can call you just to say hi, can't I? Everything isn't an emergency."

Wasn't it? He released a slow breath as his shoulders slowly relaxed. "I know. I'm sorry. How are you? How's Elise?" Elise, his deathly ill ten-year-old niece.

"She's . . . okay."

He heard the hint of a lie in her voice. But he understood—"okay" was relative. It was personal. Okay for Elise was someone else's worst day. "I wish I could be there with you. I wish I could do more."

"Are you kidding? Without your help, Elise would . . ." Lauren choked up and couldn't finish the sentence. Her next words were breathless and tear-filled. "I can't thank you enough, Braden. But what has this cost you?"

"The cost doesn't matter."

Didn't she understand that he would pay any price to save Elise?

Any.

Price.

He'd wanted to be the hero and spare his sister the truth, but he had no alternative explanation for leaving her alone to go through this with Elise. Again. Alone. Her husband had died in a work accident. Then Elise had fallen ill, and Braden had been on the other side of the world in the middle of a high-risk mission involving multiple US and foreign diplomats—a mission that had gone very wrong. He instinctively touched the old scar along his jaw, hidden beneath his stubble.

He hadn't been there for Lauren and Elise. The loss of that job after covering for someone else and taking the blame might have gutted him at first, but in the end, he counted it a blessing. He was then able to stand by Lauren's side, holding her up and being both uncle and father figure to Elise. So he'd had to tell Lauren that Octavia required this of him—to secure a chance at survival with an experimental drug.

"It matters, Braden. It matters to *me*."

"You don't need to worry about it. You just be there for your daughter. You take care of my niece. She's precious to me too."

Lauren had resigned from her job as an up-and-coming attorney to be with Elise. And with Rick's life insurance policy, they had a nest egg, but that wouldn't last forever.

This situation couldn't continue on like this for infinity. *God, please let the medication work. Please save Elise.*

Braden couldn't be sure if this experimental drug was the answer, God's answer, or if he'd taken things into his own hands and allowed himself to be manipulated by a master.

"Can I talk to her? Is she awake?"

"Sure. That's why I called, actually," Lauren said. "But first I wanted to make sure you were in a good place to talk."

He was never in a good place to talk anymore. Then again, he would always make time for Lauren and Elise.

"Uncle Braden." Her sweet voice came through the cell. He squeezed his eyes shut, listening to her, hoping to remember every part of how her voice sounded in case she didn't make it. Hoping to hear any pain she was suffering but too afraid to tell anyone.

"Hi, sweetie."

"I miss you. When are you coming back? When can you come and see me?"

Braden worked to keep the pain from his voice, enduring the acid rising in his gut.

"I miss you too, honey," he said. "You know I would be there right now, today, and never leave, if I could, right?"

"I know."

"Just remember that I love you. I'll come visit as soon as I can." *I'll come live close, again, as soon as I can.*

Elise continued talking, sharing with him about a man who made her laugh by making balloon animals when she was at the hospital getting her infusion. Then Elise grew tired, and Lauren said goodbye.

How had it come to this? The agony was almost unbearable. He hated Octavia for this. And at the same time, he couldn't be more grateful that she had made this possible and given Elise a second chance at life. Still, everything about this situation felt completely wrong. But maybe it was due to the simple fact that he lived in a fallen world. Nothing was as it should be.

He blew out a breath and tried to refocus on his current situation. The sooner he completed his task here, the sooner he could get back to the people who mattered most.

Lauren and Elise.

And what about Cressida? She hadn't been far from his thoughts even while he talked to his niece. Braden didn't like leaving her alone in the cabin, but Remi assured him she would make sure she had a place to stay at the lodge. In the end, it was Cressida's choice.

Dreading the next call, he stared at his cell.

Braden contacted Octavia and, as expected, got her voicemail. He didn't leave a message because she'd asked him not to. She would recognize the number and return the call. Next, he returned Trent's call and got his voicemail. He grabbed a quick lunch at the sandwich shop next door, then returned to the reports app, which allowed him to review the information they had and connect dots if possible.

He needed to upload the recorded statement into the database and include a written transcript. He wanted to listen to it again. Listen, in case he missed some nuance in her tone or answer. Braden turned on the recording and got up and paced as it played. He struggled to listen to the pain in her voice.

This wasn't what he signed up for, and he was furious at Octavia. The woman managed to offer favors and pull strings in the most unexpected places. In Braden's opinion, she was working overtime to keep her daughter clueless or at a distance.

Why not give Cressida a call and talk out their differences? Why send Braden into this situation, while also leaving him in the dark? Leaving him clueless was one thing—and he would get those answers—but her daughter was another matter.

Octavia had done something to alienate her daughter, and she had her reasons. Braden couldn't fathom any reason would be worth losing your daughter. He would go to the end of the earth for his family—all he had left were his sister and niece, and he had done everything he could for his niece. And now here he was.

People had a way of justifying their position. Like right now, he justified his own position—owing Octavia and following through with her demands. And he could see no end in sight.

After a few hours working on the reports and research, he closed his laptop.

Trent finally called Braden back. "We got no one on the CCTV. No man going in or out."

"Okay, then let *me* see the footage. Her attacker could have had an accomplice. Someone else could have been working with him, stealing her laptop while someone else was trying to drown her and leave her for dead."

"You might want to ask her what she has on her computer or in that bag of hers that someone wants. What's she involved in to bring this on?"

Trent and his detective instincts. "She's the *victim*, Trent. Don't twist it around to sound like she's guilty of a crime. Anything else?"

"I canvassed the beach again. A couple saw a man hiking up the trail from the beach, looking like he was in a hurry. He fit the description Cressida gave, but that's all I got."

"You could have led with that," Braden said.

"Anything else you need?" Trent asked. "I have to respond to a fender bender, oh, involving a motorcycle. Dude's okay in case you're wondering. But you should watch your back out there. Tourist season is in full swing."

"Thanks for the advice." He needed to get footage from the surrounding area up and down the only highway in and out of this region, tourists stops, and gas stations. He'd get that himself, so he ended the call.

A text from Remi came through.

> Cressida received a package today—a journal.

He thanked Remi. He would love to talk to Cressida about the journal, but he wouldn't give Remi away. He needed a good reason to contact Cressida and hoped to finally reach Jo Cattrel, who worked as a freelance forensic artist for law enforcement around the state. Jo also worked part-time at Cedar Trails Lodge.

Fortunately, this time Jo answered her cell. "Braden, what's up?"

"Did you get my message that I need you on an investigation?"

"I just finished with a client, and I'll be back on the coast on Wednesday morning. Can we meet then?"

"That's perfect. I'll make the arrangements."

He grabbed his county-issued rain jacket and headed out the door. He'd prefer to take his Ducati, but the blue skies had given way to rain, and he'd left his leather jacket with Cressida. He hadn't had the heart to ask her for it because she'd been through so much. Before heading over to see

Cressida, he'd make those stops where security camera footage could be obtained. Maybe he'd get actual footage of the guy who had attacked her.

Later in the day, after getting the footage, he finally parked at the lodge. He made his way to her cabin and knocked on the door. Nothing. Braden knocked again but got no answer. He hiked over to the lodge—a centuries-old structure built from the surrounding trees—and scanned the small gathering at the tables near the panoramic window overlooking the rocky cliffs. The kitchen served up the special of the day in the evenings, and a few people still lingered at those tables.

Lodge patrons came here in the winter to watch the spectacular storms—waves crashing on the rocks. This was summer, and with an hour of daylight still left, even in the rain people were combing the beach, searching for tide pools. He was relieved when he spotted Cressida at a table with one of the baristas and an older couple.

Remi sidled up next to him. "I don't have to guess why you're here. She's doing well for someone who was attacked this morning. I joined them earlier."

"Oh yeah? What are they talking about?"

"She's asking questions about their lives. Just good old-fashioned conversation. The kind people used to have instead of staring at their phones."

"They can't really do that here, can they?" He referenced that lack of cell reception.

"Maybe conversation was all she needed. Just a sense of normalcy after that horrible welcome she got when she arrived in Hidden Bay."

He started forward, and Remi gently pressed her hand on his sleeve. "I wouldn't."

"Excuse me?"

"I don't mean to interfere with an investigation, but unless you have specific questions or something important to share, I'd give her some time before you start charging in again."

Charging in again? Is that how Remi saw him? Cressida seemed relaxed and happy, though he could still see the strain of this morning in her eyes. Maybe Remi was right, and he'd give Cressida a break for today.

If Cressida was anything like her mother—and so far she seemed to be—she would face her fears head-on.

And look out, anyone who got in her way.

Good guys . . . or bad.

7

The next day—Tuesday—it was late afternoon before the rain finally stopped. She'd spent the day resting, eating snacks supplied by the Cedar Trails Lodge store, revisiting her notes over the last many months of research.

The clouds crossed over like waves, and at the moment, the sky was crystal clear. Cressida walked along the shore, but she anticipated another rain shower before she finished her outing. Though she didn't expect any trouble, she'd prepared for it. Just in case, she always carried her small Glock 26—unloaded and secured in a lockbox in her duffel. Her concealed carry permit wasn't recognized in Washington state, but after what had happened, she wasn't about to travel without protection. So she'd slipped it into her waistband and taken her chances. If necessary, she'd lean on the kind of political pull her estranged mother still wielded—pull that could smooth over the paperwork, or make it disappear entirely. The thought of asking her mother for anything sickened her. If only she'd kept the Glock with her that first morning in Hidden Bay. Still, she'd been caught off guard.

Families, couples, singles combed the beach. Laughter

erupted as two kids chased their dog, trying to grab onto his leash. Though she'd experienced trouble arriving in Hidden Bay yesterday, the world kept turning. Time hadn't stopped. Life continued.

Earlier in the day, before she'd taken to the beach, a close friend had put her in touch with a therapist—as in, the therapist had taken Cressida's call to her direct cell *immediately*. Unfortunately, such special treatment reminded her of her mother, which had a negative effect on Cressida's mood. Connections were everything, Mom always said. And Mom always made sure those connections had strings on them.

The thought disturbed Cressida.

But she wanted to do what was needed so yesterday morning's attack wouldn't hang over her and prevent her from finishing Dad's book. While she remained in Hidden Bay, she needed to focus on gathering research for his incomplete manuscript. Remi had given Cressida privacy, allowing her the use of the landline in her office for both calls.

That had turned into a long conversation with Anne Crighton, LPC, who was big on exposure therapy—in other words, she helped her clients face fears in locations or scenarios tied to trauma—and that had been just what Cressida needed. Still, maybe Cressida had taken her counsel further than the therapist had intended when she decided to come right down to the beach to face her fears. Several miles south of the marina, this beach wasn't the exact place where she'd been attacked. The lodge rested on top of the cliff, and the beach beneath was at the edge of the bay, near rougher waters—all this so the guests could watch the dramatic storms and crashing waves. From here, Cressida could barely make out the liveaboard boats bobbing out in the bay's calmer waters. They called themselves pirates—all fun and games, of course.

Pirates.

She snorted a laugh.

Her soft shoes pressing into the wet sand, she tried to avoid the areas with larger pebbles as she weaved her way through the mass of big white tree trunks—Pacific red cedars that nature had transformed into driftwood.

Gripping her waterproof Nikon, relieved it had remained in her duffel, she faced the vast Pacific Ocean and searched the waters. No Coast Guard. No actual pirates.

And definitely no *Specter's Bounty*.

Would she even recognize it if she saw it? Dad had sketched an image in his notes. With the rusted-out hull and cranes, it looked like a salvage ship from decades ago. Where had he gotten this idea for the picture? He must have seen it somewhere, but he left few details about it in the notes— unless information was in the missing pages that had been ripped out before she'd gotten the journal after his death. Dad's notes included a warning surrounding the boat—"a crewless vessel that serves as a cautionary tale of the dangers of the deep"—the kind of detail that often fed superstition surrounding vessels with mysterious histories, adding to the local folklore. And a question—"Does Evelyn Monroe know?"

Know what, Dad? Know what?

The question and lack of information surrounding this last vessel to be included in his book made it that much more mysterious.

She lowered the camera. Though no one had followed her out to this part of the beach, she shouldn't take too much time. She had a reason for coming. Evelyn Monroe's mansion sat on the top of the cliff. She'd hoped to get a good look at it from the *Mariner's Gambit*, but she'd been sidetracked. Peering up at the rocky cliff face, she spotted a barely visible set of steps that led to the top.

Interesting.

She could only see them if she stood at just the right spot.

They'd been built for privacy. If she climbed those, would she find herself at Mrs. Monroe's back porch?

She could be shot for her intrusion. After all, the woman hadn't agreed to an interview.

Cressida shook her head. She'd have to keep trying. Her father had mentioned her in his notes for a reason. Talking to Mrs. Monroe could be key to learning more about the *Specter's Bounty*. She could try again another day. She'd been accused of being a workaholic, and maybe that was true, considering her never-give-up attitude on the very day after someone had tried to drown her.

The simple truth was that Cressida could not allow someone else to hold that much control over her life. She wouldn't let the attack destroy her plans. Talking to the therapist had been the kick in the rear she had needed. But she had no intention of tackling those stairs to Driftwood Manor—Mrs. Monroe's residence—this evening.

Nor intruding. *I'll come back for you, Evelyn Monroe.*

In the meantime, she could at least talk to Diggins, like Malloy had suggested. Cressida turned around and headed back the way she'd come, knowing she still had steps to climb—those that would take her up the cliff to the Cedar Trails Lodge.

The sun finally setting on the horizon, the bright pinks and oranges took her breath away. She had plenty of sunlight left to light her way back to Cedar Trails, just over a mile away. Her body was starting to ache in places that hadn't hurt earlier.

A flash of pain in her scalp and she was gasping for air. Underwater.

No. No! I can't let him get the best of me.

Just calm down.

She breathed deeply. In and out. In and out. Took in her surroundings.

The present moment was her reality and not events of the past. Up ahead, other beachcombers remained to watch the sunset, reassuring her that she wasn't completely alone. No dense fog closed in to make her feel isolated.

All her positive thoughts did nothing to assuage the fact that a singular figure emerged from the others enjoying the shore and hiked in her direction.

Past the steps she was aiming for that would take her back to the lodge.

Not strolling. Marching with purpose.

She palmed her gun, an unreasonable panic rising in her chest. She'd never been one to back down, but maybe she could have given herself more time to recover from yesterday's attack, at least psychologically—and physically, given the way her chest constricted and ached.

Her shoulders too.

Cressida turned and hurried back. Another quarter of a mile and she'd be at the private steps again. Breathing hard, she moved as fast as she could without appearing to be in an all-out sprint. Somewhere in her psyche floated the rule that running from a predator only caused them to give chase. Right or wrong, she maintained a controlled escape.

Finally, she made it to the stairway that would take her up to the top. A glance back told her the figure was closing the distance.

Okay. I'm climbing these stairs up this cliff. For all she knew, the steps simply led to another park and not necessarily Driftwood Manor.

Cressida started up the staircase. Taking one step at a time, she didn't look down. Didn't look back. By the time she made it to the top, she struggled to catch her breath. This climb might have been easy for some, but not for her.

She peered down the steps and saw no one climbing after

her, and she released a heavy sigh of relief. Maybe she'd panicked for nothing and could have kept walking on the beach to the Cedar Trails Lodge steps.

But now she was here, and she'd have to find her way back to the lodge.

She moved away from the cliff and assessed her surroundings. And yep. She was on the property surrounding the mansion.

Cressida tried her cell. Maybe she could get Remi to send someone to pick her up. But she had no bars. What did she expect?

As a journalist, she liked to set up interviews with willing interviewees, but this wasn't a perfect world. And she was no longer a journalist. She was simply completing her late father's book. While she was here, she might as well try to set up an interview in person. To get to the drive to the house, she had to walk along a trail through a beautiful meadow outside the main gate. The path coursed along next to a thick growth of spruce and red cedars.

Cressida followed the trail toward the house. It was a big old mansion that belonged in a gothic novel, especially when you factored in that—on the one side—it sat right on a cliff, overlooking a rocky beach.

Evelyn Monroe was an enigma herself. Cressida had taken a shallow dive into her backstory, learning she'd moved to the area approximately twenty years ago and bought the old manor from someone who'd moved here from Baltimore and built it at the turn of the century. The place had a history of its own, but she suspected Evelyn Monroe also had an interesting story.

As she approached the house, dusk was well and truly falling, and she wanted nothing more than to get away from the darkness edging the trail. She pressed her hand on the G26 at her side. Maybe not the best way to approach the house. But it was still quite a walk. A long private road led to a circular drive at the front.

Near the manor, a shadowed figured slipped from a corner of an outbuilding and crept to the house.

Cressida froze.

Those weren't the actions of someone who had come to the mansion for aboveboard reasons.

Did she have time to warn Mrs. Monroe? Would she, too, be seen as an intruder? One who approached wielding a gun?

What should I do? Rush forward and pound on the door to warn the residents? Tugging her cell out, she prayed for a signal. It was worth a shot. And she got one bar here, standing in this exact spot.

Cressida pressed the number for Detective Sanders. Of course, he didn't answer. He could also be in a place without cell service. She didn't have a radio to reach him.

Should I leave a message? Not like he could help me right now if I did.

Then again, if she ended up going missing, someone needed to know where she'd been last, so she left Braden a quick voicemail. "Listen, I'm at the Monroe place—Driftwood Manor? I climbed the steps from the shore. Someone's sneaking around the house. Can you get here fast?"

Her gun easily accessible, she rushed forward, keeping her eyes on the area around her. The shadowed figure—a man, if she was going by height and build—had gone to the back of the mansion, closer to the cliffside. She could bang on the front door. Two old classics—a Mercedes and a Jag—sat in the drive. Somebody was home.

Cressida approached the double door with the lion's-head knocker. Another classic. She would love a picture of that and to document this entire experience from a journalist's point of view, but later. Grabbing the lion knocker, she banged on the door, and she also pressed the doorbell many times as she stared at the doorbell camera.

Bang.

Bell.

Bang.

Bell.

Nothing. Nada.

Her palms grew slick. Had someone already gained access to the house and started wreaking havoc? Causing harm took mere seconds.

She banged again and spoke into the camera. "This is Cressida Valentine. Please open up. It's an emergency."

The door creaked open, and a tall, trim woman literally looked down her nose. Or maybe that was Cressida's perception.

"May I help you?"

"Hi, I apologize for the interruption. I saw an intruder. Someone creeping around the house."

"Are you referring to yourself?"

"Me? No. I . . . I was walking the trail and approaching when I saw someone."

"We have security cameras. I saw you approaching and no one else."

"Whoever crept to the back of the house probably knows how to avoid the cameras." Cressida frowned and shook her head. "I'm sorry, I didn't get your name."

"Madeline Chase."

Oh! "My name is Cressida Valentine, and we spoke recently. I'm hoping to interview Mrs. Monroe." And now might be a great time to use the fact that her mother was Octavia Dane, but really, no one outside of political circles knew that name. And if they did, she'd embarrass her mother with this intrusion. Besides, Cressida would never use her mother to help her. Ever. Again.

Madeline huffed like a pro. "I told you that Mrs. Monroe wasn't available, and now you show up here using an imaginary intruder as an excuse. I'm calling the police."

"Please, call the police," Cressida said. "Someone is creeping around your house. Sneaking in the shadows."

The woman started to swing the door closed, then the sound of glass shattering came from inside. Madeline hesitated, her eyes wide as she looked back at Cressida, failing to keep her composure.

Before Madeline could shut her out, she stepped into the house, weapon drawn. "We need to protect Mrs. Monroe."

"She isn't even here. She isn't due back until later this month."

Despite the weird situation, a little hope danced around inside. Maybe that was the sole reason that Mrs. Monroe couldn't see her for an interview. Mrs. Monroe wasn't even here. But Madeline had failed to communicate that information. She was a protective assistant, and Mrs. Monroe probably chose her for that reason.

Gripping her gun, Cressida eyed Madeline. "Then let's get out of the house and call the police, just like you said."

"Is that necessary?" She gestured at the gun. "Do you even know what you're doing? You said nothing about being law enforcement."

"Shh." Cressida took some joy from shushing Miss Smug. She opened the door for their escape. "Let's go. We can call the police to check the house. Going back in isn't safe."

"You're wasting my time. It's probably nothing." Madeline held the door for Cressida to leave.

"I'm not leaving until I know you're safe." Was this one of those too-stupid-to-live moments? Well, if this woman was too stubborn to listen to her about an intruder, she couldn't leave without doing what she could. "Do you have a safe room where we could hide?"

"No. You're leaving right now. I insist."

Cressida ground her teeth, but she had an idea. "I can't force you into safety. But instead of waiting in the house, can you please give me a ride to Cedar Trails?"

"Call a cab."

The door slammed in her face. Cressida stared at the lion knocker. How could anyone be so callous, so rude? Then again, Madeline could see Cressida as an obnoxious gun-wielding trespasser, and she'd just blown any chance she had with Madeline of coordinating an interview with Evelyn Monroe.

She'd had her self-justifications for taking those steps, and now here she was on the porch of a house where an intruder had entered. She let panic take over and checked her cell again. Cressida was ecstatic to have three bars at the house and called 911 to report the intruder and her location.

The dispatcher was reassuring. "Is the intruder still in the house?"

"Um . . . I'm not sure."

"Find a safe place to wait."

Okay. "I'm actually outside." She cringed. "This isn't my house. I saw someone break in. I tried to—" Cressida stepped out from under the eave, and her connection immediately dropped.

What? Of course. Just as well, or she would have gone on to detail that she'd been kicked out of the house. She kept her gun at her side. Just in case. She had no plans to hike along the trail through those dark woods, then down the steps at night. Getting a bar again near the porch, Cressida called the Cedar Trails main number to ask Remi for help.

Bright white lights from an approaching vehicle lit up the drive, and emergency lights suddenly flashed as well. She hadn't expected such a fast response in this large county that was only covered by a sheriff's department almost an hour away.

The vehicle screeched to a halt on the circular drive, and someone jumped out and rushed forward, his familiar protective demeanor flooding her with relief and warmth.

"Cressida! What on earth? Are you okay?"

I am now.

Braden Sanders to the rescue.

8

He gripped his 9mm Smith & Wesson at his side. When he'd gotten her message, his pulse skyrocketed. This incident was the perfect example of why he needed to stay closer to the bay instead of going into the county seat. The town of Forestview might not be close enough.

Cressida blinked up at him, relief clear in her gaze and the drop of her shoulders.

"I got your voicemail. Then I heard a call for assistance on the radio. Are you okay? Where's the intruder?"

She gestured over her shoulder. "Someone crept to the back of the house. I knocked on the door and spoke with Madeline. We heard a noise—sounded like glass breaking. But she didn't think it was anything to worry about and shut me out."

Braden approached the double doors and rang the doorbell. "This is Detective Sanders of the Timberbrook County Sheriff's Office."

A few seconds ticked by. Braden waited patiently. The place was big, after all. Finally, the door opened to reveal a tall, slender woman who glanced first at Cressida before her gaze landed on him. She appeared visibly perturbed. Not shaken by a supposed intruder.

In case she hadn't heard, he introduced himself again. "And you are? I need your name for my notes." He kept his tone warm and friendly but held that edge of authority. This woman exuded the kind of air that told him she might want to challenge him.

"Madeline Chase," she said. "I work for Mrs. Monroe."

"We received a report of an intruder."

"It was a false alarm, Detective. There's no intruder here."

"Is Mrs. Monroe available? I'd like to speak with her."

"She isn't, I'm sorry. She's out of town."

"Ms. Valentine, who's standing behind me, reported seeing someone creeping around your house, then she heard glass breaking inside."

"It was just a vase. I left it too close to the edge of the table in my rush to stop her from knocking one more time."

Braden kept his features neutral. The woman was definitely perturbed.

"Would you mind if I checked your perimeter to make sure whoever was lurking is gone?" Might as well give Cressida the benefit of the doubt.

"You're wasting your time. We have security cameras," Ms. Chase said, "but go ahead."

"With motion detectors?"

She blinked, hesitating a second. "Of course."

Most of them did. He'd wanted to test her knowledge. "Have you looked at the security feed? Was an alarm triggered?"

"Detective, as I said, you're wasting your time."

On you. "You have a good evening." Braden dismissed her with a nod and turned his back to her before she could shut the door.

"Oh, Detective," she called after him.

He turned. "Yes?"

"Please make sure that Ms. Valentine leaves the premises. She's the only intruder of which I'm aware."

He said nothing and turned to walk toward the car, gesturing for Cressida to join him. He held the passenger door open for her.

Cressida hesitated, her eyes narrowing.

"You need a ride?" he asked.

"I do, thanks. Are you going to check the perimeter in spite of her claims?"

"Yes. I believe you." He held her gaze, making sure she understood. "You can wait in the vehicle, safe and sound, while I do. Lock the doors."

Once Cressida got inside, he eyed the surrounding area and made quick work of the grounds near the house. Noted the cameras. Since they were easy to spot, they would be easy to avoid. Using his flashlight, he found no obvious footprints, but he could be messing them up if they existed.

He jogged back to the county vehicle and got inside. Started it.

Cressida watched him. "Well? Did you find evidence of an intruder?"

"It's dark, so I could have missed something, but no."

"What about the windows at the back? Did you see anything broken?"

"No." He steered around the circular drive. "Listen, I believe you. I'll have a deputy drive by again tonight and make sure the woman's okay."

She blew out a breath and settled into the seat next to him.

"But I have to ask," he said. "What were you doing here? You must have walked since you have no transportation."

"Yeah, about that. I was on the beach below the house, and I saw the steps. They don't say they're private, so why not?"

"Fair enough. I came by the cabin earlier and you weren't there, so I looked for you on the beach, but I must have missed you."

"You were looking for me? You must have had something to tell me. What did you learn?"

"I have a forensic artist who can meet with you tomorrow."

"Oh, good. Anything else?"

"Not yet. I'm surprised that you went back to the beach so soon. You're resilient, I'll give you that." He remained concerned. "Remi said you got a package."

"My journal was returned. I must have left it on the boat. Captain Malloy had made it clear that he was leaving the area, and it surprised me. He had to have come back to give the journal to me."

"Did he say why he was leaving?"

"He hadn't wanted to come to begin with. I paid him a lot to bring me."

"And why would you do that? Why not find another charter?"

"My dad somehow ended up with him. I was just following his exact journey. Oh, but Malloy left a note with the journal, reminding me to watch my back."

Cressida should have contacted Braden immediately, but she hadn't, and that unsettled him. "At what point did you decide it was a good idea to go back to the beach? I'm assuming you went alone because you're here. Alone."

"Well, when you put it that way . . . but it wasn't like that. I talked to a therapist on the phone, and I felt encouraged. I believed that I needed to get outside. Get fresh air and clear my head. If I sat in that cabin alone with my thoughts, with the memories of the attack, things would only go downhill. I need to finish Dad's book. I'm not going to let that jerk who tried to drown me interfere with my mission here."

Braden admired this woman. She was made of strong stuff. And maybe that made her overconfident or push too hard. He wasn't sure yet. He turned onto the road to Cedar Trails Lodge, steered down the long drive, then finally parked. Cressida started to get out.

"Wait." If only he could be up-front with her about who he was. Why he was here.

She sat back and looked at him. "What?"

"We'll get this man who attacked you, okay? Until then, please don't go anywhere alone."

"Don't worry. I won't." She sighed. "On the beach, I thought someone might have followed me. But there were a lot of people, and I could have been wrong. So that's why I ended up taking those steps. That and, well, I also need to interview Evelyn Monroe. Except I blew any chance I had tonight of ever getting past her gatekeeper, Madeline Chase. Did you get the feeling she didn't like me?"

"She doesn't like anyone." Probably not something a detective should say. Needed to keep it professional.

Except he was already in this for personal reasons, having been coerced into being here in the first place. "Let me work on that interview for you. I might know someone who can help."

They got out of the vehicle and started walking on the woodsy trail toward her cabin. He didn't like this one bit. Maybe he could press her to move without any pushback. "I think you need to stay in the lodge."

"Braden!" Remi called and hurried across the parking lot. She slowed on her approach. "And Cressida. Your room at the lodge is ready now. A couple checked out early. You still want it?"

"I've grown to like the cabin, but—"

"She'll take it," Braden answered for her. "I advise you to take it for your safety."

Cressida looked between them, hesitating for a moment, then, "Thanks, Remi. I'll just go get my stuff from the cabin."

"I'll help," Braden said.

"I'm in too," Remi said.

"Guys. I'm good. I only have a duffel and an empty computer bag. Oh, and your leather jacket."

Whatever. Both Braden and Remi assisted Cressida with her move from the cabin to the room on the second floor of the lodge, and he got his jacket back.

She gasped. "A room with a view. This is fantastic. I can't thank you enough."

"She also needs to interview Evelyn Monroe. Can you help with that?" Braden asked Remi. "Since you know her well."

"You know her?" Cressida's eyes brightened.

"She's my boss. I'll see what I can do," Remi said. "Find me tomorrow and let's talk. I'll need to know more before I ask her."

"Sure, that's great. I appreciate it."

"Don't thank me yet," Remi said.

"You should be safe here tonight." Braden would make sure of it.

Remi and Braden left Cressida alone, and he followed the lodge manager down the steps, then tugged her aside. "I'd like a room. I know it's your busy season, but please tell me that you have something available."

She arched a brow. "Oh? This doesn't sound like regular county sheriff's office procedure. Is it something more?"

"It's not what you think." He shook his head. "I'll pay full price, of course."

"A room is opening up tomorrow. Just talked to a couple who has to leave in the morning. Her mother is in the hospital. As soon as it's available, it's yours."

"I appreciate that."

He left Remi and exited the lodge. Checked the grounds, the cabins, and the campground, which had opened for the summer. He could have borrowed an RV to park at the campground, but then again staying in the lodge was closer to Cressida and his mission. Cressida might not like him there, but she didn't even have to know.

Darkness had settled at Cedar Trails. Campfires lit up the area near the cabins and campground, and security lights at the lodge gave off enough light he could see. He stood at the top of the stairs that led down to the rocky beach and looked up at the stars. He could see so many more here than in the city. The clouds had cleared away. If he waited long enough, and let his eyes adjust, he might even see the Milky Way.

He wasn't looking forward to what came next. Octavia hadn't returned his call for whatever reason, but he would call her again. She was three hours ahead of him on the East Coast, and probably asleep.

Fortunately, she answered.

"Braden?" Octavia sounded groggy.

He'd woken her. "Yes."

"You wouldn't call without a reason," she said.

"I called you earlier today. Why didn't you call me back?"

"You didn't leave a message."

"You told me not to. That you'd call me back. What's the reason you sent me here? I want to hear it from you."

She grumbled, then gasped as though finally waking up to the realization. "You've seen her, then."

"Your daughter is here, yes." Maybe he should have held back to hear what more she might have told him, but he wasn't going to play games. "She was attacked on the beach."

"Oh no. Braden. Please, tell me my baby is all right."

"Yes. Someone left her for dead and stole from her." With the words, the pent-up anger boiled to the surface, but he reined it in . . . to a point. This woman had saved his niece's life. "Why not tell me so I could be prepared? Why not talk to her so she could know she's in danger? Because she is, and I have a feeling you know what it's about. Now I need you to tell me."

9

ressida opened her eyes to strange surroundings.
Memories rushed at her, and for a heartbeat, panic
set in. Her pulse soared.

Oh, that's right. Last night she'd moved into Cedar Trails
Lodge instead of the cabin. She was safe here. Nothing to
fear. She took in a few long breaths to let her heart rate
slow, then rolled over to stare out the open window that
faced west. She felt rested, which surprised her after the
last couple of days she'd had. Unfortunately, her body still
ached, and she was sure she'd find a few new bruises this
morning.

But she wouldn't let the pain stop her.

She listened to the mesmerizing lull of waves lapping
the beach, some crashing on the rocks. Maybe the soothing sounds of the ocean were the reason she'd slept. Pulling herself from the bed, she looked out over the vast blue
water. How had she ended up in such a beautiful place? The
original cabin was great but couldn't beat this.

Thank you, God.

He was looking out for her. She just had to trust that. To believe it.

She grabbed her camera and peered through, using the zoom feature. She searched the horizon but couldn't get beyond the thick cloud of marine fog rolling in again. Did this happen every morning, then burn off in the afternoon?

Just once she'd like to see the *Specter's Bounty*, but given that was a rare event, she was holding on to false hope. She'd been able to secure a guided scuba dive tour down to a couple of shipwrecks for Dad's book and could adequately write the details and experiences. But the *Specter's Bounty* remained floating, lost in an endless cycle of currents that carried it around the Pacific, so it wasn't a wreck she could dive down to see. Still, it must have a history—that included both truth and lore—the stories people built around the mystery. Cressida was here to learn more.

She put her camera away and got ready. After breakfast, she was supposed to meet Remi in her office. If her laptop wasn't retrieved soon, she would need to get a new one at the nearest store so she could work. She would use her digital wallet on her cell to buy it. She'd never much appreciated that feature until this moment.

She hadn't heard the exact time she would meet with the forensic artist, but she would remain here at Cedar Trails Lodge for the morning, and Braden could track her down. The rental car company had left her an email informing her about a delay in getting the rental car to her, so it might be tomorrow before she got one. Not a problem. Having Braden take her to the museum or show her around could be productive. She could learn more about the area and feel safe with him.

In researching shipwrecks or ghost ships for Dad's book, she followed his travels and also used his tactics. Instead of trusting she could find all the answers online, she interviewed the locals. Visited marine history museums. Cressida had a list of local places, but often once she got out and looked around, she found shops or pictures that weren't listed online. Visiting in person was always best. All in all, there was much information to gather. Notes to keep. Thoughts to get on the page. The journal was important, but she still needed a computer.

After dressing, Cressida headed downstairs, then stood in line to order her coffee and a breakfast sandwich. While waiting, she moseyed over to the photographs and sketches on the wall near the panoramic window.

The photographs of the ocean were breathtaking. Someone had actually caught what resembled a monster's face, maw wide open and menacing. In another shot, the waves formed a woman's face, or at least that's how it appeared. How long had the photographer had to sit and wait to capture these phenomenal images? How many photographs were taken before these few incredible shots were captured? This photographer really stood out to Cressida, and she should know. As an investigative journalist, she'd spent plenty of time with incredible photojournalists.

Her breath caught when her gaze landed on one specific photograph. Thick marine fog . . . and there, just inside the fog, a rusted vessel appeared. Though blurry—barely there, really—she could still make out the shape, and it looked much like the image in the sketch that Dad had stuck in his journal. She searched for the credits, the photographer's name, but found nothing.

The barista approached and handed her a coffee cup.

"Who took these?" Cressida asked.

"You'd have to ask the manager, and there she is. Hey, Remi . . ."

Cressida turned as Remi approached with a smile.

"Just the person I was looking for," Remi said.

The barista left them and headed back to her counter.

"It's nice she brings us coffee, and we don't have to stand around and wait for it."

"I'm pretty sure she called your name." Remi chuckled.

"Oh, wow. Well, this won't let me go. Who took it?"

Remi flicked her gaze to the picture. "The photographer chose to remain anonymous for a reason."

"I'd really like to talk to the photographer. If you know this person, maybe you can pass my information to them."

"We'll see. Why don't we head to my office, and we can talk about that interview."

Inside Remi's office, Cressida sat on the sofa, and Remi sat in a side chair. This had the feel of two old friends drinking coffee and catching up. Remi was obviously well-suited to her job in hospitality. Cressida shared the details about her father and why she wanted to finish his book.

"And the *Specter's Bounty* is the last boat to be included in the book. I have so much information on everything else but not nearly as much on the boat depicted in that photograph on your wall. I'd love to know more. Anything at all you or anyone else can tell me? Something I can't find in a museum? I understand fishermen and sailors can be superstitious, so there must be some talk around the Hidden Bay area about the *Specter's Bounty*." She kept to herself that she hadn't been to the local museum yet. But one thing at a time.

Remi sipped her coffee and stared at Cressida over the rim, possibly giving herself a moment to digest everything Cressida had said.

Cressida continued. "So you can understand why I'd want to speak to this photographer. I'm here to talk to everyone and immerse myself in the area, the Hidden Bay culture. And then, voilà, I find a photograph—an actual photo someone took—at this lodge. I'd say that's fortuitous."

"Fortuitous?" Remi's laugh sounded warm and friendly. Good-natured.

"Yeah, I kind of slip into my father's way of writing and thinking at times. That's a word he loved. I want to keep his voice as I continue with the book."

"Ah." Remi nodded, then said, "To be honest, the photographer has no issue with sharing her name now, but in the past, sure. I didn't want anything to draw attention to myself."

Cressida stared. "*You* took the picture?"

"I did."

"I'm impressed. You're quite accomplished with running a lodge like this and taking such exceptional photographs. With that kind of patience and talent, you could work for—I don't know—*National Geographic.*" Cressida could potentially reach out to her contacts in her world . . . except that wouldn't do anyone any good. She was now well-removed. Besides, she knew nothing at all about Remi. The woman could very well have been working for a magazine as prestigious as *National Geographic* before she came to Hidden Bay. She'd mentioned that in the past she wanted to hide. Interesting.

Cressida set the coffee mug on the side table and opened her notebook. "Do you have time to talk about your photographs now?"

"What's there to say?"

"What about the *Specter's Bounty*? When did you take that shot? I'd love to hear the circumstances. Did you know what you were looking at when you took the picture? I guess I need to schedule a longer interview with you."

Remi smiled. "I think that's a good idea. For now, let's stick to the reason you want to speak to Evelyn Monroe. You're here about the *Specter's Bounty*, so why the interest in Mrs. Monroe?"

"You sound like her gatekeeper, Madeline." Cressida wanted to keep things light and friendly. She leaned forward and held Remi's gaze. "I want to talk to her because my father had her name in his sparse notes of the vessel. He had one question—""Does Evelyn Monroe know?" No other notes. She got the sense it was all tacked on to his otherwise well-organized plans.

"What? You think she has a connection to the ghost ship?"

Cressida lifted a shoulder. "That's what I hope to find out."

Remi pushed to stand. "She's eccentric and keeps to herself for the most part, but she's generous beyond imagination. I'd love to know more about her story as well. Honestly, this might be harder than I thought."

Remi pursed her lips and paced. She was overthinking, and this could be bad for Cressida.

"Listen, don't worry about it," Cressida said. "I spent years in investigative journalism, and I can find another way to talk to her."

"No, no you won't. She's an enigma, and she rarely leaves her house. I just didn't realize there might be a possible connection between her and the *Specter's Bounty*, and now you have me intrigued."

"Weren't you curious at all about it before? After all, you took the photograph."

Remi lifted a shoulder. "I guess. Maybe. I let my curiosity go because everyone has so much fun with the fact that a few have seen an actual ghost ship, an abandoned boat appearing in the fog, and it looks so creepy and adds to the atmosphere."

"Of this storm-watching lodge, too, I'd imagine."

"That's fair. And I guess now that you're here bringing it to my attention, I'd like to know what it's about. What happened to the crew? Why has it been left to float out there? The answer is probably at the museum. But if there's anything unknown about it, you're going to find that out for us, aren't you?"

"That's the plan. I have to talk to the right people first. Mrs. Monroe's assistant told me last night that she was traveling and not at home."

Remi's face tightened. "I'll look into things and see if I can get you that interview. If I can't, I'll let you know, and you can work your magic as a journalist. It's all I can offer."

"That's all I can ask. Thank you very much, Remi. And I'd still love that interview with *you*, so can we set that up?"

"Of course." A knock came at the door, and Remi rushed to open it while saying, "Let's talk in a day or two. I'll carve out some time for you."

The door opened, and a woman with long dark hair stepped inside.

"Hi, Jo," Remi said.

Jo's eyes landed on Cressida. "I was told I could find Cressida Valentine here."

Cressida stood. "And you did."

Stepping forward, the woman thrust out her hand. "I'm Jo Cattrel, and I'm a forensic artist." She glanced at Remi. "Was I interrupting anything? I can come back, and we can work together at another time."

"No, this is fine," Cressida said.

"Great. I have an art studio here on the grounds. Follow me, then." Jo smiled. To Remi she said, "I'll see you later."

Cressida perceived that they were friends, and she started to relax, if only a little. Though she'd been attacked on the beach and warned to watch her back, then Madeline had been nasty, there were still some solid and kind people around. She'd count Braden in that group as well.

And she wouldn't forget his urging that she shouldn't go anywhere alone.

Jo led Cressida away from the lodge and toward the woods. "I have a special cabin that serves as both my quarters— because I continue to work with Remi at Cedar Trails—and my art studio as well. I've been working so frequently as a forensic artist, though, I'm not sure how much longer I can work for Remi."

As she talked, she led Cressida through the thick and beautiful woods, not so far that they couldn't see the lodge, though.

"I'm so sorry that you were attacked on the beach. I know that had to be terrifying. Hidden Bay is for the most part a peaceful and safe place." Inside the cabin, Jo motioned for Cressida to have a seat in a comfortable chair across from where she sat with a sketch pad. "Any danger that comes is usually brought here from the outside."

"You mean people bring danger with them when they come?"

"Yes."

So you have to ask yourself—what danger did you bring with you? Jo hadn't said the question out loud, but Cressida had the feeling she was thinking it.

10

Waiting, Braden stood next to a tree near Jo's cabin. He assumed that she and Cressida were still at work on the composite sketch. Remi had explained they left the lodge less than half an hour ago. So he'd give the two the time they needed.

After what he'd learned from Octavia last night, he'd been furious. He'd taken a ride on his bike on the dark, rain-slick roads. Even then, he'd still needed to cool off.

Octavia had known that eventually Cressida would show up in Hidden Bay for the simple reason that Cressida had taken on her father's project. Though Octavia hadn't told Braden, he fully expected that she had somehow been following or keeping track of her daughter. She'd tried to warn Cressida away from this project, but after sinking Cressida's career over an exposé she'd been working on, Octavia had no more say in her life.

Cressida refused to speak to her mother.

The only connection Cressida still wanted was with her father—and he was dead. Braden understood that she'd thrown herself completely into finishing this book for him as a way to get through the hurt and pain. Still, he couldn't imagine, for any reason, not speaking to family. But what did he know about it?

Octavia Dane was brilliant. Manipulative and powerful. A force to be reckoned with. He wanted to ask her why sinking the exposé had been worth risking her relationship with Cressida, but he'd cross that bridge later.

He thought back to the conversation.

"I'm concerned that her father was killed because he ran across delicate information." Octavia had sounded like she might choke up with tears.

Braden didn't know if that was an act or if she could actually show sincere emotion.

"Delicate?"

"Dangerous."

"I'm going to need more," he said.

"He came back to see me. Cut his trip short, leaving Washington state. But he died before he could talk to me. I think it was about whatever he discovered in Hidden Bay."

"You *think*. There's nothing that you *know*?" Why had the man believed he needed to talk to Octavia about his discovery?

"Braden, please, just trust me."

Trust her?

"Cressida's caught in the middle. I was right to listen to my instincts and send you there. I'm so relieved that you . . ."

Complied. Like he had any choice. "I'm here. What more can you tell me so I can navigate this and protect her?"

"I've told you everything I can. Protect her, and maybe seeing this through with her will help you to discover what it's about."

"Everything I can."

Braden had instincts too. And his instincts told him that Octavia Dane already knew exactly what it was about, but she had to stay hands-off and keep her distance while she let him get his hands dirty.

After the call and the ride, he'd worked late into the night, following what few leads he had. Captain Everett "Salty" Malloy had delivered Cressida's father, Alaric Dane, to Hidden Bay. He'd also delivered Cressida with a warning. Braden had learned that Malloy had previously been a Navy guy who specialized in salvage operations, which didn't send up any red flags, but Braden would continue to dig and also try to get ahold of the guy so he could question him about his warnings to Cressida. Braden also learned by looking at Malloy's social media that he belonged to a Facebook page for a group who dressed up like pirates. Not to be confused with the Hidden Bay liveaboard pirates. What had happened on the *Mariner's Gambit* per Cressida's statement regarding Malloy's almost run-in with a speedboat?

The door opened, pulling his thoughts to the moment. Fiery-haired Cressida stepped out, along with Jo, both still deep in discussion.

Braden started toward them. He ignored that awkward feeling that suddenly rose in his chest at the sight of Cressida. Uncertainty gripped him, which he also ignored. Was his unease because he might be a little bit taken with her, which was ridiculous, or was it about the secret that weighed him down? A secret that, if she found out, would be the end of them.

He shut down the thoughts. *Get a grip. I'm a cop. A detective. Former DSS agent.*

And he was just doing his job. Mid-conversation, Cressida tore her gaze from Jo to look at him. Her striking pale eyes grew wide, then a warm, hesitant smile brightened her face. In that one look, he caught something he hadn't expected. She was glad to see him . . . on a personal level.

Or was he reading her wrong? He shoved the utterly un-professional thoughts away and approached.

"Ms. Valentine." He nodded with a grin, then looked to Jo. "Jo. It's good to see you."

"Just Cressida, please. We talked about this," she said. "I don't like anyone to call me by anything else."

He hadn't wanted to be that personal in front of Jo. "How'd it go?" he asked them both.

"Come inside and see the sketch." Jo led them back inside to her art studio, where she handed off the sketch.

He took a picture of it with his cell. "I'll make sure this image gets out to law enforcement. Can you stick this in an envelope for me so the hard copy gets to the office and you get paid?"

"Sure." While Jo found an envelope, Braden studied Cressida, who was taking in Jo's amazing art.

She lifted her face and caught him.

"Are you okay?" he asked. "It can't be easy having to go through the details of the man who attacked you all over again."

"I'm one step closer to justice," she said.

And you're a survivor. "What do you have planned today?"

She angled her head so that her long, curly hair fell to the side. "I thought I'd find my way down to the marina."

"Sorry, guys, I have to take this." Jo answered a call on her radio.

Cressida waved goodbye. She and Braden exited the art studio.

The marina, huh? Not without him. "I can take you."

"Detectives don't usually chauffeur people around, do they?"

He adjusted his jacket, letting his gaze scan the surround-ings. "I was going that way anyway. I thought we could talk about the case. Besides, I have a surprise for you in my car."

Eyes wide, she sucked in a breath. "My laptop?"

Oh, he hated to disappoint her. "Not yet. But I do have your bag with your stuff. We've already searched for fingerprints and found nothing."

He'd confirmed her ID—Cressida Valentine Dane—per protocol and for the record.

"Let's go, then." She walked with him back to the parking lot and to his car.

He handed her the bag, and she dug through, looking as thrilled as he would expect.

"Still want to go to the marina?" he asked. "My offer still stands."

She glanced up at him, looked off, then back. "What if you get called out on another crime?"

"I won't. This investigation and your safety are my priority." Push too hard and she would get suspicious. In fact, those gears were already turning behind her gaze. Brilliant like her mother. She'd have his number before he knew it. But she wouldn't find much about him in the usual places on the internet. Octavia had made sure to scrub what little was out there—for her own protection.

"If you're sure, I'd love a ride," she said. "I have some questions for you too, and I want to go first."

Uh-oh. He hadn't expected that. She'd pulled herself together quickly, and that impressed him.

With the forensic sketch tucked in a file folder in the back seat, Cressida Dane buckled in the front, and the information Octavia had shared with him last night rolling around in his head, Braden steered out of Cedar Trails Lodge and Resort.

He drove slowly to give them more time. "You said you had questions."

"Captain Malloy suggested I talk to Diggins about the *Specter's Bounty*. Malloy says he's one of a group of people who live on their boats out in the bay that call themselves pirates. *Pirates.*" Her eyes grew big in exaggerated incredulity as she repeated the word. "Do you know about them? Do you know Diggins?"

Everyone calls themselves pirates around here. Braden had investigated the boaters after an incident last year and questioned them. "I know a few things about him. For one, Diggins is his nickname. His real name is Jonas Daggerty. The liveaboards call him their captain, or rather 'pirate king.' Their name is for fun, and it works really well with the upcoming Hidden Bay Pirates' Bash. And he's like a bazillion years old but gets around like he's a very lively seventy."

"How did he earn the name Diggins?"

Braden scratched his temple as he turned onto the picturesque descent into Hidden Bay. "I couldn't tell you with any certainty, but it might have something to do with him digging into the past. It's not something you can find on the internet. Decades ago, he captained a commercial fishing vessel, and his boat was impounded for allegedly smuggling illegal artifacts. He avoided jail. I don't know all the details."

"How did you find out?"

"Through law enforcement connections, archives." He cracked a grin. "And he told me most of it."

"That was really honest of him."

"He claims he has nothing to hide, that everyone knows about it, so you have a good idea of what you're going into."

"You know, sounds like I could write an entire book on the characters who live in Hidden Bay, outside of this book I'm trying to finish for Dad."

And once she learned about Braden's background, she would either blast him in that book or erase his existence—to her—altogether. Like she'd done her mother.

"What else can you tell me?" she asked.

"He was the first one to live on his boat anchored out in

the bay and brought in others. Couldn't afford the moorage, or didn't want to pay for it. I'm not sure."

"And who knows," she said. "With his background, maybe he really was a pirate. Could still be."

"I shouldn't have said anything. He's a nice guy. Warm and friendly. He's an old guy, and what's past is past. He could have been innocent." Why had he told her that story? To win points?

"I hear you," she said. "As for living out in the bay and not paying moorage, he's a bit of a rebel?"

"That's my opinion. Nice guy and rebel."

"I usually don't do this," she said.

"Do what?" he asked.

"I usually like to walk into a situation knowing very little about a person so I can make my own judgments," she said. "I'm sure that's atypical for journalists."

"I don't like to talk about people either, especially sharing their background," he said.

"Sounds like the voice of experience. I don't know why I asked you, because what you've told me will color any opinion I have." She angled her head, a smirk in her eyes.

"An experience we've all been through."

"I agree one hundred percent." She offered a soft smile.

"You know the bad, now let me share the good. Diggins mentors those who can't afford to live on the land. Teaches them how to live on their boats. I admire that about him. He's helping others. Sometimes the laws of the land are just too much, too hard, and a burden for the little guy. There's a group of liveaboards in Puget Sound as well. Marinas have rules and restrictions, and a lot of the boats, well, frankly, don't measure up to the required standards. Expensive insurance. No one wants to insure a wooden hull, that sort of thing."

"Is that your opinion too? They don't measure up?"

"No, I'm sharing what I've heard from the locals, though

honestly, there aren't a lot of people who complain. Hidden Bay is probably a perfect spot for the liveaboards. Only a couple of mansions looking out over the ocean, and they're both situated on either end of the bay, almost like sentinels. Bottom line is that, at the end of the day, these people are certainly not pirates in a criminal way."

"But in a character way? Like maybe a salt-of-the-earth kind of way?"

"Maybe in a salt-of-the-ocean kind of way." He cringed. "Bad, huh?"

She chuckled. "You get points for trying to make me laugh, because it worked."

"I can come with you to talk to Diggins if you want."

"No offense, but you're a cop, and I don't want him to withhold information."

He frowned as he parked at the marina. "I'm exactly the person from whom people should *not* withhold information. But I get it. Unless he's at the marina or comes ashore for some reason, you'll need to take a boat out to talk to him. After what happened, do you really think it's safe?"

"Of course not. I admit that I made a mistake even going out for a simple walk on the beach. Don't hold that against me. I'm not stupid."

"I would never say that. You're a survivor, and you're on a mission."

"I have an idea," she said. "Malloy said that Mavis at the chandlery could tell me how to talk to Diggins. I'll find out from her, then I'll come back and tell you."

"Mavis is also the unofficial harbormaster, so don't let her tell you she doesn't know how to reach Diggins."

Cressida tilted her head just so and smiled, her eyes so serious. "Thank you for that."

You're welcome. "Once you find out, then we'll talk about how to proceed. Deal?"

"Deal," she said. "Maybe we can talk about it over dinner."

"Sounds like a plan." Except the dinner part. He could never have a personal relationship with her because, one, he was investigating her case, and two, he was working for her mother, unofficially, and once she found out, she wouldn't speak to him again. And if he told Cressida all of it . . . would Octavia discontinue her assistance with Elise? Braden simply couldn't risk it.

The woman had put him in a precarious position.

That was her modus operandi, and if he didn't watch out, her daughter would do the same to him. He had the feeling she was trying to do just that without having a clue.

11

Cressida left Braden by his car, relieved he hadn't resisted her plan so far. The sun shone bright on the water, but the cool bite in the wind reminded her she was in the Pacific Northwest. She strolled along the planked walkway toward the Bayfront Chandlery. A large portion of the boats in the slips were older, some in need of repair. Many slips were completely empty. She might not have noticed if it weren't for Braden's tale about the liveaboards out on the water.

Officials were preparing for the Hidden Bay Pirates' Bash. Nautical elements—fishing nets, barrels, treasure chests, wheels, anchors, and more—were set about on tables. A couple of guys erected large tents and, sure enough, pirate flags. Someone was stringing twinkling lights about the area. A big sign advertised sea shanties sung by a local band, skits, and treasure hunts.

And her favorite was a game called "Walk the Plank."

She had every intention of attending the event to enjoy the local maritime culture and perhaps learn more about what the locals had to say about the ghost ship. She could add more to her father's book.

Oh, Dad, it would have been fun to be here with you.

No time to get melancholic. How far had Dad gotten? Had he talked to Diggins before cutting his research short? She couldn't wait to meet the guy, especially after Braden had described such a colorful character. When she was done talking to Mavis about communicating with Diggins, her next business was to secure another laptop.

She pushed through the door to find Mavis behind the counter today. Her smile was big but faded slightly when she realized Cressida had entered her domain.

Cressida, the woman who'd committed the crime of being a victim, and that news could scare away potential tourists.

"Good morning," Cressida said.

"What can I do for you?" Fear and suspicion laced her words.

Hello, I'm the victim! But she wouldn't use that to her advantage. She'd take the high ground. Did Mavis actually think Cressida would cause her trouble? "I'm looking forward to the festivities."

"Oh, you're staying around for the Pirates' Bash?"

"I wouldn't miss it for the world, but there *is* something you can do for me. I'm working on completing my father's book. He passed away last year." Yeah, she was using the sympathy angle, and why not?

"Oh, I'm sorry for your loss." Mavis's attitude shifted slightly. Who couldn't relate to losing a loved one? "It's wonderful you're taking the time to finish what he started."

Cressida relaxed a little, finally making a connection with this woman. In fact, before she left, she would make a big purchase as a show of goodwill. "He was a maritime historian," Cressida continued. "I'm here for research, and I would love to chat with Captain Diggins." Cressida brightened her eyes. "I'm sure he has so many stories to share."

Cressida glanced through the big windows to focus on

the group of boats floating deep in the bay, then back to the woman.

Mavis's demeanor once again shifted as she narrowed her eyes, but then she forced a smile. She hadn't learned how to school her features. "I have no idea how to contact him."

"Oh, but don't you?" Cressida didn't believe her, and Braden had warned her. "He owns a boat in the bay and must frequent your shop. I hear you're kind of the unofficial harbormaster."

"He comes and goes. Lots of people do. I don't keep their contact information in an old-fashioned Rolodex."

"Will he participate in the Pirates' Bash? Seems like he and the others would since they call themselves pirates."

"I'm assuming so, but I can't know that."

"Can you at least get him a message for me?" Cressida pulled out her business card, relieved that her bag had been returned. She laid the card on the counter, then pushed it forward.

The woman lifted it. "Cressida Valentine."

She wasn't sure the woman had remembered her name from two days ago. "Yes. My cell number and email are on the card. You can do that for me, can't you?"

"Of course. I'll give it to him if I see him."

Emphasis on *if*.

"And please feel free to call me if you learn of a way I can contact him directly." Cressida smiled. "I'm going to browse your shop now."

She left the counter to look at all the boating paraphernalia and supplies, touristy gifts, and a couple of grocery aisles. Along the top of the wall, black-and-white photos depicted fishermen, boating activities, sea lions, and a breaching whale. Everything one would expect to see.

One of the photos caught her attention and included a signature at the bottom, as if from a famous actor. Jonas

"Diggins" Daggerty. Cressida took a photo of it. Now she knew what he looked like in general, but this photograph was definitely a man much younger than a bazillion years, or even seventy.

Cressida searched for something to purchase and stayed near the photographs. And there she found it. A few historical photographs of the marina from years before, including a fully intact dock and building—the Hidden Bay Museum that had burned. The image wasn't overly large, but at fifteen by thirty inches or so, it wasn't easy to carry to the counter. "I want to buy this, but it doesn't have a price on it."

"Because it's not for sale."

Cressida wanted to make friends. "Please. I see you have another picture of the museum. I would love to include this in my father's book. I'd love to own it. This is my last stop before I start compiling the manuscript. Name your price." She wished she hadn't added that last part.

Mavis stared at the image, pursing her lips. "I don't know. A hundred bucks?"

"A hundred bucks it is."

The woman's smile seemed genuine. Cressida smiled too, feeling equally as genuine. The purchase was well worth it to earn this woman's trust and cooperation. Whatever it took. "This will be perfect. I can't thank you enough. You can have the frame though. Just stick this in a bag if you have it, or a large envelope. Anything."

Mavis disappeared into the back room and, a few moments later, appeared again and handed off the gently wrapped photograph—at least the image was on hard card stock.

"I'll contact you as soon as I pass your card along," Mavis said, "so you'll know."

Progress.

"Thank you, Mavis. I'll be here a few days, and I'll see you again soon."

Thrilled that she'd accomplished her task, Cressida left and strolled the sidewalk, taking in the salty, fishy smells and the chirps of seagulls fighting over dinner. In the distance, honking, noisy sea lions relaxed on a rocky outcropping. Holding the photograph under one arm, she lifted her cell to take a picture, wishing she'd brought her good camera.

She found Braden walking the planks—pacing back and forth, actually—and on his *cell*? He eyed her as she approached. Even though he spoke into the cell, his bright-blue eyes were sharp and took her in like he focused on her alone. Her heart sped up.

He ended his call. "Well?"

"I want to know how you got a cell signal."

He looked at his phone. "Sometimes you get lucky. So how'd it go?"

He glanced at the package she held.

She shrugged. "She's going to pass on my contact information. I'll give it a day, and then I'll just have you take me out there. Not sure if I need to rent a boat or if you have one." She gestured to the docked boats.

"I'll take care of it. What next?"

"What about that museum you mentioned? I bought a picture of the museum when it was here at the marina. If possible, I'll include it in Dad's book."

"Let's grab a quick lunch, and then . . . Hidden Bay Museum, here we come."

12

I n Forestview, they grabbed a quick sandwich at the local Subway, then headed to the Hidden Bay Maritime Museum. Once inside, Braden wasn't sure what he'd expected. Considering the building was new, he was surprised at the overwhelming scent of salt water and burnt wood permeating the place. The builders must have brought some of the old in with the new.

A woman in her sixties welcomed them at the entrance. "Good afternoon. My name is Sheryl. Tickets are fifteen apiece. We used to be free, but with the fire—"

"Oh, no need to explain." Cressida smiled. "We're more than willing to pay. I'm paying for two tickets." She looked at Braden as if to make sure he was okay with her paying.

He said nothing. This was her show.

"Do you want a tour?" Sheryl asked.

"I'd prefer taking my time going through, and then, if I have questions, will you be around?"

"Until two o'clock." Sheryl glanced at the clock, then smiled at Cressida. "We close early today."

Way to let them know that Cressida couldn't really take her time, at least not today.

After Cressida paid, Sheryl stepped aside, and Cressida led the way into the first room, filled with all things nautical. "I'm surprised to see it so packed with artifacts. After a fire, I wouldn't imagine they would have salvaged so much."

Cressida's eyes were bright and beautiful, filled with hope and possibilities. He'd never been interested in history. Marine history in particular. Maybe that's because his dad had been a fisherman out of a small town in Maine and died in a storm when Braden had only been ten. He didn't need the reminders. His mother raised him and his sister, Lauren, while working as a waitress. He didn't relish remembering those hard times. Still, that experience growing up taught him how to work hard.

His throat tightened as they entered, and the images accosted him. He'd give Mom the credit for instilling in him a sense of responsibility and loyalty through hardship. He definitely knew how to prioritize family—and he'd do anything for Lauren and Elise. He supposed, if anything, he should be personally fascinated with Hidden Bay's history—like Cressida was.

Octavia's words from last night came back to him. *"I'm concerned that her father was killed because he ran across delicate information . . . Cressida's caught in the middle . . . Protect her, and maybe seeing this through will help you discover what it's about."*

Her words turned this into an unofficial investigation into Cressida's father's death, or rather a search for why he was killed and if his death was somehow connected to Hidden Bay. To Braden's knowledge, Cressida remained unaware of her mother's suspicions the man might have been murdered. This museum visit could hold answers. Good. He'd found the justification he needed to ignore the memories and focus on the present.

And in this current moment, Cressida's expression as

she took in marine artifacts made him smile. She was a distraction for all the wrong reasons.

"This place is amazing," she said.

Just looked like the normal stuff to him, so he kept his mouth shut. A sextant, a ship's wheel, a boring piece of hull timber. Whaling harpoons and nets. An old nautical chart of Hidden Bay, expanded to cover an entire wall. He continued following Cressida, letting her take her time as she explored. What, specifically, she was looking for that could tie into her research on the *Specter's Bounty*, he wasn't entirely sure. Would the museum even have information on the lost vessel?

She paused in front of a huge anchor belonging to some old ship—the *Sea Fortune*—and looked at him. "The dim lighting and the real wood floors are just the right ambience, don't you think?"

"Hmm?"

"The historical feel. Even though the place is new, someone went to a lot of trouble to make it feel old and build on that setting to take visitors back."

If you say so. "I see."

Sheryl remained in the room, hovering nearby but not too close. Guarding the relics? Available to answer questions?

Cressida continued through the museum, and she talked about various artifacts like she'd been an expert all her life. For all he knew, she had—her father, the maritime historian, would have kept her informed. A display case of barnacle-encrusted planks, brass fittings, and a compass caught her attention. Ship logs. Journals. Faded documents in protective cases. Maps. Charts. Photographs of local ships and ports, and even of Hidden Bay. Then they found the partially burned relics.

Charred remains.

He glanced at his watch. Twenty-two minutes until Sheryl would kick them out.

Cressida read out loud to him about the history of Hidden Bay. "'A remote, small fishing community, founded in the late 1800s, turned out to be ideal for smugglers during Prohibition, while Forestview developed into a thriving local lumber supplier. But the area remains isolated and is known for artists and reclusive retirees.'" She looked up at him to make sure he was listening, then continued. "'The Hidden Bay marine fog lends to the haunted beauty.' I can relate to that. It feels eerie and could be the reason a person gets attacked and nobody sees it."

Before he could respond, she continued. "Look at this. Five years ago, the fire swept through the marina and destroyed a couple of historic boats and part of the museum."

Nothing she didn't already know. Braden continued reading along with her. "Says the case was filed an accident, but whispers of arson lingered."

She glanced up at him. "You're the detective. You don't know about this?"

"I've only been here a few months. Joined the county sheriff's department in February."

She blinked. "I didn't realize that."

She suddenly turned her back on the documents and gave him her full attention, and that could have knocked him over. "What brought you here? I don't know much about you. I mean, not that it's any of my business, but I'd like to know. Where are you from, Detective Sanders? I detect a bit of a New England accent."

She smiled, and he might tell her anything she asked if he wasn't careful.

"I grew up in Maine. My dad was a fisherman."

Her mouth made a perfect O. "So this is old school to you."

"I wouldn't say that. Dad died on one of his trips. As soon as I could, I went into the Army. Not the Navy, mind you." He shrugged. "End of story."

"But still, why are you here?"

He glanced at his watch. "This place closes in fifteen minutes. We can talk about me, or you can learn everything you need to learn while there's still time."

"Oh, you are so right."

He'd dodged the proverbial bullet.

"In fact, I can come back for the history later." She glanced over Braden's shoulder. "Excuse me."

Sheryl came forward eagerly. "Yes, what can I help you with?"

"I'm here to learn more about the *Specter's Bounty*. Do you have any documents or related artifacts?"

The woman chuckled but with a warm smile. "Of course. We have an entire section dedicated to that more recent deserted vessel." She led Cressida and Braden to a far back corner.

To his way of thinking, the local ghost ship story should be front and center.

Sheryl stood next to the photographs of locals and their tales, some handwritten. A photograph or two of the vessels in the fog, like the photograph Remi had taken that was up at the lodge.

"*Endeavor Spirit*?" Cressida read the name, then looked to Sheryl for an explanation.

"Yes. Connected to the *Specter's Bounty*. Begin here for the full story. Built in 1980 for the Harborstone Shipping Company as a state-of-the-art salvage ship. You can read all the details, but I'll skip to the high points since we're closing in ten minutes. Normally, I'd stay late, but—"

"Oh, please, we won't keep you. I can always come back tomorrow. I might come back every day this week."

"I appreciate it. I have to babysit my grandbabies." Sheryl's smile was heartfelt. She turned serious again and continued with her practiced spiel. "The *Endeavor Spirit* was sold to a private shipping company that supposedly was tied to organized crime. Smuggling goods. Weapons. Pharmaceuticals."

"Oh no."

Sheryl nodded. "Rumors only, mind you, but adds to the mystique. In 2010, the *Endeavor Spirit* left Hidden Bay. One of the fiercest storms we've had in the area hit, and it never arrived at its destination. All contact was lost. Originally it was believed to have sunk."

"And the *Specter's Bounty*?" Cressida asked.

"Never saw it again until about ten years ago when suddenly, locals claimed to have seen a salvage vessel drifting aimlessly in the fog, almost unrecognizable as the *Endeavor Spirit*. Then more rumors of secret, mysterious cargo. The Coast Guard boarded it—no one was aboard. They towed it, but another storm hit, and it broke away and was lost again."

"Lost?"

"And renamed. Fishermen and locals in Hidden Bay claim to see it now and then. And it has since been renamed the *Specter's Bounty*. Some believe it carried a mysterious treasure that was stolen but most especially a warning that these waters are dangerous." Sheryl acted as if she practiced telling her grandchildren ghost stories. "You can read the legend here."

She led them over to a big plaque written in an aged, slightly weathered-looking font, giving it an old-world maritime appearance, that said, "The Legend of *Specter's Bounty*."

Sheryl read the tale out loud to them. "'*Specter's Bounty* carried cargo valuable enough that men would kill for it. In

2010, she sent out a single, garbled distress call and then vanished without a trace. No wreckage. No bodies. Just silence. Some say she was hijacked; others believe she was lost to a freak storm. But the strangest stories came later. Fishermen claim to see her massive hull on foggy nights—just beyond the breakers. Some even say they've heard distorted radio transmissions—an eerie SOS from the long-dead crew. If anyone dares to go after the ghost ship, their instruments fail and the *Specter's Bounty* disappears before they get too close. So word is that she is still out there, trapped between worlds, the crew searching for something—or someone—to set them free. The warning is that if you see her lights in the fog, turn back. No one follows the *Specter's Bounty* and lives to tell about it.'" Sheryl's face had grown serious as she put all her energy into the tale, then she smiled and winked. "Fishermen love their tall tales and superstitions."

"That they do," Braden said.

Cressida was here to learn the truth about the *Specter's Bounty* so she could add that to her father's book. But how did they cut through all the fiction? More distressing was the prospect that her father could have been murdered over information he'd learned while on this last part of his trip—per Octavia.

He had to ask, though. "Hold on, an entire crew simply lost at sea, and no one knew about it?" Braden wished he hadn't said the words because he just sounded incredulous and much too emotional. His father had in fact been lost at sea, and he still grappled to understand it. To believe it.

As a kid he was given all kinds of explanations. An entire crew vanishing in a severe storm wasn't unheard of. The more sinister explanations had tortured him as a kid—piracy or hijacking gone wrong. In the case of older vessels, stories of mutiny and foul play took hold. Someone could have kidnapped the crew and left the ship behind.

"I know it can be hard to understand," Sheryl said.

"This is a bit of what my father dealt with in his research," Cressida said. "He shared a story with me about a more recent cargo ship carrying rare earth elements. It reported navigation system failures, then it went completely radio silent. When they found it, the crew was gone. So was the cargo. On international waters, getting answers can be a big problem." Cressida suddenly looked away.

He knew exactly where her mind had gone—to her mother, who was all about international waters. Octavia Dane started out as a protocol officer working in the Bureau of International Organization Affairs. Basically, the State Department. She worked to coordinate and facilitate meetings involving officials who worked with the IMO—International Maritime Organization—an agency most people had never heard of and had no idea the role it played in creating global shipping laws, safety protocols, and environmental regulations. Octavia eventually worked—or manipulated—her way into becoming Deputy Assistant Secretary for Maritime Affairs. That put her in the perfect position to call in favors using the secrets she'd collected.

Given Octavia's position and Cressida's research, maybe there was something to be discovered here after all—something related to a lost ghost ship.

Cressida shuddered slightly, then focused back on Sheryl, who glanced at the clock. "I've been working on my father's book, and not all the so-called ghost ships have an end to their story. This one fascinates me."

"You're looking for the end, then? To solve the mystery?"

"If it's possible, yes. I don't understand how it can be left to just drift out there and endanger other boaters. Isn't the Department of Natural Resources involved?"

"I'm sure it's a complex issue, but you're better off asking the DNR." Sheryl looked at her watch. "I'll tell you what. You come back again this week, and you can get in for free, no charge. Do all the research you want, but I really have to go. I'll see you out."

Cressida seemed preoccupied as they exited the museum, and she got into his vehicle. She turned to him, clearly wanting to talk out her thoughts, and he welcomed that.

"What is it?"

"I'm just thinking through the possible reasons the *Endeavor Spirit*, or *Specter's Bounty*, is still floating around. It wouldn't be the only recent abandoned boat. I could list a few."

"Please don't. I believe you."

"Supposedly it was already towed and escaped during a storm. Weather patterns could have sent it out to the high seas and out of reach. Dense fog could keep it hidden. You name it. The Coast Guard patrols a specific region with their goals in mind—capturing drug runners, for instance. With their priorities, their resources are probably stretched thin, and if *Specter's Bounty* didn't pose a threat, it would be a low priority."

"You mentioned the DNR."

"Yes. If other agencies can't solve an issue surrounding a vessel, they often reach out to the DNR, but that's more local—state, county, and harbor kind of local. It doesn't sound like the *Specter's Bounty* has stayed local long enough for the DNR to be called in."

"What's really bothering you?"

"My overactive imagination, that's all."

"Let's hear it."

"I was thinking, what if someone doesn't want it to be found?"

"You mean someone intentionally sabotages the discovery? Or provides false leads? Why?"

"Like I said. Overactive imagination."

Try, she was more aware of the world in which her mother operated than she was willing to admit.

"At any rate, maybe it's not considered a big threat," she said. "And it's not a pressing concern."

"Not a pressing concern? People are missing," he said. If he ever got closure on what happened to his father, it wouldn't be soon enough—but that mystery would never be solved.

"I know this topic is a reminder of what happened to your father. I'm not sure the authorities—whoever towed the boat to begin with—don't know what happened to them. We should keep digging."

"And in the meantime, we have the folklore surrounding a ghost ship warning people about the dangers out in the deep sea. I'd say that authorities could even dismiss any sightings of it, except for Remi's pictures." He'd admired her photographs the first time he'd seen them at the Cedar Trails Lodge.

Cressida nodded and turned to stare straight ahead as if dismissing their conversation.

"I should get you back." On the drive, Braden gave Cressida her space. The same space he needed to process the information they'd learned. Octavia had insisted he see this through, but to what end? What could he and Cressida discover that her father, Alaric, might have also uncovered—something dangerous enough to get him killed? Octavia's request confused him. She had to know some of the truth, if not most of it, and she had to realize that continuing on this path could put him and Cressida in more danger—and Cressida was already there.

Same as her father.

And Braden was walking a very thin line, keeping what little he knew from Cressida.

Finally, he parked at Cedar Trails Lodge. He was unsure how to inform her he planned to stay at the lodge tonight, or if he even should.

She looked at him. "Thanks for today, Braden. The rental company is bringing me the car tomorrow. A day late, but at least they're bringing it. So you don't have to babysit me."

Her smile seemed forced.

And her words were not what he wanted to hear.

"I need to get a new laptop tomorrow, so I'm going to town," she added.

"Please be careful. I'm still concerned for your safety. Someone tried to kill you. Aren't you concerned at all about what you're digging into?"

"You're going to let what Sheryl said creep you out?"

Well, it was more than that, and he needed to tell her, but the problem was, he didn't exactly know *what* he needed to tell her. Had her father stirred up danger that somehow got him killed? He would contact a friend in law enforcement and see what he could learn about Alaric's death.

But before he did that . . . "Have dinner with me tonight?"

Yeah. He went there. She'd brought it up earlier, after all.

"Dinner?" She twisted her lips around as if exaggerating that she was thinking hard on the question. "You have more questions about this investigation? Or is it something . . . else?"

If only it could be something else. He was playing with fire. "I want to hear more about this book you're writing. You have to eat. I have to eat."

"I'm tired. Too many thoughts rattling around in my head. Rain check?"

"Tomorrow night, then?" he asked. "I might know more by then, too, that I can share with you."

"You're an unconventional detective." She got out of the vehicle.

He did too, and she stood there, her bright-red curls frizzing around her face in the humid Pacific Northwest. Freckles and striking bright-green eyes. He shouldn't notice them . . . in the way he noticed. This wasn't the first time he'd had the thought, and he feared that it wouldn't be the last.

I am losing my mind.

"I'll have dinner with you, Detective, tomorrow evening. You can take me there on your motorcycle."

He had no words.

"Meet me here at six," she said.

She left him to stare after her as she headed into Cedar Trails Lodge. He couldn't breathe. He rubbed his jaw hard, then his neck. She had so much of her mother in her, and that terrified him, but in just a few short encounters, this woman had him tumbling around on the inside.

Her father *might* have been murdered.

She could be in danger.

And his niece's life could also be on the line. He had zero business getting involved with her. Zero. Business.

Braden started the car and drove all the way back to the sheriff's office at the county seat almost an hour away instead of his apartment so he could look into how her father died. Put some distance between them—that should work. He texted Remi to ask her and her helicopter-tour-guide husband, Hawk, to keep an eye on Cressida for him. They'd gone through a few things together, and he could consider them friends, in the loosest sense. They didn't eat together. Or talk much.

But weirdly, they had each other's backs. He could trust them.

Unlike other people.

When Octavia had asked Braden to stay here and wait and work undercover so he would be in place for . . . something, that had been in the vaguest of terms. Octavia could have led with the possible murder of her ex-husband because of something he'd learned in Hidden Bay about a derelict boat. She could have led with how she feared her daughter might fall victim to the same fate.

13

Thursday morning, Cressida slept late because her brain hadn't shut off last night. At some point she'd finally fallen asleep in the early morning hours—right when the dawn brightened her room. Thoughts of the museum visit kept her tossing and turning and thinking about the *Endeavor Spirit*, aka *Specter's Bounty*.

Then her mind had drifted to Detective Braden Sanders. He wasn't like any investigator she'd ever known—and that wasn't saying much since she hadn't known that many. Still, she'd interacted with them on occasion during her journalistic investigations and usually irritated them. They were matter-of-fact and never forthcoming or talkative. Then again, his investigation was about *her* and not about her attempt to pry information from him, which was a completely different situation. Braden had gone out of his way to stick close to her. Yes, to protect her, but she sensed there was more going on.

After getting dressed, she went downstairs to the lobby and grabbed coffee and a breakfast sandwich. Sitting at one of the tables, she enjoyed the panoramic view of crashing waves while she waited for the rental car to be delivered.

Journal in hand, she flipped through the pages and reread her notes from yesterday, comparing them to Dad's notes. One question continued to dig at her—why had Dad cut his trip here short and gone to DC? She hadn't been on speaking terms with Mom at the time and had only seen Mom at Dad's funeral. They shared niceties for the public eye—a place Cressida had lived far too long, and she was done with it. Just like Dad had finally been done with it. Mom and Dad had been divorced since Cressida was twelve.

But Mom might know why Dad had come back to see her. Cressida had learned that much. He'd flown directly to DC and taken a cab to talk to her but had been hit by a taxi while walking across the street. Did it really matter why? Still, something that could pull him from his research had to be important, and Cressida found herself growing curious about it. She should have questioned this all along.

I need to call her.

But I don't want to talk to her. Her heart ached. It wasn't that she didn't love her mother, but the woman had put her job and her own life ahead of Cressida for the last time, betraying Cressida. Destroying her hard-earned career.

She'd enjoyed writing for *The Pinnacle* because the editors had considered her an elite investigative reporter and gave her room to explore and expand her horizons. Mom had demanded that Cressida stop digging into a story about environmental damage from sunken vessels without telling her *why*, and she'd refused. The next thing Cressida knew, she was let go from *The Pinnacle*. She hadn't been told in so many words why, but she knew. Oh, she knew. Mom had pulled strings to get her way like she'd always done.

Cressida was an award-winning journalist and liked to believe she had earned her way into the upper echelon of journalistic venues. And it was pure torture to think for even one moment that her mother might have influenced those doors that opened for her long ago. Regardless, after she was let go, with her accolades Cressida could have gone to any other magazine—*The New Yorker*, *The Atlantic*, *Vanity Fair*—so she'd tried, but editors who once sought her now ghosted her.

Those doors had all closed. She didn't bother confronting her mother. What was the point?

Cressida shut the journal. She hadn't been looking at it anyway.

Finally, the car arrived. A blue Nissan Versa. The rental driver entered—a guy in a red shirt and cap—and pulled her from her morbid thoughts. She should put them completely behind her. Except . . . that nagging feeling at the base of her skull that Mom knew something about Dad that she hadn't shared with Cressida.

But she would worry about that later, after she was done here in Hidden Bay—her last stop before compiling, editing, and polishing the book for publication with Anchor Point Books.

In the rental car, Cressida drove south, steering through two small towns until she finally landed at a big-box store, and that had taken her a good hour and a half of driving.

Maybe she could get a laptop there. Just something to keep her in business.

She preferred to spend as much time as she could out in the community. People were so interesting, and she loved to observe, to talk and get their stories first, but she needed to get online too. She could transfer her notes and do some research to dig deeper into what she'd learned at the museum.

Cedar Trails Lodge had no cell service or internet and therefore no Wi-Fi. Even BYOIS—bring your own internet service, such as Starlink Mini portable—was frowned upon.

After all, it destroyed the whole theme of getting back to nature. Still, she'd taken the time to stop and smell the proverbial roses in each place of the globe she'd visited to finish up Dad's book.

She wasn't at Cedar Trails to unplug, and so she traveled with her own mini satellite. However, she still needed a laptop to make things work.

After purchasing the most powerful laptop they sold—which wasn't that great—she stepped out of the store and made her way over to her vehicle. She'd go back to her room at the lodge, set up the laptop, and connect to her notes in the cloud. She had completely written off her old laptop—it was gone forever, and she didn't care. She had all she needed with her.

Now that she had the journal back.

And later this afternoon, she'd have to get ready for dinner. She smiled to herself. What had she been thinking to bring up dinner and then later *agree* to dinner with Detective Braden Sanders? And then she'd had the nerve to ask him to take her on his motorcycle?

Seriously.

At the thought of him, heat flooded her entire being as she paused to fumble for the fob and unlock her car. In the window reflection, she spotted a face she'd seen at the marina.

Not the man who'd attacked her. Someone else. Who knows? Maybe he'd come here to get a laptop too. Except he was watching her.

Definitely watching her.

I'm watching you too, dude. She lifted her cell to grab a selfie and made sure he was in the photo, then climbed into the vehicle. She sent the photo to Braden, then sped away. It wasn't like she could escape the tail. If he was watching her and he was following, he already knew which road she would travel back to Hidden Bay and Cedar Trails Lodge.

Before she'd been attacked, she might have approached him to ask what he was doing and get some answers. That was the old investigative journalist in her. In her experience, it took action to get answers.

Fortunately, she saw no one following her on the touristy two-way highway that was jammed with traffic driving up and down the coast and the only path through the Olympic Peninsula.

Almost two hours later, she was finally back at the Cedar Trails Lodge, and she stopped at the coffee kiosk to grab an iced coffee, then took a picture of the photograph of the *Specter's Bounty*. She lingered at the big panoramic window and asked lodge patrons hanging out if anyone had ever personally seen the ghost ship.

Negative.

She noticed a text had come through while she'd been driving. It was Braden asking about her safety. She sent him a quick text—hoping he'd get it—that she was at the lodge, safe and sound, and would see him at six tonight.

Coffee in hand, she made it to her room, unpacked the laptop and the mobile satellite, and set everything up. She'd laid out her journal and notes on the bed and desk.

She'd been to the museum and gotten the dark story of the *Specter's Bounty*, but she had more questions than answers. What happened to the ship and the crew? And what did Evelyn Monroe know?

At five fifteen, she woke up sprawled on her bed next to the journal and notes and yawned.

I can't believe I fell asleep!

She bolted from the bed. She had to get ready for her not-a-date with Braden. Did she want it to be a real date? Sure. Yeah. She'd admit it to herself. Did she think he wanted a date with her? Yeah, sure. She'd admit it for him.

Cressida hadn't been on a date in three years, and that

was well before Dad had died. Back then, she'd even been talking to Mom. Until her own mother had sabotaged her career, and as a result, that guy Cressida had dated, Gavin Ashford—someone her mother had introduced her to— ghosted her.

Fine, Gavin. I don't need you. I don't need anyone.

So, yeah, she was done, so done with dating. At least anyone in *her* world. But here she was as far as a person could get from DC, and Detective Sanders—Braden—was there on the beach.

Intense steel-blue eyes and just . . . looking good all the way to his bones and in every way that mattered. She had a feeling he had a good heart. She could sense it. After what she'd been through, dating a down-to-earth, middle-of-nowhere detective was the best idea she'd had in a long time. Now, if she could just fully bring him into *her* investigation, *her* research, that could be an extra layer of protection for her.

She sounded like a manipulator even to herself.

And maybe in that way she was much more like her mother than she'd ever want to admit to anyone, especially herself. But she wasn't harming anyone. Hiding the truth or taking down careers.

She could learn everything about the *Specter's Bounty* and hopefully talk to Evelyn Monroe all while finding out who was behind the attack, and that would be a win-win for everyone.

Cressida cleaned up, putting on her least-wrinkled blouse and jeans. She'd be riding a motorcycle, so no point in wearing the one dress she'd packed. She brushed her crazy hair that she could never get under control, then finally gave up.

Staring in the mirror, she scrutinized her face. She'd never worn makeup and preferred her freckles to be in full view.

A text came through on her cell, surprising her. Like

Braden had said—sometimes you got lucky. Cressida didn't recognize the number, but she passed her card out frequently and expected unknown numbers.

8:30 at the Sea Reaper. Daughter of Alaric Dane deserves answers. I'll give you half an hour. Captain Diggins.

I'll be there.

Heart pounding, she smiled to herself. But it was strange. Dad's notes didn't reflect that he'd spoken with Diggins. How did this man know Alaric Dane was her father? Though she was pleased with the news, the way he stated she deserved answers made her wonder if she even knew the right questions to ask.

14

The only time he hated the low rumble of his Ducati was when he navigated along the woodsy, serene private road of Cedar Trails Lodge. Patrons visited this region to escape the rest of the world. Remi—through Evelyn Monroe's direction—even insisted that her husband, Hawk Beckett, operate his helicopter-tour package out of Forestview, though it was part of the lodge's offerings.

Guests came for the sounds of nature—wind, rain, and crashing waves—nothing more.

Braden was unapologetic as he pulled into a parking spot.

Unfortunately, he had no news to deliver to Cressida regarding the identity or capture of her attacker or discovery of her missing laptop. But through his connections, he'd learned that her father had been hit by a taxi while crossing the street. That wasn't a fact Cressida expected to hear from him. She had to know that already. But what he couldn't figure out was why Octavia thought her ex-husband's death was suspicious. Braden was waiting on the report from the ME for more information about Alaric's cause of death, because there was more to this story.

Sliding off his bike, he removed his helmet and set it next to the extra one he'd brought for Cressida. He didn't think Sheriff Thatcher would approve, but who was Braden to turn down such an adventurous proposition.

Cressida had nailed it when she mentioned that Braden was an unconventional detective.

You have no idea.

He was fortunate he even had a legitimate reason to spend time with Cressida due to the investigation into her attacker. At the end of the day, Cressida was his whole purpose for being here, and if he had to ignore professional etiquette—like having dinner, taking her on his motorcycle—he would do what had to be done.

He was beyond caring about decorum.

Take that, Octavia.

He would do whatever it took to protect Cressida from unknown danger potentially related to her father's research because he was here in this situation under peculiar circumstances, and he could get no definite answers from her mother.

Striding toward the lodge, he adjusted his leather jacket.

All good reasons to be here. But . . . maybe he was here for himself too. In fact, he'd be here if for no other reason than to take this woman for a ride on his bike. His better self warned him . . .

Get answers and get out. That's your only play here, dude.

He entered the lodge and glanced around the mostly empty place. Everyone was outside enjoying what remained of this glorious day. The kind of day created for the perfect bike ride. Remi smiled and approached from behind the registration counter.

"*Detective.*" She emphasized his title.

Was she onto him? Thinking he might be personally interested in Cressida? Did she, too, believe he was playing with fire? "Remi. Any news on Cressida's interview with Mrs. Monroe?"

"It's Cressida now, is it, Detective?" She blinked in a sarcastic way.

Braden said nothing to that. She might twist anything he could say into something else. He was obviously already in trouble. He glanced up the stairway. *Where is she?* Then looked back to Remi to wait for her answer.

"No. She's out of town, according to her new assistant, Madeline Chase."

"Yeah, about her. What's your impression?"

"Are you working? Is this detective business? Because you look like you're on a date."

"I wear this when I ride my motorcycle."

"Ooh, a motorcycle date."

He wasn't escaping this. Cressida had suggested dinner. He'd brought it up again. Then Cressida had been the one to suggest the motorcycle. One thing had led to another. As for her other question . . . "I'm always working. So . . . Madeline Chase?"

"I'm not sure what I think of her yet. I haven't had that much interaction with her. She's definitely a gatekeeper. Very formal and unemotional and distant."

"So you don't like her," Braden said.

"I didn't say that."

"Didn't you?"

Braden didn't hear anything else Remi said as he focused on the woman coming down the open stairwell—all bouncing red curls and intense bright-green eyes dancing around the room. Then they landed on him, and the air rushed out of his lungs. And she hadn't even smiled yet.

He kept his expression flat. Hardest thing he'd done in a while. Though he felt like he'd known her for well over a year now, he'd only just met this woman, and he had to shake off the effect she had on him. He didn't know her. She was a stranger. So what if he'd seen that photograph in Octavia's office?

Cressida approached and stood next to Remi as she smiled at Braden. She looked nothing like a woman who'd been attacked four days ago.

You look beautiful. That's what a guy would say on a date. But not here and not now, in front of Remi.

And this wasn't a date. Was he lying to himself?

"Have you heard anything from Mrs. Monroe?" Cressida asked Remi. "The sooner I get the interview, the sooner I can get answers and get out of your hair."

"You're not in my hair. We love our guests. But no, not yet. She's traveling."

"Do you know when she'll be back?" Cressida asked.

"I'll let you know when I find out." Remi smiled, then excused herself.

A confused frown emerging, Cressida watched her walk away, then glanced at Braden. "I take it she isn't fond of the gatekeeper either. Well, there are always other ways to get through." She smiled again. "Are you ready?"

Couldn't be more ready.

"Let's go." He walked with her, opened the door for her, then at his motorcycle, he handed off the extra helmet.

Cressida put it on like a pro. "Are we going to eat first? Or are you taking me for a joyride?"

He grinned. "Which would you prefer?"

"A short joyride, and then we can eat. Our time is limited, I'm afraid."

Well, she might have just taken all the joy out of it with that.

This isn't a date, remember?

He got on the bike, and she climbed on behind him, and the space was tight. Then she wrapped her arms around him, and he tried to ignore his pounding heart.

What was he doing?

Protecting her. The only way he knew how. Getting close enough to do it was a huge issue. He was glad they'd planned this, considering she texted that someone had followed her and watched her in town. The Timberbrook County Sheriff's Office was processing the image within the limits of privacy laws. If that got him nowhere, he might send it through DSS channels—this was Octavia Dane's daughter, after all.

Braden took the twists and turns at reduced speeds. Enjoyed the blue sky, the thick evergreens lining the road, and . . . the feel of her arms around him. Yes, he enjoyed that too. Having her riding with him made him realize just how lonely he was.

For too long he'd been living life as a bachelor. Unfortunately, just when he found someone who took his breath away, the relationship was over before it could truly begin. Someone stood between Braden and Cressida.

He hated to end the joyride, but it was time to head over to the small mom-and-pop café—Lucio's Bistro—in Forestview. At least he could still look forward to sitting across the table from her and learning as much as he could about her, and possibly more that could help him protect her. Anyone who could walk away from a person like Octavia Dane, especially as a daughter, deserved his utmost respect and admiration.

15

The bistro at the end of the strip mall looked cozy and quaint. Cressida pulled the helmet off and flipped her hair around to get out the kinks. Braden took the helmet from her, then secured them both with a locking clip on his bike.

She never would have imagined she'd ride on the back of a detective's motorcycle in the middle of an investigation into an attack on her life.

Stranger things have happened.

And maybe this situation was strange, but she'd count it as a good thing too. For months now, she'd been working hard on Dad's book, and now and then a girl needed to have fun—like that old eighties song. Except she wasn't sure that having dinner with him would be fun, and she didn't think this was actually an official date.

On the sidewalk, Braden waited on her, and the look he was giving her increased her uncertainty about this not-a-date.

He opened the door for her, and she smiled and entered. The cute brunette hostess talked to him like he frequented the place, then ushered them back to Braden's "usual" table. He took the seat that would let him keep his back to the wall like Cressida would expect from law enforcement.

There was something about his actions, his mannerisms. Cressida couldn't put her finger on it, and maybe she already had enough to figure out that she didn't need to spend energy on solving the enigma that was Braden Sanders.

But neither could she simply let this go.

Who are you?

She needed to get to the bottom of him. But that could take some time. Yes, he'd grown up in Maine. His dad had been a fisherman. But what more?

Water and menus were brought, and after a quick perusal of a limited menu, she decided on the lasagna instead of something hard to eat like spaghetti and meatballs. Food ordered, she clasped her hands on the square table with a red-checkered tablecloth. Italian dining music softly played in the background, making conversation easy.

"You come here a lot," she said. It wasn't a question.

"Once or twice." He hitched a grin and sat back.

She gave him a pointed look.

"Okay, it's my *favorite* place."

"Because it reminds you of your favorite place?" In Maine?

"What's *your* favorite place?" He hadn't answered her question.

She went through a list of restaurants where she'd eaten in the last year of her travels—in Bermuda, Scotland, Namibia, and Micronesia. "But there's a little place in DC, a small place that reminds me of this. They serve the best Reubens."

"I wouldn't have pegged you for a Reuben kind of girl, or even a sandwich girl."

She lifted her shoulders. "I wouldn't have pegged you for a Ducati kind of guy."

And that made him laugh. He had a great laugh.

So what that she'd shared her favorite place in DC with him? Maybe she was holding on to false hope that he wouldn't learn her mother worked for the State Department, because if the investigation went on long enough, that would be an eventuality. Then again, her mother's position in the government could be meaningless to him. Just a government employee. She wasn't exactly sure why it should bother her. Maybe she was concerned that he would contact her mother and inform her of the attack, and the next thing Cressida knew, DSS special agents would be stalking her to protect her.

Having dinner with him might have been a bad idea, opening the door to more questions that she didn't want to answer. They continued talking about nothing too important as if they both danced around the truth, whatever that was.

The food arrived. Finally. She slowly released an anxious breath. "I'm ravenous."

After the waitress left, Cressida put her napkin in place and lifted her fork.

"Wait," he said. "Can we say grace?"

"Sure. Of course." She set her fork aside. Bowed her head and closed her eyes.

He said a quick prayer over the food and thanked God for it and also prayed for the investigation. Dad had been a Christian and raised Cressida to believe, and maybe that's why this distance between her and Mom was eating her alive. But how did she forgive? She pushed the thought away. She didn't want thoughts of her mother to overtake this time with Braden.

Cressida focused on Detective Braden Sanders . . . the man.

"So, tell me more about your father's book," he said.

"Shipwrecks and ghost ships—the ones that fascinated him. He's written a couple of other books for this publisher, and they agreed to look over this work and possibly publish it too, trusting me to complete it in the same fashion and style that he would have. I plan to include a special 'in memory of' section." The pain of tears erupted behind her eyes, but she blinked them away with a smile.

"And you can write like him because you're a writer."

She shrugged. "I'll do my best to write with his style and flare, but my voice is different." She looked off into the distance, picturing her father. "He wasn't what some people might think of as a boring historian. He had a way about him that added magic and life to old stories."

"Like what? Give me an example."

"Like, he really loved World War II history and got into sharing the danger and intrigue of it. Details about German U-boats and the many sunken ships and how they were sabotaged. It might not sound interesting to you, but he had my full attention, and those who attended when he lectured at museums to talk about his latest book. You should check out his books. I should have asked the museum if they carried them. I should have looked, but I didn't want to draw attention to him in that way, just yet."

"I'll be sure to do that." Sadness edged his voice.

From that, she assumed that his memories of losing *his* father still ran deep and he didn't enjoy revisiting maritime history—yet here he was, stuck with Cressida. The pain of the loss of her own father remained fresh and raw since he'd died just over a year ago, but she relished submerging herself in his world before she lost that feeling forever.

Eventually, those memories would fade, and while they remained, she would wrap herself in them. But she didn't like the sad Braden who sat across from her now, so she changed the subject.

"How about we talk about the investigation? Have you learned anything about the man who attacked me now that you have the sketch?"

"Nothing yet."

Cressida glanced at the clock on the wall and tried not to make it obvious, but he caught her. He didn't say anything.

Time to explain. "Listen, I got a text from Diggins. He wants to meet me tonight at eight thirty on the *Sea Reaper*, that's his boat. It's the old trawler floating to the immediate south of the group. Easy to spot, he said. It'll still be light."

Braden stopped chewing and stared.

"Before you tell me I'm not going, you should know I have no intention of going alone. I didn't *have* to tell you." She bit into the last of the bread.

He wiped his mouth with the napkin, then laid it on the table. "I'm going with you."

"That's the idea. If you have the time."

"I wouldn't miss it. I sense a 'but' in there."

"I want to be smart. I don't sense anything nefarious here, but after the attack, I have to play it safe. So maybe you can just hang around nearby or something. I have thirty minutes with him and that's it. I don't want him to hold back on me because you're there."

"Do you know what you're going to ask him?"

"I have a lot of practice at this, so yes. I'm old school, and I wrote up a list of questions in my notebook. One other thing. He . . . um . . . mentioned that he's giving me the time because my father deserves answers. That really threw me. Dad hadn't put any notes in his journal about meeting with Diggins."

"That's interesting that he would know who you are and about your father," Braden said.

"That he knows the connection is strange. I hope he has some answers since my father cut his trip short, his research, and left. I don't know why, but he went back to DC to talk to my mother, and then he died. I only know he was going to talk to her because I overheard her mention it at the funeral."

Staring at her, Braden had the strangest look in his eyes.

She was good at reading people, but she couldn't read that look. "What are you thinking?"

"Nothing that you aren't already thinking."

"I don't know what to think. I'd love to know what would cause him to cut his research short." *Mom knows.*

I have to call Mom.

But I can't! How would that conversation even go? How did a person overcome the wall they'd built?

"Thank you for telling me and letting me go with you in case something goes wrong. I hope it doesn't. I hope you find out what you need to find out from Diggins. You got a laptop today, but I assume you haven't been able to get online much to do more research."

She chuckled and explained about her portable satellite. "Still, I don't like to research online before going in."

"Excuse me?"

"I follow in my father's footsteps"—it was hard not to bring up her family ties—"in talking to the locals and forming my basic knowledge that way before I read anything out there on the internet. He wasn't a journalist per se, but he was a good researcher, and he did much of it on his book, well, before he died. There are four basic methods—observation, conversation, interviews, and research. I chartered the boat so I could get a distant view, observe the coast from the ocean while talking to Malloy. That's what Dad did."

"You mean you want to get the perspective from the locals. Their thoughts on the ghost ship kind of thing before reading about it. You're coming at it with different context than most."

"Exactly. I'll observe and have conversations, and really, that's all my interview will be. I'm just having a conversation. What does Diggins know about the *Specter's Bounty*? That's what I want to learn."

"Because Malloy mentioned him."

"Yes."

"I enjoyed the museum with you yesterday. I'd like to learn more about the *Specter's Bounty* too. What more can I do to help you finish this book?"

And that's what she wanted from him. Still, it surprised her. Cressida tilted her head, studying him. "I appreciate your offer. Can I ask . . . *why* so interested?"

He didn't shift uncomfortably at her direct question. Could mean he was well trained. She wanted to know his background—everything about him—and maybe they had already crossed the professional lines into personal. She wasn't exactly sure because despite that, she wanted to have fun—a ride on a motorcycle, a nice dinner with a handsome, interesting man at the end of the day . . .

I'm not ready for that. So. Not. Ready.

This detective . . . this man sitting across from her was definitely giving her the interested vibes, though she sensed that he was holding back too.

"Why am I so interested? The sooner you finish your research, the sooner you can get home where you'll be safe."

"Sounds like you want to get rid of me." *Oh boy.* She stared at her plate. *I need to stop flirting and pulling him into my web and acting like Mom.* The last thing she wanted to do was become Octavia Dane—a master manipulator.

Pursing her lips, she glanced up at him. She hadn't wanted to see his reaction. Cressida needed to shift gears.

Now. Before it was too late. She wished she hadn't suggested the motorcycle. She liked this man too much to play games.

His smile, those huge dimples . . .

Cressida had to look away.

"I appreciate your concern. I do. Really."

"But?"

"There's no but." She held his gaze. She had to think about her next words. This experience in Hidden Bay was strange at the very least, with the attack and the warnings and the stonewalling of her interview with Evelyn Monroe. And she certainly hadn't expected to have a detective in her life. A man she liked and might want to get to know better. But once this was over, she was going home.

"Given the attack on you, I think the sooner you're done, the better," he said. "But Cressida, I'm not trying to get rid of you. Not at all."

He hadn't needed to add that last part, and she could feel that message he sent enveloping her. Maybe he hadn't intended to reveal himself, but she was definitely reading him now.

Arms on the table, she leaned forward. "I'm not one to play games or hold back, but in my experience as a journalist, I have to play all the pieces at the right time, let's say. I guess what I'm saying is that I want to put all the cards on the table with you tonight. Here and now."

He remained expressionless, which told her that on the inside he was reacting to her words.

"I'm listening."

A laugh escaped, and she stared at the table. *I'm really doing this.* "I don't know why someone would target me. I have no idea why I was warned. I've been on this research journey to finish my father's book for about eight months now." She lifted her shoulders. "I'm glad you asked me to dinner tonight because having you around is an extra layer of protection I never thought I'd need. I worked as a journalist in the past, and got into some awkward situations, but honestly, I've never almost been drowned. I've never felt so vulnerable."

In his eyes she could see so many questions, passionate emotions, and something hidden. Something else. So Detective Braden had his own secrets.

Before he could respond, she continued. "Maybe I'm not supposed to say that, or what I'm going to say next might put you in an awkward position, but I confess . . . I like you."

She held her breath.

16

nd I like you too. He couldn't have been more relieved when the waitress suddenly appeared to take their plates and ask if they wanted dessert. Or more relieved they had somewhere to be immediately after dinner. Dessert would have to wait.

A text dinged, and he would normally have ignored it, but he glanced at his smartwatch.

Octavia.

He was thankful his sleeve covered it from Cressida's view. He'd gotten himself into this.

He wanted to respond to Cressida's statement. Say the words out loud. But he would just dig a deeper hole, and the fall into that hole was already going to be painful. He might have secrets that he couldn't share, but he couldn't speak bold lies to her face. Some believed an omission counted as a lie. But a life depended on those secrets, a life was on the line.

Cressida waited for his reaction to her statement.

"I like you."

This one was strong and determined. She might be a force

to be reckoned with. With those striking light-green eyes alone, she held power over him that he couldn't understand. Her crazy red curls and all those freckles. Appearance and allure aside, she was a fighter on the inside. A survivor. And that stirred him all the more. He wished he could tell her that he had liked her the first time he'd seen her in a photograph.

"I think you know the feeling is mutual," he finally said, "but you don't know me. Not really." He didn't back off when her expression shifted, her chin lifted. "And by the time you get to know me, you won't like me anymore."

There. He'd told the truth.

Now was the moment to steer this back to where it belonged. Octavia's text had been perfect timing, as if she had been reading his mind. The woman reminded him of his digital life—Alexa and Siri and social media. He could have a thought, and the next thing he knew, an advertisement appeared like someone had read his mind. Though it wasn't out of the realm of possibility that Octavia could be—somehow—watching him, he didn't think that likely.

"You sound sure about that."

What? That she didn't know him? Or that she wouldn't like him when she got to know him? "Oh, I'm pretty sure." He grinned. "And you're leaving Hidden Bay when you're done."

His statement could have been taken in a couple of ways. He demanded it of her. Or he was simply making an observation and offering his strong assumption of her plans.

"I don't know how long the research is going to take. This is the first vessel for which I've had to do all the research. If my father knew anything, he left nothing for me. All the others, Dad had stayed the course and recorded the details."

She crunched on the ice left in her glass. Dinner was over. They'd declined dessert. And yet they were still here.

"Let's make a deal," she said, "you and I."

Those words hit him wrong. They were the exact words her mother spoke to him. He tried to hide how much he disliked them, and yet coming from Cressida, the words were much more palatable.

"You're some kind of negotiator." He hadn't even heard her terms.

"It comes naturally."

"Let's hear it." He leaned back in his seat.

"You do your job as a detective and focus on finding the guy who attacked me. I'll *continue* to research, interview people about the *Specter's Bounty*, do what I do, and you can accompany me if you believe it's relevant to your investigation."

She'd turned things away from their "liking" each other.

He opened his mouth to speak.

"I'm not done." She cut him off. "And we'll just be natural with each other. I don't want things to be awkward between us."

"That's why it surprises me you even brought *it* up." The liking each other part.

"Well, no point in dancing around what's obviously between us." Her grin was a spin on incredulity and flirting.

He'd never seen anyone do that.

"And what's between us?" He unwrapped the complimentary mint and popped it in his mouth.

"You know. It's there," she said. "Now it's on the table."

"Honestly, I kind of liked the dance."

She smiled. "Oh, we can keep dancing. Don't worry."

Then her gaze drifted up and zeroed in on something over his shoulder. Nothing was behind him except a mirror.

"What?" He stared out the window to see what the mirror reflected.

"That's the guy who followed me. He was at the store where I bought my laptop."

"I see him." Hackles raised, Braden watched the man. What was he up to? If he was following Cressida, he might not have realized that Braden was law enforcement, or else why tail her so closely, even wait for her in a small parking lot?

The guy was six foot tall, which Braden had guessed from the image she'd sent him. Dressed in jeans and a brown jacket, the man leaned against a silver crossover SUV and talked on his cell. The region had a small population but lots of tourists. Could be coincidental, though Cressida sounded convinced he'd followed her, and now there was the fact that he was here at this strip mall.

And so was Cressida.

"Aren't you going to do something?" she asked. "Question him?"

"I'm going to watch him and see what he does."

"You don't believe me?"

"I absolutely believe you." She believed he was following her. And likely he was.

"You work for the county sheriff. You could ask him for ID. Something."

"And if he gives me a reason, I will."

"What? *I* gave you a reason."

"Which he could brush off."

She pushed the chair back to stand. Remaining seated, he caught her wrist and stared at her. "I want to know why he's following you and who he's working for. Let me handle it my way."

"Well, you'd better make it quick because we have to get to the marina. I'm meeting Diggins."

"I'll get the check." He still wasn't sure if this was a date, and at the look on her face, he added, "It's part of the investigation. I can write it off."

Right. Okay. He paid, then at the door, turned to her. "Maybe head into the ladies' room. Let me check him out. I don't want you to be in danger."

She frowned. "I'd love to watch and listen in on the interaction."

"Fine. I'll record it for you."

"This isn't how I like to work."

"You usually walk up to possible danger and face it?"

"Every situation is different. If he was going to hurt me, he would have already. So, yeah, I want to face him. Ask him if he's following me and why. Come on, you'd be standing right there."

He lowered his voice. "You'll get your chance. But you were attacked. Someone tried to kill you."

"Fine." She turned on her heel and headed to the ladies' room while he strolled to the front of the restaurant. Braden stepped outside and casually walked over to his motorcycle. The guy was leaning against his vehicle, cell phone to his ear?—pretending to be on his cell?—right next to Braden's ride.

Braden stood next to the Ducati, waiting for Cressida to come out. Washington wasn't a "stop and ID" state, and he needed reasonable suspicion. Right now, her claims simply weren't quite enough. He needed more. Only a little more, but more. The guy put his cell down and looked at Braden, giving Braden the opportunity to memorize his face, though he already had an image.

"Great day for a ride," the guy said, all friendly like.

"It is. But this time of year, it's hard to enjoy the roads. Too many tourists."

The man shrugged. "I'm one of those tourists, I'm afraid."

He turned and got in his vehicle.

Braden let him. He got zero weird vibes about the guy, and he usually trusted his instincts. He got the license plate, and he'd run it based on reasonable suspicion. He sent the image to the support staff at the office.

Cressida stepped outside, the expression on her face plain. She was furious. But she said nothing, walked up to his bike, and put on her helmet he'd released from the locking clip. He could have said something. Should have . . .

But then she sent him what he suspected was her best if-looks-could-kill stare. "You can tell me later. I got another text from Diggins. Says he can't make it."

"Then where are we going?"

"To the marina. You're taking me to the *Sea Reaper*. No-body stands me up."

17

The Ducati rumbled to life, and she wrapped her arms around Braden. Wind whipping around her as he accelerated out of the parking lot, she tightened her hold on him. This model didn't allow a lot of room, and so she was pressed against him as close as humanly possible.

She could feel the muscles in his back and his core.

She tried to think about something else. Braden wouldn't like what Diggins's text said, so she'd paraphrased and then left off the last part . . .

"It's too dangerous."

Those words only fueled Cressida to want more information. And on the ride to get that information, she enjoyed the stunning display of God's creation—sometimes speeding by in a blur, and other times, when Braden slowed, she enjoyed the view of the ocean through the trees.

With Braden to assist and protect and discover, she would finish Dad's project. She'd prayed for God to help her when she'd been floating, pretending to be dead. He'd answered her prayer, and she had a feeling that maybe Detective Sanders was part of that help.

He steered through the marina parking lot that was being transformed into the Pirates' Bash, opening Friday—tomorrow—and running through the weekend. The chandlery, the burned-out museum, and the collapsing dock on the far side and the rusty older boats docked at the newer part of the marina gave Hidden Bay an uncommon charm hinting at times gone by.

And actually, now that she thought about it, she felt more comfortable here than at the other modern marinas with fancy yachts only afforded by millionaires and billionaires who reminded her of the elites and the circles her mother often ran in. She wanted no part of that group.

As usual, thoughts of her mother sent pain stabbing through her. She hadn't spoken to her in too long. Yes, she was still angry and hurt, but she missed her mother. She just didn't know how to get over it. How to reconcile.

Lord, I'm sorry that I feel the way I do about my mother. Help me to work through it.

The motorcycle slid into a parking spot, and Braden shut off the engine. She hopped off first, then Braden followed. He secured their helmets like before, though if someone really wanted them, it wouldn't take much to steal them.

He gestured toward the chandlery. "We'll need to rent a skiff."

"The county doesn't have a dedicated boat?"

"We don't have an official marine department. But even if we did, would you really want me to take you out there in the county sheriff's official marine department boat? I thought you were afraid my presence would prevent you from learning more." He didn't wait for her answer and started toward the buildings.

"That was the initial plan." She stared off at the cluster of boats as she kept pace with him. What was the best way to go about this?

At the door of the chandlery, he paused. "Before we head out, I'd like to know if there's something you haven't told me."

Oh, he'd picked up on that, had he? He was good. In her experience, talking to people in a relaxed environment, getting them to open up without the threat of law enforcement or reprisal wasn't easy to do, and she'd prefer if he didn't have to be with her.

"It's getting late. We need to make this happen." Tonight. "We can hash through everything else later."

He subtly shook his head, then opened the door, and she stepped inside first. Kit was on tonight, and she quickly rented Cressida the skiff. Braden handled the single-engine skiff like a pro as she watched the constellation of anchored boats out in the middle of the bay for movement. Would the *Sea Reaper* pull anchor and head out to the ocean if Diggins spotted Cressida and Braden heading his way?

"I'd like to know if there's something you haven't told me."

"Braden?" She wanted to make sure she had his full attention. That he could steer a small boat and talk at the same time.

"Yeah?" He kept his eyes on their destination.

"You need to know that in his text, Diggins didn't want to meet because he thinks it's too dangerous."

She expected Braden to react. But he remained focused.

"Well? Aren't you going to say something?"

"I figured," he said.

"How could you possibly figure that?" And really, she should ask if there was something he hadn't told *her*.

"Not to be cliché, but this isn't my first rodeo."

"About that. What did you do before?" She should look him up. Research him. Find out more. But her father's old-school methods had grown on her. She actually *enjoyed* learning about someone naturally and organically without any preconceived information she pulled from an internet search. She'd never used that strategy before in her journalism. But there was something to this method, she now saw after reviewing Dad's work, that offered a better perspective.

They neared the collection of liveaboard boats, and Braden still hadn't answered.

"Do you know which one is Diggins's? The *Sea Reaper*?" she asked. "I don't see it anchored where he told me he would be."

"I know the boat. I've interviewed him before," he said, and steered them around the clustered boats until he found just the one.

He navigated until the *Sea Reaper*—clearly painted on the stern—appeared, and then slowly piloted to the lee side of the trawler. That would protect them from the wind and minimize drift. As if he practiced this maneuver every day, he floated up next to the trawler. She could reach out and touch it.

"All this trouble and he might not even be here," he said.

"I had to try," she said.

"And you're not concerned it's dangerous?" he asked.

"I have you with me, so . . . no." She hadn't expected the look he gave her. He liked what she'd said. "Honestly, I'm surprised you didn't turn us around. Or, if you suspected the text I got, that you even agreed to this."

"I know that you would have gone without me," he said.

"I'm not stupid." She wouldn't have come under these circumstances without Braden, or someone of equal authority and ability.

"I know that too."

"Text him and let him know you're here," Braden said. "Tell him that I'm with you, in case he doesn't already know."

She texted Diggins. "Now what?"

"We wait."

"It's darker out here on the water than I would have thought."

Beautiful and yet creepy, and the wind had picked up. She was glad for the windbreaker. Cressida glanced at the wide Hidden Bay beach. She wasn't exactly sure where she'd nearly been murdered. The fog had truly disoriented her that morning, and the images were now beginning to blur. That was a good thing. And here she was, pressing onward and forward. She must have nerves of steel.

Like mother like daughter.

A figure appeared at the railing and let down a ladder. Cressida and Braden climbed up, and Braden secured the boat to a cleat on the trawler. "That'll have to do for now."

Then he turned to the man Cressida could only assume was Diggins—with his white hair and weathered face. With a genuine smile, Braden shook the man's hand.

"It's nice to see you again, Diggins," Braden said. "Thanks for agreeing to see Cressida."

Diggins released Braden's hand and dipped his chin, looking at Cressida. "I didn't agree. You shouldn't have come."

The man rubbed the back of his neck, and his hand came back with blood on it. He grimaced.

Shock rolled through Cressida.

"What happened?" Braden and Cressida both asked.

Diggins glanced around the area, looking at the smattering of nearby boats floating with the setting sun as their backdrop. He glanced to the bay, then finally motioned them to follow him. Slowly, he led them across the deck, leaning into each step as if negotiating an unseen current, then down a set of short steps leading belowdecks.

"You need a doctor, man," Braden said.

"Ain't trusting no doctor. I'm fine."

He gestured for them to take a seat, and Cressida followed Braden's lead, sliding into the booth behind a table.

"I'll make coffee since you insisted on talking. We might as well make this conversation worth the risk."

"What's going on?" Cressida asked. "Why is it dangerous to talk?"

"I'll get to that, eventually. Why don't you ask your questions. The faster we're done, the better."

"Shouldn't we take care of your head first?" Braden asked.

"It's just a bump. I'll handle it when we're done."

"You never said what happened." Braden had shifted back to his detective tone.

"I don't know," Diggins said. "One minute I'm warming up leftovers, and the next minute I'm on the floor."

"Did you slip and fall?" Cressida asked.

"Uncertain." He frowned. "What did you need to talk about?"

He would shut down sooner than later, and she should make these moments count. Get to the point. "Captain Malloy delivered me to Hidden Bay and suggested I talked to you about the *Specter's Bounty*. What can you tell me that I didn't learn about at the local museum? Do you believe the lore that say these waters are dangerous?" Shut up, Cressida, and let him talk. *Did you meet my father?*

He scoffed. "Just an old boat, like the museum says. Nothing more to know if . . ."

Diggins let his words trail off and gave her a look she couldn't misread.

If you want to live.

18

Braden wanted to focus on the conversation, but Diggins was stalling, if he even truly knew anything. He clearly wasn't going to say, and that could very well be because Braden was here. He remained suspicious of that bump on the man's head.

Though he was no forensic pathologist, it looked to be in the wrong position to have happened from a fall. His instincts had already kicked into high gear.

He wasn't operating with the same protocols he would have used while working in the DSS, but these circumstances were precarious at best. If he followed those rules, he probably wouldn't even be here now.

So while he half listened to Cressida argue with Diggins about what he did or didn't know about the *Specter's Bounty*, Braden took in the cabin, the lack of dinner being warmed up like Diggins had claimed. Braden hovered near the door to go above deck and slowly crept up those steps, his instincts telling him that danger lurked nearby, to add to the fact that Diggins said as much.

Cressida could hold her own and could very well get the

answers she sought without Braden in the room. He was fortunate she chose to include him. And if he wanted to continue to be included, he needed to roll with it, let her do her thing.

The door to the lower deck remained open, and through the opening above him, Braden spied the skull-and-cross-bones flag—a literal pirate flag—flapping from the mast. And yet a well-worn Bible rested on the counter, flipped open to the book of Psalms. While those themes seemed contradictory, Diggins's flag wasn't the usual call sign of a pirate but rather the banner of brotherhood of the people he'd taken under his wing. Drifters, wanderers. Those who couldn't afford a home on land but found life on the waves.

But tonight Braden would wager someone had hit Diggins on the head. Was the camaraderie, this tight-knit community, breaking up?

"The whole idea of a mysterious ghost ship, seen a time or two, and the warning that developed over stories told at campfires is what keeps the lore alive, that's all." Diggins's raised voice brought Braden back to the moment. "People make up all kinds of stories. You're trying to make it into something more. Why do you even want to know?"

Braden remained at the top step looking out above deck and listened.

"Why?" she asked. "I'm finishing the book my father wrote. He died, and I lost my job, and it just seemed that God opened the doors. The time was right. There's more to the story or my father wouldn't have added this boat."

Braden stepped down again, getting a look at Diggins.

The man leaned in, shadows turning this friendly "pirate" menacing. "Your father is the only reason I agreed to see you, and then I told you not to come."

"You said I deserved answers. And I'm here, but you're not giving them to me. My father wrote detailed notes, and there's no mention of you." She shook her head, a slight frown showing her confusion. "But there were a few pages torn out of his notes after the last shipwreck he researched."

Really? Interesting. Braden hadn't heard that from her.

"I can't explain why he didn't take notes about our conversation, unless he wrote them on those torn pages, and in that case, he didn't want anyone to see what he wrote. I enjoyed talking to him. He knows his history."

"So you *did* talk to him. What did you tell him about the ghost ship?"

"Same thing I told you."

"Which is nothing more than I learned at the museum. Malloy told me you knew something. He didn't tell me to go to the museum."

Cressida asked the questions whose answers she already had after going to the museum. He supposed her tactic was to get Diggins's perspective, which could be different from what the museum claimed. Since her father had been a historian, she might have an insider's view on published history versus the truth.

"I'm looking for the *hidden* truth."

Diggins scoffed.

With the rocking of the ship and the constant creaks, Braden couldn't be sure he hadn't heard footfalls above deck, so he maintained his stance on the stairs, his hand pressed to his gun.

"You found me," Diggins said. "You came for me, against the danger warning, so I give you points for that. But I don't know anything. I think Malloy was just trying to appease your active imagination."

"On that point, why is coming to talk to you dangerous? Or are you stonewalling me? And if so, why? Is it because you know something that I won't find at a museum or anywhere else? Something you alone know?"

With that, Braden was duly impressed.

Cressida showed her true professionalism in refusing to be detoured from her goal. Not surprising was her ability to coax words from people with her sincere expression. "Look, my father died before he could finish. You said you met him. You met with me because of him. Help me to finish this book. It'll be his legacy. It'll be this maritime historian's tribute to those lost at sea. I just want the truth about the *Specter's Bounty*—it was important enough to him to include in his book. I'm trying to do this for him and to do this tale justice." She leaned in. "Tell a story that possibly no one but a few have ever heard before."

Watching Cressida, maybe Braden finally understood how Octavia coerced and manipulated so many people, and that should serve as caution for Braden to stay away from Cressida when it came to anything beyond this covert operation arranged by her mother.

And Diggins, too, might have fallen for Cressida's gift, because he shifted forward. "I have a proposition for you. There's something I need. You get that for me, and I'll tell you what I can."

Stalling again?

"You'll tell me what you know about the *Specter's Bounty*, something that I can't find anywhere else?" Cressida asked.

Her father had not included his conversation with Diggins in his notes, then he'd taken the next flight out to DC. Diggins knew something, and Cressida had caught on to that from the start.

Diggins's expression turned dark. "I will."

"I have the feeling you think I won't be able to meet your requirement. I promise you, if it's not illegal, I'll make it happen."

A boisterous, incredulous laugh erupted.

"Name it," Cressida demanded.

He cocked his head. "Don't this feel a bit like you're walking the proverbial plank?"

"Nobody's walking a plank, metaphorical or otherwise." Braden stepped down so he could see the two of them, warning Diggins he should avoid threats.

"Name it," she repeated, her expression determined.

Diggins didn't even offer Braden an acknowledgment but kept his piercing eyes on Cressida. "I need something from Evelyn Monroe. And if we're abandoning plank metaphors, let's shift gears—you're Dorothy in *The Wizard of Oz*."

Cressida narrowed her eyes. "Are you saying you want me to steal something from the Wicked Witch of the West? Evelyn Monroe is *not* a wicked witch."

But Diggins? He was the man pulling the strings from behind the curtain.

Braden couldn't have imagined this exchange and was riveted, but another noise up top drew his attention. The waves or the wind or something nefarious?

He wanted to hear Cressida's response, but he couldn't wait. He crept halfway up the steps again while trying to listen to their conversation. Intuition warned him of imminent danger, leaving their discussion behind to head above deck.

Bright pinks and oranges on the horizon stunned him like the sunrises had on the East Coast decades before when Dad would leave on his fishing expeditions. Braden focused on his surroundings. Taking in all the sounds—the wind rustling through the boats, some with sails, the ocean lapping against the hulls. Seagulls and their endless calls.

Though they were anchored in the bay, the chop was rough as the wind picked up. Braden palmed his gun, and from the shadows, he took in everything. Others on the nearby boats hung around outside doing chores. Someone whistled an old sea shanty. The aroma of grilled fish wafted toward him.

He didn't feel comfortable walking around the boat and leaving Cressida and Diggins exposed down below, so instead he would remain at the entrance. Let danger come to him. He was prepared.

A creak.

Then another.

The hair on the back of his neck stood on end.

He held his handgun at the ready. The sun cast the last rays, and the shadows were long. He sensed movement and shifted to face his attacker, aiming his S&W. "Freeze."

Pain sliced across his back. His knees buckled and he dropped, then rolled away from the dark figure standing over him with an iron rod. Braden fired his weapon at the same time the man dodged away, expecting to be fired upon.

Braden scrambled to his feet, ignoring the pain.

Footfalls pounded on the steps, and Diggins and Cressida appeared above deck.

"Go back down," Braden commanded.

Cressida took a couple of steps down, but Diggins came all the way onto the deck, holding a shotgun.

"I'm not going down below," he said. "Come on. You and I will chase them off. Gotta get them off my boat."

He growled. Determined, he stomped around, looking down the barrel of his shotgun.

On the horizon in the facing sunset, Braden spotted a speedboat slipping away. He couldn't exactly go after them in his skiff. Was that the assailants getting away?

"They're gone now. No catching that," Diggins said.

Braden started for the skiff.

I can't let them get away.

"Braden, wait," Cressida called. She'd come above deck. "Are you okay?"

The care, concern in her eyes, when she looked at him pulled him back from the edge.

"Yeah. Just . . ." The throbbing in his back wasn't something easily ignored, after all. He never should have allowed someone to get at him like that.

"We need to get you to the hospital." She looked at Diggins. "I don't know how far it is."

"I can fix you up," Diggins said.

Braden wasn't entirely sure that was the best idea, but he'd take immediate attention and then deal with the rest later. "It's just a bruise, but you can check it to make sure it's not bleeding. And we'll look at your head too, Diggins."

"Fine," Cressida said. "But what if they come back?"

"They're not coming back tonight. Come on." Confident, Diggins started belowdecks.

"They? You know who they are, then?" Cressida asked.

Braden wanted that answer too.

"If I knew, I would tell you. Didn't I warn you? Didn't I say it was dangerous? I wasn't joking."

Diggins continued down the steps, and Braden would have followed but Cressida had a look on her face. Something more had happened. Something else. The pure anger and hurt in her eyes rattled through him.

He gripped her arms. "What is it? What did he say?"

"He said . . . I'm not sure your father's death was an accident." She pressed a hand against the rail.

Coming from her, those words slammed into him.

He wanted to tell her everything. Right now. His cell dinged, and maybe he should have ignored it, but it was his excuse to wait. He had to think about this. Figure it out. Convince Octavia that telling her daughter was for the best. He followed Cressida down the steps as he answered his cell. The words he heard chilled him to the bone.

19

My father's death wasn't an accident?

Someone had *murdered* him? Cressida wanted to shake the rest out of Diggins. And right now, her gut was churning.

Cressida struggled to wrap her mind around Diggins's words, and she stumbled to keep up with Braden, who got a call and suddenly paced the deck. Out here in the middle of the bay, she was surprised he could even get a signal. Diggins could have positioned his boat in the exact right spot.

Braden's grim expression as he held his cell to his ear scared her.

She couldn't get enough oxygen. Holding on to the rail, she leaned out and looked over the water, sucking in the cold, briny air. A hand pressed her shoulder and gently pulled her back. She dreaded looking at Braden but lifted her eyes.

He grabbed her hand and tugged her toward Diggins, then said to him, "You were attacked today."

"Attacked?" Cressida studied Diggins to see his reaction to Braden's statement. "So the bump on your head wasn't because you fell?"

"And they came back a second time." Braden's face was grim, his eyes hard.

"I can handle myself," Diggins said. "You don't worry about me."

"Who are *they*? Why did they attack you?" Braden asked.

"I'm not pressing charges," Diggins said.

"They attacked *me*, a detective, so charges are being pressed. I want to know who they are."

Diggins shook his head, his features equally determined. "I don't know. Even if I did, that wouldn't do you any good."

"I'm asking you a direct question—as a detective—and I want answers now."

While Cressida wanted those answers for Braden, he was about to destroy her connection with Captain Diggins—a man she believed had answers she sought. Answers to a question she hadn't even asked.

"Braden, maybe—"

"I'll get the answers, Diggins, but I'd prefer that happened with your cooperation." The sudden shift in attitude startled her, but she admired him all the more.

"I *am* cooperating, Detective Sanders."

Braden pursed his lips, clearly not convinced.

"I'll be back to check on you," Braden said. "Maybe by then you'll have come to your senses and tell me who the assailants are."

Cressida was surprised that Braden gave up the battle with the stubborn self-named pirate. If he hadn't gotten that phone call, would he remain here and pressure Diggins? She wanted answers too. But that wasn't happening. Braden urged her toward the ladder so they could climb down to the skiff.

She hated leaving Diggins, but she had a feeling that he could, in fact, take care of himself. The man had struck a deal with her almost on par with emotional blackmail and showed his years of practice at withholding information, using it as a bargaining tool like someone who was accustomed to a world where secrets were currency.

Not unlike the world in which her mother thrived.

She shuddered at the comparison but had no time to think on it as she focused on descending the rickety ladder into their skiff that rocked on the choppy water a little too much for comfort. Once Cressida settled in the skiff, Braden started the engine and navigated away from the anchored liveaboard boats, then sped toward the lights of the marina.

Maybe now wasn't the time, but she had to know and turned to look at his tense features, eyes focused ahead, lips flat.

"Braden. Tell me what's happened." She had to raise her voice over the wind and the boat's motor.

"Madeline Chase. Evelyn Monroe's assistant? Mrs. Monroe claims that Madeline tried to kill her."

Air whooshed out of Cressida. She pressed her hands over her mouth.

"Is she all right?" Cressida finally managed.

"Yes, as far as I know."

"But what more? There must be more."

"There is. But it's an ongoing investigation. I can't talk about it. I shouldn't have shared what I did, but meeting her is important to you. I'm trying to prepare you for the fact there might be a kink in your plan."

His jaw worked as he focused on his thoughts and getting them back to the marina. Cressida held on as Braden steered them across the rough water on an otherwise beautiful night. With the blinking lights and decorations for the Pirates' Bash opening tomorrow, the rustic marina looked homey and welcoming, and Cressida needed that. Still, she knew better than most that looks could be deceiving, and if her father had been murdered, she believed his death must be due to something he discovered here—why else would Diggins claim to know anything at all about a death that happened all the way across the country? Her attack also related to that discovery.

Oh yes, she could see through those twinkling, dancing lights at the marina—a growing shadow of danger hung over Hidden Bay. Braden docked and moored the boat, and they returned the keys by dropping them in a box since the chandlery was closed, then they walked in silence to his motorcycle.

As much as she had pretended this wasn't a date, all while wishing it was, now her time with Braden was coming to a harrowing end. Still, she knew she hadn't seen the end of him.

This was only the beginning.

"I assume you're taking me back to the lodge," she said.

He gently gripped her shoulders, forcing her to look him in his serious face, his steely blue eyes intense. Demanding. "Promise me you'll stay in your room tonight. Don't leave the lodge. Please, just . . . watch your back."

"I'm more worried about both Diggins and Mrs. Monroe than I am myself. Is this . . . typical in Hidden Bay?"

"What? Crime?"

"You know what I mean."

"Crime is everywhere, Cressida."

"It feels like it's all connected."

"I agree." With those words, he donned his helmet, and she did too.

She climbed on behind him and held on again. This time, all the rush of adrenaline and excitement drained away, replaced with a dread that weighed on her. Maybe the reality of her near-death experience was finally hitting her—and if that was the case, she'd had a delayed response.

After Dad died, she had promised herself that she would

live one day at a time. That's what he'd always told her, but she found that fear of the past or dread of the future ate away at that promise. Still, in this moment, she savored the feel of her arms around Braden. Even though Braden's presence was temporary in her world, in this moment, living one day at a time, she was with him, and he was the rock she held on to.

In the waning light, he ascended the road to the top of the cliffside—which was a bit terrifying. She struggled to recall how carefree she'd felt just a few days ago on the *Mariner's Gambit*. Her life had been upended the first few moments in Hidden Bay. But she still had breath and was still strong, and she would stay the course—like any seaman fighting the greatest storm of his life.

With a few miles of road behind them, Braden parked next to her rental vehicle in the Cedar Lodge lot. She hopped off, removed the helmet, and handed it to him.

"You keep it for next time." He didn't get off his motorcycle.

Next time? "Braden."

"Yeah." His tone said he was preoccupied. She understood.

"You be careful," she said. "You were hurt tonight. Maybe your boss should give you time off. Please tell him what happened on Diggins's boat."

He suddenly got off his bike and removed his helmet, then gestured for her to walk toward the lodge, which she did.

"What are you doing?" she asked.

"I'm seeing you inside," he said.

"You don't have to do that." *But I'm glad you are.*

"Your friend is here," he said.

"What friend?"

He gestured toward a vehicle. "Recognize that car?"

"Oh. The guy who followed me. The guy you didn't question at the restaurant earlier."

"Yeah, well, now I'm going to talk to him."

"What about Mrs. Monroe and Madeline?"

"Your safety is more important." Braden entered the lodge with her.

The overwhelming urge to forget about finishing Dad's book rushed through her. Could she do that? Actually let it go? Or what if she simply left off this last one—the *Specter's Bounty*? She could still finish it. But too many questions needed answers, and she had never been one to back down, especially now that her father's death had come into question. She just had to be careful. Be smart.

And Evelyn Monroe could have all the answers. She needed to talk to her, and she needed to get what Diggins asked for. And maybe Diggins would then tell her why he believed her father was murdered.

That just couldn't be. Her mother would have made sure that her father got justice if that was the case. Mom was many things that Cressida disliked, but she was still a woman about justice, and despite the divorce, her mother had still loved her father.

Braden grabbed Cressida's hand, again bringing her focus back to the moment. He tugged her down a long hall where he pulled her into Remi's office. The door was open, and Remi and Jo stood with two men. Braden motioned for the men to follow him out of the office and instructed Cressida to stay.

He closed the door, and the three men left Cressida with Remi and Jo.

"What was that about?" Jo asked.

Where did she even start? "Apparently Mrs. Monroe's assistant—Madeline—tried to kill her. I don't think he was supposed to tell me that or say anything at all. So maybe

I shouldn't have told you, but you both know her, don't you?"

"Oh no!" Remi pressed her hands over her mouth. After a few moments, she dropped them. "Please tell me she's okay."

"I think so, yes." Cressida sank down onto the sofa and rubbed her head. *And Dad might have been killed . . . but why?*

Jo and Remi bombarded her with questions. "Look, I don't know anything. I was with Braden when he got the call."

Remi sat at her desk and stared at her hands, and Jo sat on the sofa next to Cressida.

"I take it Braden's investigating," Remi said. "What did he need our guys for?"

"Your guys?"

"Oh," Remi said. "Well, the lumberjack-looking guy is my husband, Hawk, and the other guy that looks like him only taller, slimmer, is his brother, Cole, and Jo's fiancé."

"So . . . do you know what he wanted?" Jo asked. "Or why he wanted you to stay here?"

"I have a stalker, for one thing. Someone has been following me, and his vehicle is in your parking lot. Braden was headed to work on the investigation, but I suspect he wants to run interference on this guy."

"Oh, Cressida," Remi said. "Let me know whatever I can do to help you remain safe. You could stay at our place. Hawk and I have a house not far from here. It's on the property. You'd be safe there."

Wait. What? "I won't be safe here in the lodge?"

"I'm not implying you won't be safe here," Remi said. "I'm just saying that's an option if it would make you feel more comfortable."

"Thank you," Cressida said. "I appreciate the offer." Why were these people so nice? She wasn't accustomed to such kindness. She sat forward and rested her elbows on her thighs. "Listen, I know this is kind of morbid for me to ask in the middle of everything that's happened. But I really need to talk to Evelyn Monroe. Talking to her is going to give me some big answers. Tonight Braden took me out to talk to the so-called pirate king, Captain Diggins. He won't answer my questions unless I get something from her."

Remi narrowed her eyes. "What do you mean 'get'?"

"I don't mean *take*—of course not. No, no. I plan to talk to her. But now that Madeline has tried to cause her harm, me requesting an interview sounds so insensitive. I'm sorry."

"Cressida, what exactly did Diggins ask you to get? What does he want from Evelyn?"

"I don't know what it means. He simply said that he wanted the truth from her."

20

On his motorcycle, Braden raced to Driftwood Manor. He hadn't wanted to leave Cressida behind, especially after what she'd learned from Diggins. The man had a lot to answer for, but one thing at a time.

Braden had left Cressida in good hands.

Since taking on the position in the county offices as detective a few months ago, Braden had worked with Hawk and Cole on an investigation surrounding Jo, and he could trust them to watch out for Cressida. He'd had the bright idea a couple of months ago to enlist them as reserve deputies, so they essentially worked for the county sheriff's department when needed, holding full arrest powers.

The beautiful night had turned stormy, fitting for his mood. He put all his focus on the slick, curvy two-lane road that wound through a black forest, finally steering up to Evelyn Monroe's mansion on the cliff. An ambulance along with two county sheriff's department vehicles were parked on the circular drive at the front of the house.

Braden arrived just in time and bounded up the steps. No

crime-scene tape to secure the area or official log-in system to slow his entry, but this wasn't exactly a busy intersection. He stepped inside and took in the immaculate foyer, and beyond that, a sweeping staircase. He was curious to know more about someone who would choose to live alone in this gothic fortress overlooking the ocean.

The voice of an older woman speaking in both an authoritative and strained tone drifted to him as he continued into the living room to the left, where a stone fireplace made a grand statement. The silver-haired woman sat in a deep-blue velvet chair. And his gut clenched. Evelyn Monroe. Had to be. He'd never met her, but this was her home. And now part of it was a crime scene.

Braden hung back at the edge of the Persian rug, surprised as Trent spoke with her. Trent? Thatcher approached from behind and touched his shoulder, then motioned for him to follow him back into the foyer.

"Where are we?" Braden asked.

"Waiting on the coroner to give me the time of death to make sure everything works in the timeline."

"What happened?" Braden leaned in to say the words under his breath. He'd withheld from Cressida that someone had died tonight.

"Monroe returned from her trip earlier than expected and overheard Madeline arguing with a stranger in a room Monroe told her was off-limits. When Madeline exited the room, Monroe was standing at the top of the stairs and confronted her. Madeline pushed her, but Monroe was able to catch herself and didn't topple down the stairwell, which could have killed her. Madeline had wanted her dead, based on the conversation she overheard."

"And what was the conversation?"

"She hasn't told us yet," Thatcher said. "That's for *you* to find out."

"Then why is Trent talking to her?"

"He was already taking her statement when I arrived."

"So what happened next, after Madeline pushed her?"

"Madeline ran past Monroe and exited the premises. Monroe grabbed a shotgun from the gun closet and opened the door to the room where Madeline had been arguing to find a man standing there. *He* then lifted a handgun, aimed it at her, but she shot first."

"She killed him?"

Sheriff Thatcher nodded. "She's an eighty-one-year-old dynamo, and it goes without saying that she's upset."

Anguish weighed on Braden that Evelyn Monroe had been put through this.

"An APB has been put out on Madeline Chase."

"Do we know who the man was?"

"I think we do. Follow me upstairs."

Evelyn continued talking to Trent in her living room, even though Thatcher had already provided Braden with what sounded like her statement. A paramedic was taking her blood pressure. Maybe Trent was there providing additional support.

Braden caught a glimpse of her as he followed the sheriff upstairs and down a long hall, past several closed doors. The coroner was in the room at the end of the hall, where he stood over a body.

Braden instantly recognized the man. Jo had sketched his face after her session with Cressida.

"Got ID on him so we finally know who he is?"

Sheriff nodded. "Gordon Collins. I'm running the information to confirm his identity and see if he has a record."

Two deputies from the coroner's office arrived to bag the body.

"Let's talk outside," Thatcher said.

Braden preferred to stay inside and take it all in. His background included protection detail and threat assessment and prevention, but as a DSS agent, he also investigated crimes against State Department personnel. Working for Thatcher, he'd solved a couple of complex investigations and believed Thatcher trusted him to solve this one. Braden might have taken the job under a ruse, but now all of it was colliding, and he suspected that Octavia had fully known Braden would need to be in a position of investigative authority.

Bile rose in his throat at the thought, and he shoved it down, pushed away the violent thoughts to focus on this investigation that was growing in complexity. The crimes suddenly occurring with Cressida's arrival were loosely connected, if not completely.

He followed Thatcher out of the house, and they walked into the misty weather. Then Thatcher kept walking away from the mansion as if he intended to lead Braden well out of earshot until, finally, they stood over the ledge and watched a sliver of moon peek through the clouds rolling in. Below them, waves raced against rocks, flaring briefly with the faint blue-green glow of bioluminescence.

Stunning. Braden wished this was a moment to take in that phenomenon. But it wasn't. He waited for Thatcher to speak first.

"You and I never talked about this. We're not talking about this now. Are we clear?"

What is *this*? "Crystal."

"Why are you here?" Thatcher asked.

"It's my job." What was he *really* asking? Braden suspected he knew.

"No, I mean, why are you here in Hidden Bay?"

"You know why. I needed a job. It's stunning. Who wouldn't want to work here?"

Thatcher raked a hand over his head. "Give me a break.

You have a top-notch résumé. You could have gone any-where."

"Exactly. So I came here."

"Months ago, I got a call from Octavia Dane, offering up her reference. I didn't ask for one. But she offered."

Braden suspected he knew what was coming next. "You hired me because of her?"

"Of course. I liked you already, but I admit I considered passing. The reasons are many. You didn't fit this way of life. You're overqualified. Then I got a call from someone from the State Department, and that meant she wanted you here. I've been wondering why for months."

"And?" Braden hoped the sheriff had stumbled across an answer for which Braden still searched.

"You tell me."

"I didn't know until her daughter showed up," Braden said. "And honestly, I still don't know." He gestured at the mansion behind them.

"You think what happened here tonight is related to the reasons Dane sent you?" Thatcher asked.

"Without knowing more, I can't say for certain." But yes, he suspected as much. "This could be a coincidence. Collins was attacking women who are alone." Braden shrugged. That wasn't uncommon. "On the other hand, Octavia sent me here to protect her daughter, who needs to interview Mrs. Monroe. She's attacked upon her arrival, and Monroe is also attacked when she returns, and the same man is involved, so yes, I'm leaning heavily on the connection. One more thing, tonight I took Cressida to the *Sea Reaper* to meet with Diggins. He'd been attacked earlier, mere moments before we arrived, and the assailants returned. They almost got the best of me but got away." With the words, the pain suddenly throbbed again, as if he could forget. "I'll write up a full report tonight. Unfortunately, the incident involved me firing my gun." Braden didn't have time to be put on administrative leave and held his breath.

"I'll review the report. Now, what else?"

"Diggins claims he doesn't know who, what, or why, but I think he's hiding something. He mentioned that Cressida's father could have been murdered."

Thatcher rubbed the back of his neck. "What more can you tell me? Why did Mrs. Dane want you here?"

"That, I'm still trying to pry out of her." And unfortunately, Octavia Dane was never involved in anything that wasn't high-stakes drama all kept under wraps—that seemed to be her expertise.

"Keep me in the loop on your investigation. All of it. Especially the part where you learn more about how this is related to Ms. Dane."

"She prefers Valentine."

"Ms. Valentine. My point is that she's your priority."

"I'm the county investigator, not a personal security detail." Braden pushed back to find out where Thatcher really stood.

"Your experience is in protective detail, and I want you to lean in that direction. Can't have the daughter of a bigwig getting hurt on my watch. The truth of the matter is that we both know that you're here for one reason—Cressida Valentine Dane. Anything happens to her, and we'll both pay for the rest of our lives."

"So, we understand each other," Braden said.

"You keep your fingers on the pulse of everything but do it all from close personal contact with Cressida Dane. You have my full support."

"She's going to ask me why."

"And you're free to tell her."

"I'm not, actually. Part of the assignment was that she cannot know her mother is involved. They're estranged."

"That's a nasty predicament, and you're a smart man. I'm sure you'll figure it out."

The coroner stepped onto the porch and drew the sheriff's attention. Braden and Thatcher hiked toward the house.

"I'll do my duty here tonight, gather all the information, write up my report," Braden said. "I'll do it from my new location—the Cedar Trails Lodge."

"I could put you on leave. Make you take vacation. But then I'd lose my investigator."

"And I have a feeling Cressida would become suspicious. I'll come up with a plan and keep you informed. The best thing we can do is solve this quickly and help Cressida finish her business here."

"Agreed." Thatcher stepped up to speak with the coroner, and Braden followed. Got the information.

Then he headed inside to talk in person with Evelyn Monroe—a well-respected but reclusive elderly woman with a good heart who held tight reins on the Hidden Bay region. She'd only ever done good and assisted those in need.

And tonight, she'd shot and killed a man.

She didn't deserve to walk into her home to this violence. They'd need her to stay elsewhere for tonight at least. Worst case, a day or two, until he could release the scene. He walked into the living room where Trent was waiting with her.

"Mrs. Monroe," he said. "I'm Detective Braden Sanders."

"Detective. I've been waiting for the moment when we would talk about our shared interests but never imagined it would be under these circumstances."

Our shared interests?

Did she, too, have an interest in Cressida Dane?

21

In her room at the lodge, Cressida stared out at the endless darkness of a cloudy night over the Pacific. The aged frame creaked as she opened the window, letting in the salty breeze, so she could better hear the unending sound of the ocean. Some waves crashed against the rocks while others swept up the sandy beach, then slid back out to sea—all of it with a rhythm that soothed her bleeding soul.

And she desperately needed that comfort. Hard enough to accept her father was gone, but to think that he could have been murdered over what he'd discovered in Hidden Bay? Diggins could have shared more with her, but he chose to keep it from her.

She almost wanted to ask Braden to haul Diggins into the sheriff's office and interrogate him. But with no evidence that her father might have been murdered—that she knew about—it wasn't like Braden could officially interrogate him. No. She'd get Diggins what he wanted, and maybe she could also get answers of her own.

What *had* her father learned? What did her mother know about it, if anything? Cressida opened up her laptop and emailed a law enforcement friend in DC. Maybe he could look into it and find out more, and she could avoid calling her mother. Even if she did go groveling back—and that's what it would take—her mother wouldn't tell her anything.

Secrets. Her mother always had them.

And her father's secrets? He told her that he learned early on that a sunken shipwreck might tell a story, but the rest of its secrets sank deeper than the wreckage. She closed her eyes and once again listened to the ocean . . . and yes . . . she could hear the thrum of the ocean as if it whispered secrets only it could know.

A strong gust sent rain straight through the window to hit her face, startling her like the good, cold slap that she needed. Cressida shut the window and stepped away.

Time to get busy and find the truth before it was too late. *Sorry, Dad.*

Things had escalated. Her research here had an expiration date.

She couldn't take the time to interview multiple people or spend a day or two or three at the museum to learn more. She couldn't take the time to feel and enjoy the reminders of her father. She couldn't just hang out at the local coffee shop and listen to the chatter, ask about the lore, or even stop to join in singing sea shanties if someone were to suddenly break out with "Blow the Man Down." Everything she'd done over the last year, following Dad's path, revisiting the places he walked so she could see and feel for herself, had come down to this one last ghost ship story. After ten shipwrecks for his book, researching them had never led her to danger.

And with the risk factor, Cressida had lost her freedom. She wanted to walk on the beach right now, even in the rain, and be alone with her thoughts. Maybe she still could. After all, she now had *two* bodyguards.

No one had actually told her they were standing guard. She wasn't a prisoner locked in her room. But she knew those two bulky guys belonging to Remi and Jo were watching over her. Maybe in the past she would have felt incredulous at the intrusion. But in the past, not once had she ever felt like she'd been in danger or targeted like she was now. So she appreciated this extra protection while she uncovered the mystery behind her attack, Diggins's and Braden's attacks, and now Evelyn Monroe's attack.

Cressida needed to read through her journal and Dad's notes with fresh eyes, if only Dad's notes on the *Specter's Bounty* weren't so sparse. If only his journal wasn't missing pages—which she now found utterly suspicious.

She toyed with her cell phone. She could use her portable satellite to get a signal for her cell.

And she could call her mother. Distaste quickly rose in her mouth, and she drank from her soda can as if to wash the thought away. She'd emailed her friend and would wait for an answer from him.

I know I'm wrong to have walked away from her, Lord, but how in the world can I face her, talk to her, after what she's done?

Even knowing that God expected her to forgive her mother, she didn't know how to make that happen. Cressida had labored for years, and her mother had destroyed all her hard work in one fell swoop. One or two phone calls and her career was dead and gone forever.

Why, Mom? Why?

And deep down, she suspected there was a story there, a reason behind her mother's behavior. Cressida dreaded that reason. She suspected that with her mother's connections, digging would uncover a truth that put her mother's life and career at risk.

But for Dad—to find out more about what happened to

him—she could talk to her mother. She could call and find out if Octavia knew anything about Alaric Dane's death. Had any suspicions. And for all Cressida knew, her mother was connected to it somehow or even in danger herself.

And then . . . then she knew.

Or she suspected. That guy . . . her *stalker*.

Cressida got up, pulled on her raincoat/windbreaker, and left her room. Downstairs, a fire blazed in the massive fireplace, and lodge guests gathered to enjoy it or mingled near the coffee station. Not far, two broad-shouldered males emerged from the shadows on opposite ends of the lodge.

Okay. Now she was definitely feeling their invasiveness. She bounded down the steps and approached the lumber-jack guy—Hawk, wasn't it?

"Hi, so, I need to talk to the guy," she said.

He shrugged. "The guy?"

Then Cole approached. She was surrounded by these big men with extremely protective demeanors. Kind of like the men who guarded her mother—DSS special agents. A thought flitted through her mind and then escaped. She couldn't capture it again. Cole and Hawk stared at her even as they continued to project fierce protection. Their behavior almost made Cressida appear like she was someone important, when she wanted to remain invisible and behind the scenes and be nobody who resembled her mother.

"People are staring," she said. "Please . . . back down."

"We're helping a friend," Hawk said. "Keeping you safe."

"You want to keep me safe? Then help me find the guy. I need to talk to him."

"Not sure that's a good idea." Hawk again. "Want one of us to talk to him?"

"Braden wants that chore." This from Cole.

Braden had his chance to talk to the guy at the restaurant. "Look, I think I know who he is." Sort of. "You can come too. It's not like I can stop you. So where is he? And don't tell me you don't know."

"Honestly, we don't." Hawk shared a look with Cole. "He left."

"What? And you didn't follow him? Seems like you would have." Maybe they were somehow tracking him. "Whatever. So is it possible I could get some fresh air?"

"It's dark and raining." Cole crossed his arms.

"Right. Fine. Okay." Cressida got some coffee and then went back upstairs to her room.

She opened the door and stepped out onto the small veranda this time. The rain had settled to a light mist, but she would get wet all the same. She closed her eyes and sighed. Once this was over . . . *Oh, Lord, please let it just be over* . . . she could actually live in a place that provided peace and quiet and was sparsely populated.

And . . . Braden . . .

Yeah, what had she been thinking, telling him that she liked him? Her time in Hidden Bay was stirring up the worst of memories regarding her mother—Cressida's career, and then being ghosted, or rather dumped, by the guy she'd been dating for six months because of her career. Was she ready to put her heart on the line and trust someone, especially someone she barely knew, after what she'd been through already? Not that their "like" of each other had gone anywhere or would go anywhere.

Before she got too soaked, Cressida moved back inside, and then on her laptop, she spotted the returned email. Her friend's email wasn't working anymore. Hmm. She blew out a defeated sigh and found Mom's cell number. This was a good number unless she'd changed it. Her finger hovering over the number, Cressida fought the surging tears and the ache in her throat. When and if she talked to Mom, she absolutely had to be in control of that conversation, and right now the emotions still ran too high.

A text came in from Braden, sending relief through her. She could put off her call to Mom.

If you're still up, meet me downstairs.

On my way.

She downed the rest of her coffee, glad for the caffeine. The day had worn her down, but a text from Braden gave her an adrenaline surge. She traveled the stairwell, searching for him as she descended. His two buddies didn't emerge from the shadows. Instead, Braden stood in the middle of the floor and stared up at her.

The look he gave her was a mix of admiration and, oddly, both fear and determination. Her pulse kicked up, and she took her time descending the stairs. When she finally approached and was close enough to see, his face looked haggard, but his eyes were as sharp as ever.

"Braden . . ." His name came out as a whisper, maybe telling him how glad she was to see him. Not what she'd intended.

And the slightest flinch in his features revealed his raw reaction. She hadn't expected that, and something deep inside stirred. She could be reading him all wrong—he'd been through a lot tonight.

"Are you okay?" she asked. What a ridiculous question.

He pulled a hand from his leather jacket. "Let's go somewhere we can talk."

She glanced around the space. "There's a table over there."

"I mean, let's get out of here."

"Okay. I just need to get my jacket."

From her room, Cressida grabbed her windbreaker and

stuffed her small wallet and cell in a pocket, then joined Braden at his vehicle.

"So you switched rides," she said. "I can't say I'm not disappointed. It was fun earlier, dinner and the ride, before all the chaos. I guess what I'm saying is that, in your official county vehicle, it feels more like business."

"Is that a good thing or a bad thing?"

Hard to say. "Probably the best thing."

Great. As if the rest of their venture together was personal. She'd given her thoughts away. To his credit, Braden said nothing more, but he was brooding. On the dark, lonely road, he navigated down the sharp drop to the marina, then kept driving in the opposite direction of the Pirates' Bash preparation and to a deserted part of the shore where vehicles could park. She'd seen a couple of vehicles earlier, but tonight she and Braden were alone.

"You want to get out?" he asked.

In the Pacific Northwest, the clouds and rain moved in and then onward before another band of clouds. At this moment, the rain had moved on, and she caught a glimpse of the night sky. "Yes."

She pulled her jacket tighter. She didn't have to pretend with him. They'd both admitted that they liked each other, but she was already having regrets. Was he having those same regrets? She wished she could take it all back. Neither of them had time for a like relationship with chaos and murder around them.

And standing out here alone with him under the stars felt like they now moved away from professional and back into dangerous territory.

"So what's happened? What's going on?" she asked.

"So much." He shrugged out of his jacket and laid it across the hood of the vehicle. "Madeline is on the run. She took off."

"So she's out there and dangerous?"

"We'll catch her. Her face is everywhere. But there's something else." The way his chin dipped and his eyes locked on her, she knew she should brace herself.

"The guy who attacked you on the beach is dead."

What? "I don't want to be relieved that someone is dead, but I wasn't expecting that. You're on the case, then?"

"I am working the case right here and now. You deserve to know the man who attacked you is dead."

And still, he had more to say. She could tell by the angle of his chin. She didn't know him well, but she knew at least that much about him. And right now, that look gave her chills. "I can tell there's more. I'm listening."

"I can't know for certain, but you arrive in Hidden Bay, and you're attacked. Diggins, who has a connection to you, is attacked, and Monroe. It feels like you're at the center of what's going on. Or rather, your research is."

"I kind of figured that." She couldn't hold Braden's stare. Rubbing her arms, she took in the stars and another set of clouds crawling toward them from out over the Pacific. "Why are you telling me this? What do you want from me?"

"I want your permission to stick close to you."

Okay. She definitely hadn't expected that. "So you can solve the mystery behind a ghost ship?"

"You bring up a good point. Solving that mystery could help resolve this, but in the meantime, I want you to be safe. I already told you it's my priority."

"And your sheriff would agree to you being my protection." This felt off to her. "Braden . . . *Detective* Sanders . . . not saying that I don't welcome the protection, and if that's what it takes for me to finish Dad's book, I'm all for it. But why are you really doing this?" *There's much more to you than you've shared, and I might need to dig deeper.*

"Thatcher insisted on it. I have his full support."

Then it hit her. Maybe it had been staring her in the face and she'd been slow to see it. She stood tall and lifted her chin. "I get it now. You're not so much concerned about *me* as an individual. It's because of who I'm related to. It's because of my mother. You've learned that much about me."

Braden lifted his hands in surrender. "I'm surprised you don't already have security detail. But let's be clear." Then he closed the distance.

Cressida might have stepped back and fallen over a log, but he caught her and pulled her a little too close. "I would be here protecting you with or without Thatcher's directive. I'm saying, regardless of your connections, I would be here, Cressida, for you . . . *You.*" Then he leaned closer, and his next words she barely heard over the waves. "Do you understand?"

Cressida couldn't move. She couldn't speak. He was close enough he might kiss her. Against all common sense, she closed her eyes and lifted her chin. *Kiss me already.*

Pounding footsteps drew near, and he stepped away, reached for his gun. A jogger ran by them a little too close.

"Sorry!" he shouted.

And the moment was broken. What had just happened? What was going on between them?

Braden took two steps back. "Watch that log behind you."

She couldn't see his eyes in the shadows, but she could feel the intensity coming off him. What would it have felt like to have been kissed by him?

Come on, Cressida, you're not some middle schooler with a hard crush.

"About Mrs. Monroe," he said. "A deputy took her statement, but I talked to her later." He hesitated, then, "She shot the man—your attacker—in self-defense."

"Oh . . ." The thought of that poor elderly woman shooting and killing someone rocked through her.

Her knees buckled a little. She hadn't met Evelyn Monroe, but the news still stunned her. She swiped at a couple of errant tears. "Is she okay?"

"She's upset. And she said some things that surprised me. I'm still thinking about them, but I got you an interview with her too, Cressida."

"But . . . I can't imagine she'd want to talk to me after this. How did you manage that? Why even focus on it?"

"She believes it's imperative she speaks with you soon. She held back from telling me, but I strongly suspect it's related."

"Okay. You're kind of scaring me."

"If it was up to me, I'd say pack up and go home. Get away from this."

"But you think I'm going to keep digging no matter the danger." She'd never let go of a story in her life. What was happening here went much deeper than research to finish Dad's book. This was a story, but she wasn't entirely sure what it was about.

"While I believe you certainly have the tenacity to continue no matter what, I think packing up and going home isn't going to make you safe. It isn't going to save you."

What did he know that he wasn't telling her? His words chilled her to the bone, because she agreed. She wanted to leave for her safety, but go where? What then? Her father—if he was murdered because of what he'd learned—had been killed in DC, which was on the opposite coast. "And you *are?*"

"I intend to keep you safe, yes. I thought I made that clear."

I can't believe I'm in so much danger this guy and his sheriff want to guard me. Not quite protective-custody danger, but maybe he knew she would never stand for that, and to find out the truth about what was going on, she needed to continue her research.

But that truth could get her killed too, if it had in fact gotten her father killed.

She felt his eyes still on her, as if he was waiting on a response from her. Oh, she had a response, all right. Her heart was pounding. It should be pounding because she was in this much trouble, this much danger, but instead, she knew it pounded for an entirely different reason . . .

The man with the steel-blue eyes who stood like a fortress between her and danger—as if she belonged to him.

22

I n all his travels around the world, his assignments, and then that last reassignment to Octavia Dane, he'd never run into such an odd set of incidents connected to or surrounding an even odder search. He struggled to believe that any of it could be related to Cressida or her father's research about the *Specter's Bounty*, but it seemed those questions stirred the waters and now they were frothing and would start to boil soon. He could feel it.

Octavia, what have you gotten me into?

He wouldn't be here now if something big wasn't brewing. His only choice was to keep moving forward—for Elise's sake, and now for Cressida's. His thoughts and prayers remained on Elise and her improvement, but maybe that's why his brain had been ignoring the warning signals going off in his head when it came to Cressida.

She was at the center, if only because she'd stirred the waters. She stared up at him, absorbing the news he'd shared. He thought she'd be happy, but under the circumstances, she was surprised Mrs. Monroe would give her an interview, much less ask to see her.

"When does she want to see me?" she asked.

"Whenever you're ready."

"I can't imagine she would be in a good state of mind after shooting someone." Cressida shifted back and forth in the sand. "Unless she thinks I'm connected to what happened."

That's what Braden intended to find out. "She shared that Madeline never mentioned you wanted an interview."

"That liar. I would love to know what Madeline was doing working for Mrs. Monroe. What is her story?"

The wind gusted and rain started up. The weather was always changing. "I need to get you back. It's late. I didn't want to talk about this where anyone could hear us."

"You can call off your bodyguards, you know."

He arched a brow. "Why's that?"

"I think I know who's following me. I can't be sure . . . I need to look into it."

"Or I could just talk to him like you suggested at the restaurant." He rubbed his chin. "I should have done it then. Let me take care of it."

"That's fine. Please do. Bottom line is that I don't want to be trapped in my room. I have work to do."

They got back in his vehicle, and he took her to Cedar Trails and led her inside.

At the top of the stairwell, she turned to face him. "You don't have to walk me to my room. I'm good now."

I should just tell her, though she might not like it. "I booked a room here too."

Fire surged in her vibrant green eyes. "But . . . what about the investigation? Don't you need to be close to your headquarters?"

"Actually, this works out better. Everything I'm looking into is here on the coast, but this keeps me close to you too. As I mentioned, protecting you is my priority, and that comes from the top." And she had no idea just how high from the top that came. Maybe he could figure out how to tell her what he'd been charged with hiding. That he was working for her mother, the currency an experimental drug to save his niece's life.

"While I don't expect you to be my personal protection detail, Braden, I appreciate it." Cressida smiled, then entered her room.

He turned to walk the hall to his own room, then spotted Hawk heading for him.

Braden met him halfway. "So, the stalker?"

"He left early on," Hawk said. "He's staying at the Forest Trails Inn in Forestview. You want us to pay him a visit?"

"Thanks for the intel. I'll meet him myself," he said. Cressida had an idea who he was working for. Braden had suspected as much, too, and would find out.

"This is my busy season with helicopter tours," Hawk said, "and Cole is heading to Spokane for a job in a few days, but if you need help, please just say the word."

"I will," Braden said.

"What's this about, really?" Arms crossed, Hawk leaned against the rail.

"I'm not entirely sure."

Hawk studied him, but Braden felt sure he understood. "I have to write up my reports, so better get to my room. I'll send them in online when I get internet."

Hawk grinned. "Yeah, about that. Secretly, I can give you the connection, which is hidden from anyone searching for it."

"Text me the information so I can find it."

Braden decided against going to his room just yet. He needed to make a phone call and didn't know if anyone could hear him through the walls, so he bid Hawk good night and said he needed something in his car. He got in the vehicle and steered out of Cedar Trails Lodge until he got a signal, and then he stopped on the side of the road. If he spent too much more time here, it might be time to get a satellite phone, but even those had issues here.

Octavia answered immediately and sounded like she was still awake. And he started right in.

"Did you send someone to follow her?" he demanded.

"Yes."

"You didn't trust me?"

"You can't work two jobs. I was getting worried."

"Well, now he has caused a problem. Look, why don't you just make up with her, and then I can tell her that I'm here for you?"

"That's just not possible. I'm sorry."

"Things have escalated. Someone was killed tonight, and we believe it's the very man who attacked her when she got here."

Octavia gasped. "You think it's related?"

"You tell me."

"Braden—"

"She needs to know everything. She needs to know you think she's in danger. Tonight, she learned from Diggins that her father could have been murdered. This is all getting out of hand. You haven't been up-front with me."

"You can't tell her about your connection to me. She'll never speak to you again."

"And that's why you sent the other guy. In case I blew it. The only problem is, she would eventually learn he was from you too. So call her. Make amends."

"You don't understand. I destroyed any vestige of our relationship."

"You want to tell me how?"

"Not that it's your business."

"Listen, her life could be in danger. Maybe if I understand

the dynamics, I can find a way around them to tell her the truth."

"I'm public enemy number one in her mind. She was working on a story that I was against from the start. Digging into places she shouldn't dig. I asked her nicely. I begged her to shut it down. I even misdirected her."

"Imagine that," he said.

"Watch your words."

"Look. You want me to have success and keep her safe. I need to know everything." *Come on, Octavia. Give me something.*

Octavia hesitated. Sighed. Then said, "I made some calls. She lost her job at a prestigious magazine, and now nobody will look at her."

Her words stunned Braden. He would give anything if he could hang up on her and never speak to her again too, just like her daughter.

"I'm guessing whatever she was investigating would lead back to you and cause you problems." He probably shouldn't have said that.

"Remember who you're talking to."

The expected threat let him know he'd hit a nerve. He remained silent rather than pressing her. Slow and easy won the game, and this definitely felt like a game he played with her—the person who held the power of life and death over his niece. His heart.

"I'm devastated, and my hope and prayer is one day she will come back around and understand my side." Her voice cracked.

The way she said "one day" made it sound like that time was far into the future.

No matter the reason for the rift, Octavia loved her daughter as much as any mother could, and until he knew the whole story, he should reserve his judgment. Still . . .

who was Braden working for? Was he working with a criminal?

"And at some point, you'll tell me what her investigation was all about too." He could possibly find out on his own, unless Octavia had it scrubbed completely from all parties and the internet. She had the contacts and the pull and therefore the power to do it. That's what made it hard for Cressida to learn about Braden's association with DSS and her mother, if she had even tried.

But maybe it would be as simple as Cressida telling him that story. In the meantime, he hated himself for keeping such a big secret from Cressida. She didn't deserve this.

"Is it relevant to why I'm here? Connected in any way?"

"Remember the deal you have with me."

Not an answer. He would take that as an affirmative, otherwise she could have said no.

Was Octavia so coldhearted that she would pull her assistance? He couldn't believe that about any person. Regardless, he was a man of honor. "Yes. I owe you, and I'll keep up my end of our deal as long as Elise is receiving the treatment she needs." His heart lurched at the thought of his niece and all she'd gone through. "I'm simply trying to know all the moving pieces so nothing falls through the cracks and I'm not caught off guard. If I know *everything*, then I could see connections in places that you can't."

"I'll grant you that, Braden—and it's why I selected you to help me."

In addition to the fact that she could hold something over him, but he wasn't in a position to argue.

"Then please, tell me something you haven't told me yet. I know that you're holding back."

Several heartbeats ticked by, then, "I shut down the article because it had international implications and would only bring danger to her door. I knew she would continue to pursue it, so to save her life, I used my connections and favors and shut her down. Completely." Her voice cracked. "I love my daughter very much, and I would do anything for her."

"Why couldn't you simply tell her why she shouldn't pursue the exposé?"

"That information would only feed her story. Cressida isn't someone who can be shut down so easily, if at all."

"And now she's found a way back to that story, even if she doesn't realize it. Is that it?" He was basing that off her nonanswer earlier and throwing darts to see if he could hit a target.

She said nothing, and he thought he'd lost the connection, or . . . he'd hit the target.

"From now on, I want a daily report," she said. Another nonanswer.

Bull's-eye.

Yeah, that's not happening. Probably a good thing she ended the call because he wasn't going to say anything she would like. Now he needed to find out what Cressida was working on when she was shut down before she took on her father's book.

23

Cressida was up bright and early on Friday morning, planning to meet with Evelyn Monroe at her home. Only one room had been deemed a crime scene, and it had already been released. Her palms were sweating and her limbs a little shaky. Totally unusual for her, but with so much at stake, and danger closing in on all sides, this interview could mean everything. It could get her the answer Diggins needed. Still, with thoughts of Braden pressing in on her, memories of that almost kiss, she struggled to focus.

She'd wanted that kiss too. Had he seen her reaction? Heat washed through her, flushing her with embarrassment. The two of them were a bad combination. He was an unlikely detective and she an unlikely journalist writing a shipwreck book.

Straightening her blouse, she refocused on the upcoming interview.

Mrs. Monroe had shot and killed the man who'd attacked Cressida on the beach. The fact that the woman had asked to see Cressida afterward terrified her.

Cressida had come here to Hidden Bay for many reasons,

but a priority had been to interview Mrs. Monroe. Instead, it felt like Cressida had been *summoned* by the woman. Still, this could be the best outcome because maybe Mrs. Monroe could tell her more about why she was here. She could offer detailed answers regarding the *Specter's Bounty* that Cressida hadn't learned at the museum or through Diggins. Had Mrs. Monroe met with her father, and if so, could she tell her more about what he'd learned? And vitally important, Cressida could ask her about the truth that Diggins wanted.

The pressure built up in her head. So much was riding on this interview, and she had to be on top of her game. Cressida tried to look as professional as possible, donning black business slacks and a conservative pale-blue blouse. She'd hung them both in the bathroom to steam out the wrinkles. But steaming had the exact opposite effect on her hair, and it was a frizzy mess this morning. The salty ocean breeze and misty fog turned her red curls into every woman's nightmare. Cressida pulled the red mess into a tight bun, but she looked severe rather than confident.

I'm overthinking.

She'd always been confident in her work until her career had been destroyed. The anger rose up again, and she shoved it away. No time to think about that. She'd gotten herself together mentally and emotionally by focusing on Dad's book, and through his work she'd become confident once again. That is, until she'd arrived in Hidden Bay, and now her mission had shifted and was about more than finishing Dad's book.

I promise I'll finish it, Dad. That book was all she had at the moment.

In spite of her resolve, she couldn't shake the sense of dread, the foreboding that she was walking into a dark and treacherous alley and that once again she stood on shaky ground.

One last look in the mirror and she grabbed her computer bag and duffel, then headed down to the lobby.

Braden waited to escort her to the manor. He brought stability to this situation, and at the same time, the man shook her up inside for entirely different reasons. She needed calm right now, and she was glad he kept their conversation light this morning on the short drive to Mrs. Monroe's.

Finally they arrived, and he steered around the circular drive and parked in front. She took a deep breath. This was it.

She'd never been nervous about an interview in her life. "What do you know about her? Is there anything you can tell me?" She'd wanted to form her own opinion, but now she wished she knew at least something in addition to the limited information she'd already learned.

He turned to her. "I don't know a lot, really. But I get the feeling that she's the heart of the Hidden Bay community. She helps people who are desperate."

"What do you mean?"

"Maybe just talk to her, Cressida, and see what you think."

He was right. She would do better going into this interview to learn from Mrs. Monroe herself about who she was. "Please, just wait in the car," she said. "Let me talk to her alone."

He nodded. She got out and walked up to the door. When she turned around to glance at him, he leaned against the car, arms crossed.

Now Cressida needed to ring the doorbell. Knock the knocker. Something. She just never imagined her knees would shake at the thought of finally meeting Evelyn Monroe.

Braden cleared his throat. Nudging her? *Yeah, I know. I know.*

Before she could knock, the door swung open. Cressida

had half expected to face a new assistant—someone to replace Madeline. Unless Mrs. Monroe had hired another assistant, the silver-haired woman with a sharp gaze, a soft gray cardigan to match her eyes, tailored slacks, white pearls, and soft red lipstick—a woman who was the definition of quiet elegance—was Evelyn Monroe.

Cressida stood speechless and unprofessional by her own standards.

Mrs. Monroe's eyes held the wisdom of ages, and for a moment, Cressida thought the woman might look into her soul and discover dark secrets Cressida hadn't even known she was hiding. Then her eyes brightened, lines crinkling around them with her warm smile.

"Ms. Valentine, I presume?"

Cressida shook off whatever had gripped her and smiled. She thrust out her hand. "Yes. And you must be Mrs. Monroe."

"Call me Evelyn. My friends always do."

I'm your friend? "Thank you, and please, call me Cressida."

"Please come in." Evelyn looked beyond Cressida. "And your friend can come too."

"Oh no. He's not my friend. He's just . . ."

"Detective Sanders," she called out with a strong, loud voice. "Please join us inside."

"I don't want to intrude," he said.

"Don't be ridiculous." Evelyn looked at Cressida, a question in her eyes. "Unless you object."

"No, it's fine." She'd just ignore his presence and ask the questions she wanted to ask. Cressida stepped inside, and Braden joined her.

They hung their coats in the coat closet.

"Join me in the sitting room." Mrs. Monroe led them through the foyer to a spacious room with a view of the ocean.

Though Evelyn's smile was genuine, Cressida easily saw the sadness in her eyes, in every line of her face.

A trim, neatly dressed woman in her forties brought a tray with coffee, tea, and treats. "Will there be anything else, Mrs. Monroe? I have that appointment we discussed."

"No, nothing else, thank you."

Cressida shrugged off the feeling she had stepped back into her mother's world.

Focus on the interview. Or, more importantly, why Evelyn had asked to see *her*. Everything hinged on what Evelyn would tell her, and then she would need to convince this woman to share whatever truth Diggins needed so she could pass it on. The pressure moved from her head and built in her chest.

Evelyn poured Cressida and Braden coffee and took tea herself. She was completely poised and self-possessed, willing to serve as well, even after what she'd been through the day before. All Cressida could think was that Mrs. Monroe—Evelyn—sensed time was running out too.

"Thank you for agreeing to meet with me. I've been trying to arrange this . . ." Oh, could she be any more insensitive? "I'm sorry, I shouldn't have mentioned that, well, considering . . ." Cressida was a bungling mess, and Braden would be less than impressed. Had she *ever* been a journalist?

"Please don't apologize. I'm glad we're here. Now's the moment. Please ask your questions. I think I might have been waiting too many years for someone to finally come to my door and ask."

No pressure there. *God, please let me do this justice. Please let me ask the right questions.* But Mrs. Monroe insisting that Cressida ask her questions first made her wonder why the woman had requested to see her. Cressida had assumed she had something to talk to her about, even something pressing.

"I was told that you asked to see me," Cressida said.

"Yes. And here you are." Evelyn smiled and took a sip from her teacup. Behind her, rolling white clouds blew through a bright-blue day, and Cressida almost felt like she was in a dream.

"Is it all right if I take notes?"

"Certainly. I'd prefer you didn't record our conversation, though."

"Of course." Cressida retrieved her notebook from her bag and opened it, holding her pen, ready to take her notes. She would need to focus on every word the woman said and was glad that Braden would listen in too, since she couldn't refer back to a recording. But first, she would explain herself.

"My father died just over a year ago, and I've decided to finish his book. He was a maritime historian working on a book about shipwrecks and ghost ships. I'm here in Hidden Bay to focus on the *Specter's Bounty*. Your name was in his journal as someone he meant to interview, but he didn't supply the reasons why. He ended the trip abruptly and didn't leave more notes. I'm not even sure if he talked to you already. Either way, I'd love to hear your story." *As it relates to the ghost ship.* But the woman had a charisma about her, an intrigue, that left Cressida wanting to know everything about her. Braden's information—that she helped those who were desperate—added to the mystery.

Evelyn set her teacup down with a gentle clank, then sat back. "At the core, the story is simple. My family owned and ran a shipping line back East. My father didn't like the man I loved, and so he sent him off to work on the other side of the world, and then informed me he'd been killed."

Cressida's throat tightened. Though her circumstances were different, she could completely relate to the crushing blow of a parent's controlling actions. "I'm so sorry."

She wrote in her notebook.

"I was devastated, of course, and I did the only thing any proper woman could do."

Cressida waited for more.

Evelyn chuckled. "I told my father I was done with him, then I searched for Nick. I wanted proof that he was dead. Of course, I knew what my father was capable of, and I knew that I had to do this. I hired a private investigator to help me, and he found Nick in Jakarta. I married him and, a year later, we had a beautiful baby boy—Caleb."

"Did you try to reconcile with your father?"

"Absolutely not. I was afraid of what he might do. Part of me wanted my son to have a grandfather, but then I feared my father's influence on him. Nick was killed a couple of years after Caleb was born. I had no choice but to go back to Boston and work at Harborstone. My father refused financial assistance unless I came back. I took the job he offered and remained a single mother raising a child. Yes, I had to go back to the man on whom I blamed all my problems. Though I had no proof, I believed he was behind Nick's death. Again."

This was far more information than Cressida had expected, and she held back the tears. While she was eager to understand how this related to the *Specter's Bounty*, she would allow the woman her story.

"Then . . ." She released a heavy sigh. "Caleb. I blame myself. This is all on me. Caleb got into trouble with the wrong people. He had to disappear, and my father sent him off on a cargo ship in exchange for his safety. A boat that was lost at sea. It felt like I was reliving a nightmare. Just like he'd sent Nick away, he sent Caleb away. Except my father loved Caleb. Adored him."

Was this the lost *Specter's Bounty*? Caleb was the connection here?

Evelyn stared at her empty teacup, her expression grim. Cressida was surprised she allowed herself to be so vulnerable with a stranger. She didn't know how to steer the conversation to the ghost ship, but she wouldn't push. Mrs. Monroe had shared this story for a reason. It must be connected.

Finally, Evelyn sat up tall, composed, her mind back in the present. "You're here about your father's book and his research. There's much to know about the *Specter's Bounty*. For one, that isn't the original name the locals called the ghost ship."

"I learned a few things at the museum. It was previously called the *Endeavor Spirit*, and it was lost."

Evelyn froze and her eyes flashed. "That's the story we're told."

"So it's not true?"

"The truth is complicated. It's also dangerous. Before my father died, he sold the company—our family's company—because he had no one to take it on. I wasn't going to take it. He did, however, give me a sizable chunk of money, and by then I had grown older and wiser, and I took that money. I was a woman with a mission. Then, after he died, my biggest regret was that I hadn't forgiven him while he was alive. I still blamed him for Nick's death, and then I blamed him for Caleb's death too, though I knew my father mourned his grandson. He had to die before I realized that I needed to forgive him no matter what he'd done."

Cressida couldn't fathom why Evelyn would tell her. Still . . . "But you believe he was involved in your husband's death. In other words, sending him to his death. It was intentional. How do you forgive someone like that?" The words were out of her mouth before she could pull them back.

Evelyn's eyes grew gentle as if she sensed Cressida's deeper personal struggle. "It isn't that he deserved my forgiveness. None of us is deserving."

Cressida waited for more but then realized Evelyn had said all she would say. Embarrassed at her outburst, she focused on her notes, writing out what she'd heard.

Then Evelyn continued. "I purchased this property and the lodge . . . I sat in this big, old manor and watched and waited for my son's ship to return. I hired three different investigators to find the ship he was on that went missing, find out what happened to it at the very least. Each of them came back empty-handed and then died shortly after." Evelyn drew in a long breath, then slowly released it. She lifted her gaze to meet Cressida's, as if what she would say next was something profound. "Death seemed to surround my search, so I ended it. I never wanted anyone else to end up like Caleb. To be on the run for their life, caught up in danger they couldn't escape. So when a situation comes to my attention, I arrange for safe harbor here in Hidden Bay, but that's all I'll say on that. It's no longer safe if too many people know."

She held Cressida's gaze—her eyes intense, dark, and filled with meaning. "Do you understand?"

"Absolutely." Cressida understood she should never cross this woman.

If she didn't have to.

Cressida sat on the plush sofa, stunned at Evelyn's story—this one-of-a-kind story that she could have read in a novel. It seemed surreal. Evelyn had raised more questions. Why had she wanted to talk to Cressida? As if her story or what she would say might be connected to Cressida's search and reveal the truth about the ghost ship. Now it was her job to direct the conversation.

"I noticed the photograph of the *Specter's Bounty* in the Cedar Trails Lodge, and others claimed to have seen it. Have . . . you . . . ?" The question came out raspy.

"No. I've never seen it." Evelyn's eyes remained on Cressida, but her thoughts were far away.

"But the picture . . . I believe Remi Beckett, your employee, took the photograph. It's hanging up at the lodge."

"Yes," Evelyn said slowly. "That appears to be a picture of the salvage boat the locals call *Specter's Bounty*."

Her tone had changed and was measured now. Guarded. Like a door slowly closing. She'd been only too willing to talk about the *Specter's Bounty* moments before, even sharing deep personal secrets about her life.

Cressida had to somehow bring her back around to talk about her son's disappearance. "So your son disappeared on the *Specter's Bounty*?" She assumed he had, since they'd been discussing the boat.

But Evelyn didn't answer.

Braden leaned forward. "Wait. That's not it, is it? He was on another—"

"Shush." Evelyn's face twisted, angry lines carving deeper into her gentle features. "I've said too much already."

Had Braden picked up on some nuance that Cressida had missed?

With the release of a shaky breath, Evelyn shifted from formidable to feeble.

"I don't understand." Mrs. Monroe hadn't asked to see her to simply shut her down. Maybe recalling her own story had triggered a memory she didn't want to relive or share. Cressida ignored the surging disappointment. She thought she'd get answers from Evelyn—especially since her father seemed to put so much emphasis on an interview with her—but now Cressida only had more questions.

Investigators came back empty-handed and then died shortly after. Maybe thoughts of those who'd died on this treacherous search caused the shift in the woman's attitude. Warning signals went off in Cressida's head. One question burned inside her mind and heart the brightest—*Was my father truly murdered over this? And by whom?*

To get those answers, she needed to ask the woman one more question—about the truth Diggins sought.

"I'm sorry, dear," Mrs. Monroe said. "I fear I've made a mistake in inviting you here. I know I haven't provided the answers you were looking for in terms of completing your father's book. There's another darker secret behind it all, and perhaps it shouldn't be unearthed. I—"

A loud thump resounded from upstairs at the same time the lights flickered.

24

Braden ushered Evelyn and Cressida away from the window.

"It's just the wind," Evelyn said. "Takes the power out at times."

"I'd agree, except for the thump upstairs. Is anyone else in the house?" Braden had watched her assistant drive away.

She slowly shook her head.

"I need to check that out." The manor was too far from the tree line for the wind to have blown a tree over onto the house.

"Cressida?" Braden shifted toward her as he grabbed his 9mm gun and headed toward the door. "Close the door and lock it."

"We'll be okay here," she said.

He'd radio for backup, though it normally took entirely too long for official law enforcement backup to come out, and both Hawk and Cole weren't readily available. Braden stepped out into the shadowed hallway and listened.

Watched and waited.

The slightest creak sounded from above.

Upstairs.

Cressida moved to close the door to the room.

On second thought . . . "Come on. Let's get you outside and into my vehicle. Someone's upstairs."

"Upstairs?" Evelyn gasped. "But—"

"Let's go." He cleared the front area, then rushed them outside. He urged Cressida into the driver's seat.

She didn't question his thinking. He started to close the door, but she grabbed his hand—a spark of energy coursed up his arm. "Braden, be careful."

"I will." He shut the door. Raced back to the house, then crept inside. How could someone think it would be a good idea to "illegally" enter a room upstairs while a Timberbrook County detective, Cressida, and Evelyn were inside the house.

The only reason someone would risk it was if they were afraid that time was running out. He crept up the grand circular staircase, portraits of the ocean, Boston, the Washington coastline, and Evelyn's family lining the walls. She hadn't fully given up her legacy, bringing at least those memories—along with finances—with her to Washington. One portrait of an older man—her father or grandfather?—stared back at him, eyes seeming to follow him as he started toward the room where someone made entirely too much noise.

Tightening his grip on his handgun, he crept forward, mentally preparing to face off with a bold criminal—someone willing to risk much for what they wanted. Braden remained guarded in case others were present and tried to approach him from behind. He crept toward the room next to where Collins had been shot and gently pushed the door open. He entered the ransacked room but found it empty. Curtains flapped in the breeze of an open window. Had the intruder escaped? Or was this a ruse? Was someone still inside? He cleared the room.

At the window, he leaned out. No rope or ladder to assist

with the almost twenty-foot drop. Braden painstakingly cleared the rest of Driftwood Manor and contacted Trent to make sure he brought an evidence kit. Cressida and Evelyn had dutifully waited in his car the entire time. Clouds moved back in, and the sky decided to unleash a torrent on them to add to the drama of the day. He ushered them both back into the house and explained what he'd found to Evelyn. Evelyn had never given him any details about the argument between Madeline and Collins.

"A deputy is coming out to dust for prints that could tell us who was in your house today. Are you sure you didn't hear what your assistant and Collins were arguing about?"

Evelyn's face paled. "I didn't hear the words, only the tone."

He suspected she knew what this was about. "Today someone was in the room next to where Collins was shot, searching, while a county detective and investigative journalist were in the house with you. That's a big risk, if you ask me. What was so important? What were they looking for?"

This woman was held in high regard by everyone. She went out of her way to assist those in need—a very particular need, that is. So why was she hiding something?

"No!" Evelyn hurried toward the stairs, abandoning her usual grace as she bounded up each step with a speed that took him by surprise.

"It's a crime scene now. Again." Whatever. "Please don't go in there," he called after her.

But he wouldn't physically stop her. He followed as she entered the room—without him even having to show her which one. She stood in the center of the room, taking in the destruction, a look of horror on her face, then she sank down on the edge of the bed and held her chest.

Cressida's face was panic-stricken as she shared a brief glance with him, then sat next to Evelyn on the bed. "Evelyn, are you okay?"

Braden moved to stare out the still-open window and shut it so the rain wouldn't blow into the room. He hated touching the window, but the rain would wipe away the evidence just the same. He would preserve what he could. When Trent got here, Braden would take to those woods and search, though whoever had been inside this room was long gone.

Evelyn knew something. She hadn't struck him as the type of person to hold on to a secret that could prove dangerous to others, if that's what was happening here. Then again there was the matter of her shushing him when he brought up another boat. The intruder's actions here today made it clear that someone was desperate to uncover—or bury—a secret.

The dangerous truth that Evelyn referred to, even leading them to believe the possibility her hired investigators had been killed.

Like Cressida's father?

While Cressida comforted Evelyn, he watched out the window, thinking through all he'd learned today. Evelyn hadn't actually told them anything. She raised questions that he sensed she wanted answers to herself but was afraid to send anyone into that danger.

What in the world?

Indeed. Whatever this was about was big. After all, Octavia Dane had sent him here in the first place.

International.

An abandoned salvage ship.

Murders.

Cressida's father and his research.

And now, Evelyn Monroe—the heir to the Harborstone Shipping Company fortune—in danger in her own home. *Harborstone.* Where had he heard that name before?

Braden would give anything to get Cressida out of this,

but his hands were tied. If he told the truth, he wouldn't be able to protect her. She would ghost him like she'd done her mother, who'd had to resort to sending a covert spy-protector.

He tasted acid.

He hated himself.

But he would use the time he had to get to the bottom of this.

A shadowy figure stepped out from the edge of the woods near the cliff's edge and looked at the window where Braden stood—through a rifle scope.

25

ressida wasn't sure what to do. Her instinct was to pat
the woman's back and reassure her. Evelyn seemed to
have been holding so much inside—for years, as she'd
mentioned earlier—hoping someone would ask. Well, Cressida was here to talk and listen. She wanted all the answers
Evelyn was willing to give, and even those she wasn't.

But that would have to wait.

Evelyn held her chest, not as though she was extremely
grieved but as though that grief might have sent her into
some kind of cardiac incident.

"Please tell me what I can do to help."

Before Evelyn could respond, Braden headed for the door,
calling over his shoulder, "Stay here. Stay down. Stay away
from the window."

"But I need your help."

Without looking back, he exited. He hadn't even heard
her. His tone left no doubt something else was up. Male
voices echoed in the hallway. She recognized Deputy Riker's
voice along with Braden's.

The intimidating woman next to her suddenly seemed

feeble. Concern for her ratcheted up. Was she sick? Having a heart attack?

Evelyn fumbled for Cressida's hand, found it, and squeezed.

She spoke so softly Cressida leaned closer so she could hear the words, but she still couldn't understand. "Excuse me?"

Evelyn closed her eyes and drew in a deep breath, then straightened and sat taller. Her eyes brightened, and she released Cressida's hand. She slowly stood and straightened her cardigan, composing herself, both figuratively and literally.

What had just happened?

Cressida had a few moments alone with Evelyn, without Braden or anyone else listening. Now could be her only chance to learn more if Evelyn was holding back. "Please tell me what I need to know." *While there's still time.*

Pain suddenly carved into Evelyn's face. "Please, I need to call my doctor."

She thrust her cell into Cressida's hands. "His number is in my contacts. The landline is in my room, or there's one downstairs."

Hands shaking, Cressida grappled with the phone. She wasn't familiar with this one and struggled to find the contacts.

Deputy Riker entered. "You're interfering with a crime scene. I need to—"

Evelyn Monroe collapsed against him. He grabbed her and gently lowered her to the floor next to the bed, then radioed for an ambulance.

"I'm calling her doctor." Cressida raced from the room. Instead of searching through the many doors to find Evelyn's room, she bounded down the stairwell, then found the landline phone at the base of the stairs.

Punched in the number and waited. *Come on. Pick up, pick up, pick up.*

She got the answering service. "I'm calling on behalf of Evelyn Monroe. She's collapsed and has asked for her doctor. We've called for an ambulance. Please let him know. He can call me on my cell." Cressida gave her number.

Because she wasn't leaving this woman's side.

"I'll give him the message."

Cressida ended the call. She raced back upstairs where Evelyn still rested on the floor. Deputy Riker had placed a pillow under her head and put blankets on her. Such an awkward place for her to land. Evelyn was awake but struggling to breathe. A panic attack? A heart attack?

Lord, what do I do to help her?

She dropped to her knees and grabbed Evelyn's hands. "Tell me what I can do."

"In my medicine cabinet. Glyceryl . . ." The rest of her sentence was garbled.

"Which room?"

Evelyn tried to explain, but her words were incomprehensible. Cressida bolted up and hurried down the hall and through the ridiculously big house looking for the room that could be Evelyn's bedroom. She entered what looked like the room of this grand woman, in terms of size and decor, and then rushed to the private bathroom. Swung open the medicine cabinet and found too many pill bottles to count.

What had she said?

Glyceryl. Cressida got it. Nitroglycerin was used for angina. She must be having an attack. Finding the glyceryl trinitrate, she raced out of the room, down the hall, and found Evelyn sitting up in a chair, but she still looked pale and weak. Deputy Riker stood next to her.

Cressida held out the bottle. "Glyceryl trinitrate?"

"Yes, yes. I need one. Please."

Cressida glanced up at the deputy. "A glass of water. Get a glass of water."

He nodded, then disappeared through the door.

"I can take it without water. I need it now."

Evelyn put it under her tongue, then closed her mouth and eyes, her features relaxing.

"If there's anything else I can do, anything else you need, please let me know," Cressida said softly.

"Usually, the attacks aren't so severe. This . . . this could be something more." Evelyn opened her eyes. "I think . . . I think I've made a mistake. I . . . I'm so sorry, my dear. I haven't told you the whole truth."

Deputy Riker rushed into the room with a glass of water. "The ambulance is here."

"Already?" Cressida asked.

"They came from Forestview and will take her to the hospital."

A man and woman entered with a gurney, and Cressida stepped out of the way.

"I'll ride with her, if that's okay," she said.

"It's fine with us if it's okay with her. Mrs. Monroe?"

Evelyn shook her head. Her intense gray eyes held urgency. "You stay here in this house until I get home. I won't be long, I promise."

"I mean . . . they'll probably keep you overnight." *I can't stay here that long.*

"Stay. I have documents you'll want to see. I give you permission to search for them."

"The place is huge."

She coughed and chuckled and grimaced as if in pain. "Start in this room, then move to the library."

They secured Evelyn on the gurney and took her out of the room. Cressida wanted to argue with the woman, but now wasn't the time. The paramedics carried her on the gurney down the stairwell. Cressida rubbed her arms and stared out the window that Braden had warned to stay away from. But law enforcement and an ambulance had arrived. The danger was gone. But where was Braden?

How could she stay in this house for even an hour alone? How could she stay here overnight? She wouldn't.

She headed down the steps to follow the EMTs out the front door and walked next to Evelyn. "You're going to be okay. You're going to be fine."

"I know, dear. I know." Then she grabbed Cressida's hand and squeezed again, with more strength than she should have had. "Do as I ask. Research. Read. Find answers. Then if you still have questions, I'll answer all your questions for which I have answers when I return."

"I can't. I don't feel comfortable—"

"Nonsense."

"You don't even know me."

"I know you, Cressida Valentine Dane, daughter of Octavia and Alaric Dane."

Cressida couldn't help the confused look she gave the woman.

How safe could it be in this house where the man who attacked her had been talking to the former assistant? Where someone had broken in even today?

Evelyn must have sensed Cressida's continued resistance. "You keep that nice detective with you, and you'll be fine."

The paramedics shoved the gurney into the back of the ambulance and closed the door. Cressida watched it drive away.

Where is that nice detective?

26

Rain-soaked, Braden stared out into the haze of fog hovering over the ocean.

By the time he'd made it to the spot where the watcher had been peering through the rifle scope, the man had fled. Braden had continued his search through the woods, then finally ended up at the edge of the cliff and spotted the man scrambling down rudimentary steps of the cliff face to the rocky shore. Braden followed, but again, by the time he made it to shore, the man was already in a small boat making his way toward the fog. To a bigger, waiting vessel?

He'd taken pictures of the man from a distance on his cell, along with images of the boat he could barely see in the fog. His cell phone couldn't zoom out far enough, so the images were blurry at best. He'd find someone who could figure out the name of that boat, but if he wasn't mistaken, it looked a lot like Captain Malloy's old trawler, the *Mariner's Gambit*, which had brought both Cressida and her father here on separate occasions. Braden had easily found images of Malloy's vessel when he looked into his background.

Malloy had warned Cressida when he brought her here.

Warned her against . . . himself? That made no sense. What was going on? What was the connection? Braden hiked back up the slippery steps and got a radio message from Trent—Evelyn was on her way to the hospital.

"Stay with Cressida and protect her," he told Trent, and he made his way through the dense forest that edged Driftwood Manor.

Finally, the gate and circular drive came into view. Trent's county vehicle remained parked near the front, and Cressida stood on the steps under the portico and out of the rain. Braden half jogged his way across the property, then bounded up the steps to a confused-looking Cressida. This determined, experienced former investigative reporter might have met her match in Evelyn Monroe, and she might be out of her element here in Hidden Bay as well.

Trent exited the house. "Got the prints. Dust is everywhere, though." Trent scrunched his face. "You had me dust the windowsill. How did the intruder get out the window? That's a good drop. Nobody can do that."

"Could be a trellis or a drainpipe we can't see from the window. Maybe the intruder was a free solo expert. I caught a few images of someone watching the window through a scope. Don't know if it was the intruder. Got some pictures of a boat. I'll send these to forensics at the state and see if they can clean up the images and get clarity." He looked between Cressida and Trent. "What's happening with Evelyn?"

"She had some kind of cardiac event, but she was stable when they took her away in the ambulance," Trent said. "You good here? I'm wanted elsewhere."

"Yes. Thanks for your help." He and Trent had started out on the wrong foot. Braden had learned the man had wanted the detective job that Braden had taken. Nothing he could do about that. Trent was a good man, and Braden was growing to like the guy. Liking people you worked with always helped. Right. Liking people. Braden turned his attention to Cressida. He wasn't sure where to start with her.

"Are you okay?" Dumb question.

"She wants me to stay at the house until she gets back."

"What? Why?"

"Said she hadn't told me the whole truth and that I can find answers in the room that was searched and in the library." Brows furrowed, she thrust her hands in her pockets and stared at the ground, then back up at him.

"You can't stay in this house," he said. "It's too dangerous."

She glanced up at the portico above and then dropped her face to stare at him, her green eyes warming, teasing with her smile. "She said I'd have the nice detective to help me."

"The nice detective?" He couldn't imagine she meant him, but then again, he was the only detective here. "She thinks I'm going to help you stay in this house?"

Cressida tilted her head in a way that only she could do. She'd let her hair down from the tight bun she'd secured for the interview, and now the frizzy curls clung to her face and hung over her shoulders.

"You want answers, don't you? She's giving us permission to search the house for answers. We could find answers to why Madeline was talking to Collins. I could learn about the *Specter's Bounty*. I hate to admit it, but I'm so confused right now. I've investigated serious corruption—both corporate and government, human trafficking, and organized crime, you name it—but this simple search about a boat floating in the ocean without a crew so I can finish my father's book has me tied in knots. I told her that I couldn't stay, but I was wrong. That was a lie. I'm staying in this house tonight . . . with you or without you."

She wasn't the kind of person to do foolish things, but

he understood where she was coming from—Evelyn had stayed here alone after the attack on her. Evelyn harbored dangerous secrets, and she faced fear head-on. She'd invited Cressida to stay and wasn't concerned for Cressida's safety as long as he was there to protect her. Braden, the nice detective. He shook his head.

If only either of them knew.

"Sure. I'll stay," he said. "You make a good point. So let's do this. Let's get what we need. Do you want anything from the lodge?"

"I've already talked to Remi and made the big ask for her to bring what little I have over here. I don't plan to stay longer than one night, if that, and I assured her I would pay for the lodge room even if I'm not staying in it. She has nothing to lose. And I don't want to waste any time." Cressida turned on her heel and marched back into the house. Opened the door and kept it open.

Turned to him. "Well?"

Like he could say no to this woman—investigation or no investigation.

He communicated with Trent and Thatcher to let them know he would remain at the house to search for clues per Evelyn Monroe, and also to protect Cressida. He followed Cressida straight into the massive, remodeled kitchen.

"Hard to imagine one person lives here alone," he said.

"It could just be her upbringing. She didn't know anything else." Cressida opened the refrigerator. "I'm starving, and I can't work on an empty stomach. I don't want to take advantage of the situation, but I can't imagine her telling us to stay for the night and search everything but stay away from the refrigerator and out of the pantry. If that upsets her, I'll make amends. I doubt you have DoorDash out here."

He shrugged. "I never even tried."

"Oh, look, premade meals. My favorite! What's your preference, General Tso's chicken or curried chickpeas? There's a few more if you want to look. These meals will go bad in three days. Let's eat, and we can talk about what each of us is doing while here. I'm working on one thing. You're working on another. Divide and conquer."

"Are we on the same track here?"

"Whoever attacked me must believe that my father learned something important. Valuable. Dangerous. I don't know. Did he learn something about whatever vessel Evelyn's son, Caleb, was on that disappeared?" She flicked her gaze at him, then stabbed a knife into the plastic film on the meal, making a two-inch cut. "That's right—I caught that there's another vessel involved here. This isn't about the *Specter's Bounty* per se. It goes much deeper. Diggins believes Evelyn knows the truth, and someone else must think that too."

She vented the plastic on both dishes, then stuck one of them in the microwave. "She mentioned investigators that she hired all ended up dead after looking into her son's disappearance."

"She never actually told us what vessel Caleb was on," Braden said.

She paused, her eyes shimmering in the kitchen light. "No. But somehow the *Specter's Bounty* is still connected to this. Did you catch that the *Endeavor Spirit*, aka *Specter's Bounty*, was built by Harborstone Shipping, her family's company?"

"Yes. Doesn't mean the company is connected, because the vessel was sold."

"Sold for what purpose? To do what exactly? Like the rumors said—for criminal purposes? It was supposed to be a state-of-the-art salvage vessel. So what was it sent to salvage? What cargo was it carrying when it was lost in a storm? The photograph that Remi took certainly seems to confirm that it was a salvage vessel," she said. "As for the other ship that Caleb was on, that you brought up and then Evelyn shut you down . . . we can investigate that tonight. I think that's what she wants us to do. I'm not sure why she couldn't just tell me, unless she is still looking for answers too."

"Or she's too scared. Like you said, the investigators died shortly after searching."

Cressida removed the dish from the microwave and dropped it on the counter. She shook her fingers, blew on them, then popped the next one in and set the timer. "She wanted to talk to me. She asked for me, Braden. Remember? She knows something, and she wants to tell me. It must have to do with my father."

"Let's talk about the other players here. Malloy has experience using an ROV—remotely operated vehicle—in underwater salvage operations, and Diggins allegedly transported illegal artifacts. There's a lot going on." He rubbed his temple. "I need a crime board."

"Use your iPad. A piece of paper. You'll get it," she said.

He could potentially fast-track the investigation and zero in on the crux of things if he asked her about the article that her mother had shut down. But he wasn't supposed to know about it. If he could get her talking about herself tonight, what she was doing before this project, then maybe she would tell him. Or he could press Octavia again. Worst case . . . yeah, he'd press Octavia. There was no getting around it—they needed to know the danger level.

Elevated risk?

Maximum alert?

His cell buzzed, and he pulled it out to look at the text from his sister.

Want to schedule a time to talk to Elise today? Mrs. Dane

called to ask how Elise was doing, and then Elise asked about talking to you.

He was in the middle of a volatile, dangerous investigation, but talking to Elise was a good reminder of why he had to play by Octavia's rules.

And Octavia was making sure to remind him.

27

After Remi was kind enough to drop off her things, Cressida hauled everything to the room upstairs right next to Evelyn's master suite. To Cressida's way of thinking, all the rooms in this estate were master suites. Staying here in Driftwood Manor felt all kinds of creepy and weird, but she wouldn't pass up this opportunity. Never once had she been given this kind of access.

She thought back to Evelyn's reaction to Braden's comment . . .

"Wait. That's not it, is it? He was on another—"

Evelyn had become flustered and upset and shut Braden down.

"I've said too much already," she'd said.

About her losing her son, Caleb. What was the vessel he was on that was lost? Since his grandfather had sent him out, that information had to be somewhere within the former Harborstone Shipping Company databases, ledgers, or manifests. Though Evelyn appeared afraid, she was also a woman who wanted the truth to finally be discovered and for the world to know. Or maybe that was what Cressida wanted, and she was incorporating that into Evelyn's simple request.

Regardless, Cressida intended to make good use of her time. Through the window on the second floor, she watched Braden unload a duffel from the back of his county vehicle. Maybe he carried overnight basics everywhere he went. He glanced around, taking in his surroundings, then tossed the duffel over his shoulder before heading toward the manor.

Confidence. Broad shoulders. Thick brown hair. Sharp eyes that seemed to search her until he found what he was looking for. A few days ago, he'd been a stranger, and now he was on this mission with her. He'd already told her that he liked her. That, because she'd said it first.

He suddenly glanced up to the window, almost as if searching to see if she was looking. Had he sensed her watching? If so, then he'd caught her.

In the act.

Instead of standing there and holding his gaze, she backed away from the window as if she'd been caught committing a crime. All she had to do was wave. Now she was found guilty of staring at him when she thought he wasn't looking.

Cressida groaned, then returned to the window and opened it to feel the misting breeze. The morning had passed so fast, then the event with Evelyn, then lunch, and now the afternoon was growing late, and she hadn't even started working.

Still, it was hard to walk away from such an incredible view. Though the house wasn't built quite on the edge of the cliff at the front, the back of the structure edged a cliff overhanging an expansive beach where sea stacks and rocky outcroppings could be clearly seen. She could watch the waves crashing all day long from this view.

Evelyn had mentioned spending time watching out the window for the vessel her son had taken before she never heard from him again. Those words had nearly broken Cressida's heart. Once this was over, she'd love to just relax and put it all behind her, watch the sunset on the beach.

With Braden.

She shook off the not-so-crazy thought. Fog was moving in from the ocean toward the shore, and fast. If she peered into it long and hard enough, would she see a ghost ship floating out there, waiting for her to find answers to what happened to the vessel and its crew?

Goose bumps crawled over her arms and not because this was some kind of ghost story told by the fire. The whole thing was getting to her because the danger factor was real. Cressida left the room and made her way down the stairs in search of the library, or study, where she would start first.

Braden followed her down the stairs. "I took the room across the hall from yours. But I'm not here to sleep."

"I'm not either. I'm going to start in the library and look at photo albums and journals. I'm not entirely sure what I'm looking for. I think this has something to do with the vessel Caleb was on."

"Because of her reaction."

"Yes. But I still don't know what I'm looking for."

"I have a feeling you'll know when you see it."

"That saying doesn't really work," she said.

"How about, I have a feeling you have the background and experience to weed out the noise?"

She shrugged. "Better. And where are you going to work?"

"My primary reason for staying is because you are, and I'm here to keep you safe. Wherever I work, it won't be too far away."

Braden would be close. Her heart suddenly pounded. "Well, I hope you'll leave me alone in the library so I can focus." Yeah, that didn't sound right.

He stepped closer. Her throat tightened.

"Are you saying you can't focus when I'm near?"

"Detective." She glared at him, hoping he'd buy it. "You need to remain professional at all times while you're here." Her words made no dent in his expression. "Are we clear?"

"I think I read you pretty well." He turned and walked away, calling over his shoulder, "I'll work on things from my end, but I won't be too far. Call if you need me. Scream if it's an emergency. Don't leave the house without me."

Not even for a walk on the beach?

But no, she wouldn't tease him with that, or rather tempt him. Cressida shook off the emotions tumbling around inside at her exchange with Braden Sanders—he was a distraction she didn't need but a distraction all the same. Tough being in this position—wanting help and protection from the "nice detective" and needing to steer clear of this guy who knew she liked him.

The library called to her from down the hallway, and she entered to find a desk inside. So it was a combination library-study. Just like she'd expect—floor-to-ceiling shelves covered every wall but were interrupted by a tall window draped in heavy velvet curtains. The shelves were covered with the usual leather-bound volumes one would expect in addition to just regular old books, even some paperbacks. She moseyed over to look at the paperbacks because they seemed so out of place.

"Well, what have we here? What kind of reading do you do, Mrs. Evelyn Monroe? Looks like thrillers and mysteries." She ran her finger over the spines of what appeared to be well-worn novels by Tom Clancy. She pulled off the shelf *The Hunt for Red October*, which looked to have been read multiple times.

Well, that answered one question—what Evelyn did in her free time, living in such a spacious place all alone. After returning the book, Cressida moved to the vintage globe on a stand placed at the corner of the massive oak desk, free of clutter or papers. On the desk was an old brass lamp with a Tiffany shade.

Cressida sat in the high-backed leather chair at the desk. If she were Evelyn sitting at this desk, what would she think? What would she feel? What would she see? The window offered a great view of the front and the gate. To her left, the bookshelves filled with gold-flecked classics and at the bottom, older volumes.

Aha.

Journals and photo albums could give her the deep dive into Evelyn's background and son that Cressida needed. Her reading material for the rest of her stay. She leaned down and pulled out the first journal—blew off unexpected dust. Then sneezed. Maybe she should have expected it, but Evelyn appeared so well put together that, no, she hadn't expected a dusty book, even in this massive library.

This was going to be a long night.

After skimming through at least two volumes of old photographs, Cressida opened a journal with stylish cursive writing that looked like calligraphy by Cressida's standard, which wasn't saying much. At least she could read it. Was it a diary? If so, she felt uncomfortable reading such a personal book. Still, she'd been invited to explore everything.

The cursive, at times, made it difficult to read and slowed her down, but after a couple of pages, she was pulled into the voice and world of Evelyn Monroe.

Her eyes were burning, aching, and dry when she finally noticed Braden leaning against the doorframe.

"Oh." She marked her place at about the halfway point and set the book on the desk. Blew out a breath. "How long have you been standing there?" Watching. Because he had the look of a man who had definitely been watching.

And it was dark outside.

Shoot.

I missed the sunset.

But the clouds could have prevented her from seeing it anyway. She looked at the journal, feeling the emotion and angst sweeping through her again.

"What is it? What did you learn?" He entered the room and took the seat across from the desk.

"It's a lot, really, and I'm not sure what it means for my research. But it sounds like her family's shipping operations were involved in smuggling during World War II."

He tilted his head. "Smuggling. What kind?"

"Not the good kind. Her grandfather, at least, supposedly was involved in transporting questionable cargo—though she didn't say what—during World War II. He wasn't charged because no one knew, but her father took over and built the company into an important player in maritime trade. The cargo ships transported raw materials, machinery, and even medical supplies out of Boston. Then . . ."

"What is it? What did you read?"

"I'm not sure what to make of what I read. Evelyn learned the truth about the company's nefarious legacy turned good. But for some reason, she wanted to get away from her father, except he held too much power. His reach went far and wide, and she even goes as far as to say she believed he killed her husband." Tension built in Cressida's shoulders. "Which, I mean, she kind of told us that already."

"Anything at all about her son after he was sent away? Anything about what he got involved in?"

"I have to keep reading, and my eyes are crossing. I should take a break and come back. I wish I could just take the journal with me, but I'm not going to ask her if I can have her diary. So, your turn. Did you learn anything new? Anything that helps us to figure this out?"

"I'm not sure. I went up to the room and looked around."

"What room?"

"The one that someone was searching earlier today. I looked at everything. Dug in the drawers. I wore gloves. I tell you, Cressida, there's nothing in that room. I believe whatever someone was looking for, they found. I believe that might be why Evelyn was so upset she had a mild heart attack, why she gave you the right to look through everything."

"Oh." Now, she hated hearing that. "What could someone have wanted in her room?"

"And there's something else. Thatcher called. Madeline Chase was apprehended by the state police, but she lawyered up and told us nothing." His eyes darkened.

"What else? You're holding back."

"Tonight, her *lawyer* went to see her, and she died a few hours later."

28

Cressida stood so fast the chair rocked back and almost toppled. "What? I don't understand."

"It's clear that someone didn't want her talking. It's also clear that this is dangerous, Cressida." He wished they weren't even here in this house. "I hate that you're involved in this."

"Well, I am, and it's too late to back out now. I wish . . . I wish my father was alive to finish his book. But if he died because of it, I want justice for him."

"What if Madeline was a plant?" Braden asked.

Cressida crossed her arms and leaned against the desk. "You mean a spy of some kind?"

"I don't know. I'm grasping at straws. Nothing shows up as a red flag in her background."

"Well, what do we know about Collins?"

"Trent sent me the information, but nothing connects them, at least not yet."

"I know a little bit from my work as a journalist. Sometimes people's past, their history, can be scrubbed or a fake one created, and even law enforcement struggles to find the truth." She pressed a finger on the globe and spun it slowly, as if looking for a specific place in the world.

"I assure you, we're looking into it." He wanted to reach out to his federal connections, but his gut instinct told him he should keep this very low-key. He couldn't tell who all the players were. Octavia was keeping it low-key, using *him*, and that had to be for a reason. He just didn't know what that was.

"In the meantime, I made some coffee. It's in the kitchen. Why don't you take a break and stretch your legs?"

"Actually, we missed supper." She stretched her arms.

Braden looked away, but not before he caught a glimpse of her graceful neck as she stretched. She left the old diary on the desk and followed him through the house and to the kitchen on the opposite side of the mansion.

"Maybe I can learn what it is that Diggins wants to know without having to ask Mrs. Monroe directly," Cressida said. "But I need to know what he knows about my father."

"Or I could grill him as a detective," he said.

"You think he'll tell you because you're a cop?"

"He shouldn't be holding back possible evidence regarding a suspicious death."

"Let's do it my way first," she said. "The more information we have, the better."

"Have you talked to your mother about your father?" Yes, he was going there. He needed to steer her in this direction. "Maybe she knows something about his death that she hasn't shared with you."

Cressida's face fell. He'd overstepped. She was angry but controlling it. "Why don't you look at police reports? You have connections. You can dig deeper into the fatal traffic accident in which a pedestrian was killed in DC. Maybe I *haven't* been told everything about his death." She sounded furious. Incredulous.

"My question wasn't unreasonable, and as for yours, I'm already working on it," he said.

She narrowed her eyes. "Why would you think my mother would know?"

He lifted his shoulders. "Just looking at all the angles."

Tell her. Just tell her.

But . . . Elise depended on him. He couldn't be the reason that sweet little girl's health failed her.

Change the subject. He poured coffee into mugs.

She opened the fridge. "What'll it be for you tonight?"

"I'm not hungry."

"Sure you are. I'm having the pasta e fagioli. I'll make some for you too," she said. "This seems like a soup night."

"Actually, that does sound good."

"Two soups coming up."

"You don't have to do it," he said. "I can heat them up."

"You made coffee. I'll make the soup."

"Thank you," he said. He drank the black brew from the mug. "Earlier today, after we chased away the intruder, we were all in the room that he'd ransacked. That's when I saw someone in the woods, peering at the window through a scope. Thought maybe he was the escaped intruder. It would have been about right in terms of the distance he had to run from the house. Nothing was caught on the camera, by the way. They're disabled on that side of the house. I'll get permission from Evelyn to get her cameras fixed and possibly add additional security measures."

"I remember," she said. "Evelyn was having chest pains, and you suddenly exited."

"I'm sorry. I didn't realize she was having a health crisis."

"It's fine. She got the care she needed."

"Because you were there for her." He smiled, hoping to chase away her irritation with him.

"Go ahead and tell me the rest." The microwaved soup

was ready, and she grabbed it, along with their spoons, then pushed a bowl over to him.

He paused and said a blessing over the food and was glad that Cressida joined in.

"When I got to the woods, I followed someone heading down the old steps in the cliff's edge to the beach. The ones you took before, possibly. He took a boat out to a vessel waiting for him in the fog—it was the *Mariner's Gambit*."

Cressida's eyes narrowed. "Are you sure?"

"I had the images I took analyzed." He showed her a blown-up image.

"It's Malloy's boat, all right. But I don't understand. He helped both me and my father."

"I think it's clear. He warned you and for good reason. He's involved somehow."

"But he delivered the journal back to me. It's a combination journal now because it includes both my father's notes and mine."

"Because he read it first, looking for anything that could help him. I don't see you as someone who would leave the journal behind."

"You could be right. Dax, his son, lowered my things to me in the skiff. It's possible he could have quickly snatched it without my knowledge. But you should know, from the beginning, ever since I took this on, there were pages missing from the journal."

"Do you think they were related to the *Specter's Bounty*?" Before it got cold, Braden finished his soup while they talked.

"It's hard to know, but with all that's happened, I suspect they were related. I don't know who has them now, or if they were destroyed."

"As for the journal, my guess is that Malloy or his son, Dax, read it and then delivered it back as if you'd simply left it behind."

"Isn't this all an assumption?" she said. "Circumstantial stuff."

Braden got that she really didn't want to believe Malloy could be involved. "Possibly. It's a theory. I have to have theories."

"So you're going to try to question him?" Cressida had finished her soup.

He grabbed their plastic bowls and added them to the trash he should take out soon, then washed their utensils and put them away.

"I've been trying to find him from the start. After all, he warned you, remember? I want to know why. Want more coffee?"

"Please. I need to stay awake all night, if necessary, and read as much as I can."

"I saw some cookies in the pantry," he said. "We can eat those for dessert. Coffee and sugar up so we can work through the night."

He opened the large pantry and grabbed a box of butter cookies. *Thank you, Evelyn Monroe.* At the counter, he opened up the box and let Cressida grab some first.

"In the end, all this research will help you understand more about the *Specter's Bounty*. Do you think, in keeping with your father's book, you'll stick with the folklore, or will you write in what you learned about the truth, if that turns out to be different than what is shared at the museum?"

Sitting on a stool, she leaned against the massive island and drank her coffee. Nibbled on a butter cookie. "You and I both know there's much more going on here. I'll see what the truth is and decide. This isn't the usual kind of thing. I'm not even sure what Dad would want. His books have previously been published by Anchor Point, and the editor knows I'm working on this last one. I want it to be special. Everything Dad would have wanted. But until I know how he died, whatever it is that Diggins might tell me, I'm on edge and it's hard to focus. But that just makes me all the more determined."

Yeah, he figured. He wasn't talking her out of this.

"I understand." More than she knew. He'd always been up-front and honest, and to find himself in this predicament was like being in a moral-dilemma nightmare.

Be honest and up-front, tell her, and she was gone. Done. And what about Elise?

Don't tell her now, but when she eventually learned the truth, she would be done with him. That shouldn't be a problem, except he was really into this woman and could see himself falling for her.

"I bet you were a top investigative reporter. What did you work on before you took on your father's book?"

Crunching on another cookie, she frowned. "I don't like to talk about it, but for you? Maybe it's a story you should know. The reason I won't call my mother. She's kind of a big deal in her position." She shook her head, deep lines forming between her brows and around her mouth.

He wished he could take the question back, but he needed the answer.

"She used her power to shut me down. I can't get a job working in the same world as before. So I took on this project. Afterward, who knows. Maybe I'll start a podcast."

"What would the podcast be about?"

"Exposés. See, I was looking into a story about the environment and the fishing industry when I followed the trail to toxic materials leaching from underwater wreckage. I had a source I really needed to interview, and I asked Mom for help. That's when she learned the details and asked me not to do it." Cressida rubbed her eyes while she finished talking. "I didn't stop, and the next thing I know, the magazine let me go for some made-up reason. That's when I got a clue, and I confronted her. I figured, in the end, it would somehow lead to her."

"Lead to her how?" He'd considered the same.

"She's done a lot of work with those negotiating with foreign entities over international waters. All that maritime stuff is how she met Dad to begin with." Cressida blew out a big breath. Grabbed another cookie. "They were an unlikely couple if there ever was one. Dad was quiet and laid back and into his books and history. He just couldn't fit into her world."

Their failed relationship was a rabbit trail. "So you didn't finish the article?"

"I had some roadblocks. Dad died, and then . . . I focused on this project to get me through. Who knows, maybe I'll finish it on the other side of his book."

How did he get more out of her without drawing suspicion? What kind of scumbag was he to even be here asking questions like a covert operative? He felt like it was a dark spot on his soul.

Please, Lord, let her see the connection between her article and what's going on here—if it's connected.

She angled her head. "So, Evelyn's reaction to you suggesting that Caleb wasn't on the *Specter's Bounty* but another boat . . ." She scrunched up her face—a look of confusion and incredulity. "What do you make of that?"

"I've made a note to contact the DNR to learn more about the *Specter's Bounty* and get a list of any other similar derelict boats in this region of the Pacific. It could be as simple as what Sheryl at the museum told us—it was towed but broke away during a storm and was lost again. Or it could be like Evelyn said—there's much more to the story. And maybe I can find out if they know something about another lost boat—the one Caleb was on."

If it was something far more sinister, what could it be?

She hopped off the stool. "I have an idea."

She moved around the island to stand close to him. He wasn't so sure it was a good idea.

"And what's that?" He turned and leaned on his elbow against the counter.

"We need to find the *Specter's Bounty* and board it."

He straightened. "If it was that easy, do you think it would still be floating out there?"

"I didn't say it was easy. Finding the truth can be hard, but in this case, it could be as simple as getting information out of Evelyn or Diggins. Let's find it and board it. I can add that to the book. I've dived to see sunken vessels. This is something I want to do."

"And end the folklore and all the intrigue wrapped around the ghost ship supposedly appearing with the marine fog?"

"I don't think the book or the truth will end anything. Something terrible happened, and we might never know what that was or what happened to the crew. Those untrue or fantastical stories aren't going to die, and the warning of danger the *Specter's Bounty* represents will remain. Dad used to say that the ocean remembers, and it is both a graveyard and a cradle. So we need to get out there"—she pointed west to the Pacific—"as soon as we know where to go. As for the boat on whatever secret mission that Caleb was on, we'll board that or dive to see it. Finding it is my priority. I might add one more vessel to Dad's book."

The sugar and coffee were getting to her—firing her up—but she made good points. He'd have to remember that for the future.

Before Braden could respond, the light flickered and went out, leaving them in utter darkness.

He felt the warmth of Cressida's body as she stepped closer, but even that couldn't chase away the cold chill of dread that gripped him.

29

Ugh. Not again. They'd flickered earlier today but hadn't gone out. Normally a power outage wouldn't scare her. It was more of an annoyance. But tonight, in this gorgeous, stunning, but *creepy* mansion, Cressida couldn't ignore the terror that threatened. She'd left her handgun upstairs. Her cell too.

"Probably just the wind knocking the power out." Hadn't Evelyn said as much before?

Braden said nothing. Nor did he turn on his cell flashlight. She suspected he was listening. The wind buffeted the house, stirring all kinds of creaks and groans. Were any of the sounds footfalls?

"What if it's the same intruder from earlier today?" she asked. "Maybe he came back to get what he failed to get earlier." Except Braden believed he already found whatever he was after.

Evelyn had been upset about it too, so something important had been in that room.

"We could just leave now," she whispered. She sounded like a complete coward. Then again, she was being smart.

But I can't see.

"What are we doing?" Again she whispered.

"Power outages here are common," he whispered back, his breath warm against her cheeks. "But until I determine otherwise, I need you to stay safe and quiet."

A smidgeon of moonlight reflected through a break in the clouds and shone through the kitchen window, allowing her eyes to adjust. He tugged her hand, pulling her forward to the far end of the kitchen. Opened the pantry door and stuck her inside. Then handed his cell to her.

She grabbed a jar of olives and held it up for his approval. "I can use this as a weapon." Like bringing a knife to a gunfight.

"I'll clear the house." He shut the door.

Heart pounding, she released a slow breath and tried to remain calm while hiding in a kitchen pantry with a cell phone and a jar of olives.

Dad . . . what did you get me into?

Footfalls sounded in the kitchen. Cressida squeezed back into the far corner of the large pantry, and then—of course!—she knocked into something. It rolled, then crashed to the floor. Great. She'd just given away her position.

She didn't know who was in the kitchen, but it didn't sound like Braden's cadence.

The lights suddenly flicked back on—she could see under the door. If she flipped the switch, the pantry light would come on too, but she didn't want to draw more attention to herself than she already had.

Her palm grew sweaty around the olive jar. What was she going to do? Throw it at whoever opened that door?

God, help me!

The room was quiet except for creaking—had the intruder left? She released her pent-up breath, feeling like a complete coward.

Lord, please let Braden be all right. Someone was in the house . . . and Braden missed them? Or was Braden hurt? She didn't know, and not knowing was driving her crazy.

I can't just wait in the pantry. I'm not going to die in here. If he doesn't show up in five minutes, I'll go looking for him. "Cressida," Braden said. "It's me. Don't kill me with your olive jar. You can come out now."

She burst out of the pantry, wielding the jar like she would a javelin, ready, set, aim, and go. "Someone was here, Braden. Someone was in the house."

"I just checked everything."

"The whole house?"

"Yes, though quickly." Still gripping his gun, he looked out the kitchen window.

"Well, they were here in the kitchen while you were looking everywhere else."

He still hadn't looked at her. "How do you know?"

"Footfalls. It wasn't you, okay?"

"I believe you," he said. "Someone shut the power off. I turned it back on. We're getting out of here."

"Okay. Good idea. Can we get my stuff first?"

"I'm not sure *that's* a good idea." Holding his gun, he looked wired and ready to shoot anyone who walked into the kitchen.

"What is that smell?" Through the wide arch she could see the rest of the house. The bright kitchen lights were on, and the rest of the home was dimly lit with a few lamps on here and there. But flickering caught her attention. "Braden. It's a fire. The library is on fire!"

And I left the diary!

"Let's go." He grabbed her hand and pulled her away from the windows as he ushered her to the back door, covering her as if he was well trained and had practice. She appreciated his willingness to give his life for her. But . . .

232

"What are you doing?" she asked. "I'm not a target here. Someone is burning down the library to stop us from learning what this is about!" She stopped in her tracks, causing him to stop too. "Braden—she needs protection at her hospital room."

"Already on it. She's well protected."

"But why is this happening?"

"We can talk about it later. We're leaving. I never should have agreed to this."

Braden used his radio to call for emergency services.

Cressida wouldn't argue, but staying here had been her decision, after Evelyn's insistence, and that decision hadn't been up to Braden. She hadn't hired him as security, but then again, she'd appreciated his protection. She was too exhausted to argue with herself, but she didn't feel right about leaving. They crept out the back door and stayed in the shadows.

She couldn't believe she'd left the possible answers back in the house to burn up. "Listen, we need to go back into the house to get that diary. Try to put out the fire before it's too late. It's obvious that someone doesn't want us to find those answers in the diary or other journals."

Without asking permission she didn't need, she turned and rushed back through the door. Braden would follow. And he did. She remained one step ahead of him. And, yeah, this could be stupid, but then again—what was it all for if she didn't learn what she was supposed to learn? Smoke filled the library. Flames licked the ceiling and engulfed the books.

Anguish seized her chest. "No!"

She focused on the desk. The high-backed chair and the globe would be destroyed. All the books on the shelves.

"I left the diary on the desk!" And there . . .

Braden tried to reach her and drag her away, but she

wrapped her fingers around the leather-bound diary and snatched it to her. Suddenly, strong hands gripped her waist. Braden tossed her over his shoulder and hauled her out in a fireman's carry as if he didn't trust her on her own two feet.

She'd gotten what she'd come for, and she wouldn't fight him. As he moved her through the house, smoke billowed, and flames licked the walls.

The other volumes . . . what more could they have told her?

30

Adrenaline surged through him as he carried her into the kitchen. His chest tight and breaths ragged, he set her down, and for a split second, their eyes locked. Then they both raced for the exit.

At the door she paused. "I left my gun upstairs."

"Forget it." Braden's sharp tone left no room for argument. "I've got mine, and you're not going back in."

"Fine. Let's go."

"Get behind me." He held his gun ready and prepared for anything or anyone they might face.

Braden stepped through the door, and Cressida remained close behind. He rushed her around the house. The fire on the south side lit up the night. Braden was unsure whether to head for the woods, to put distance between them and the house and danger, or for his vehicle.

Pulling the fob from his pocket, he clenched his teeth and clicked it, bracing himself. The car lights blinked on and the engine revved. His shoulders tensed as he waited for a blast or a trap. But nothing happened. His relief was short-lived since someone could be lurking in the shadows around the house or in the dark forest and creeping closer. He shined the flashlight into the woods, creating more shadows and areas of utter blackness. A few sets of glowing eyes stared back from between the trees and behind underbrush. The presence of so many forest creatures likely meant that no two-legged creatures—men—were lurking.

He grabbed her hand and tugged her behind him, booking it toward the woods. "I thought we were getting in your car!"

"Not yet. You'd better hide that journal inside your shirt or a pocket. If they suspect you got it, that'll put you in imminent danger."

At the edge of the woods, he continued to shine the light around, possibly making himself a target. Then again, he didn't want any surprises. Sirens rang out—the volunteer fire department from Forestview was only a few miles away and sounded like they'd rallied in record time, but not fast enough to save Mrs. Monroe's library. He hoped and prayed the rest of the manor could survive. Probably Evelyn could rebuild since portions of the home were built with stone. The library, however, was filled with flammable materials.

"Now that help is coming, we can start heading that way," he said.

He led Cressida toward the entrance of the manor grounds to wait for the fire crew. The old volunteer fire trucks—two of them, which surprised him—lumbered along the pavement, finally stopping at the circular drive. Still holding Cressida's hand, he glanced at her.

Tears streaked down her cheeks as she chewed on her lip, sorrow spilling out of her. She caught him looking at her and tried to blink the tears away, swiping at her face, but it was too late. "I can't stand the thought of all those books going up in flames. Evelyn's history, her heart, all gone. All those historical volumes. Not to mention Evelyn's home."

"This is a setback. But Evelyn Monroe is strong." And he could see this making the elderly woman more determined—to do what, he wasn't sure.

His own heart breaking, he wrapped an arm around Cressida's shoulder, tugging her close and tucking her tight. He might protect her from physical harm, but he wished he could shield her from the mental and emotional pain as well.

She held on to him with both arms. "Who did this? Who set the library on fire?"

"Whoever was in the house tonight. I'll look at the cameras. Maybe the working ones caught someone this time."

From a distance, they watched the volunteer fire department douse the flames, spraying into the windows they'd broken open. The outside stone was wet and wasn't burning like the library lined with wall-to-wall book-packed shelves.

"I need to talk to them." He released her.

"I'm coming with you."

"I know you are." He wouldn't dream of leaving her here alone.

Another vehicle with flashing lights emerged from the woods along the drive, then slowed next to them. The deputy lowered his window. "Get in," Trent said.

Braden got into the front passenger seat and Cressida the back, then Trent drove them the rest of the way and parked behind the fire trucks, not too close. Braden explained that someone had been inside the home and then must have started the fire.

"And he's probably still here, lurking in the woods, watching," Trent said.

"Or escaped on a boat," Braden said. "Could be the same person who broke in earlier. I need you to stay with Cressida while I search those woods."

"Braden, no," Cressida said. "I have the journal. If they find out, they'll try again."

"That's what I'd like to avoid."

"We'll be ready for them," she said.

He exited the vehicle and jogged over to talk to one of the firemen. "The house should be empty," he said. "Monroe is in the hospital. Cressida and I got out."

Then he started off toward the woods. Trent caught up with him. "Wait."

He whirled around. "I told you not to leave her alone."

"I have some news I didn't want to share in front of her."

Impatience surged. It was probably too late to find the arsonist anyway, but he would still try. "What have you got?"

"We know who broke in earlier today. I got curious about how someone got up into that room and was able to get some prints off a brick, the underside where the rain hadn't washed it away."

Good job, Trent. The guy deserved the detective job Braden had taken. Deserved this promotion. He'd get it soon enough. Braden would see to it when he left.

"And?" he asked.

"Guy's name is Derek Harlan." Trent showed an image on his phone.

Cressida's stalker? Octavia said she'd sent someone. Did he have it wrong? Was the guy working for Octavia or someone else? His shoulders tensed. "Go watch her. I'm going to find him."

He took off to the edge of the woods and shined his light around. The guy was already gone. Did he know that Cressida got the journal after all? Why hadn't he just taken it, but maybe he hadn't known its importance. Still, maybe it didn't contain the answers like Cressida believed.

He jogged to the cliff's edge. He couldn't see anything through the dark night except the light of a boat—just barely—in the fog. Could be any boat out there. He shined the flashlight beam across the slick stone steps as he took them down to the beach. This was risky business at best. Shadows danced around him, and the pungent smell of ash bombarded him, even here against the cliff face. As he descended, waves crashed against jagged rocks below, reminding him of his fate if he took one wrong step.

The flashlight made him a target for anyone with nefarious intentions, and right about now, he wished he had night vision goggles. Finally, his boots hit the pebbled beach, and he jogged forward, watching his step as he shined the beam into the thick, black night.

Nothing moved. The crashing waves echoed back to him against the cliff face, silencing any other sounds. Instinct flared. He ducked just as something heavy slid through the air where his head had been.

He lifted his gun, aiming it true. "Freeze. Timberbrook County Sheriff's Office."

But the man had run out of the circle of light. Braden had dropped the flashlight, but he could still make out his attacker running away, heading south. To a skiff so he could meet Malloy's boat in the foggy night?

Braden didn't know where he was going. Didn't care. He picked up his flashlight and gave chase, his chest burning as he sprinted after a shadow that had disappeared into the night. The dense fog grew even thicker and suffocating until the beam of his light could no longer cut farther than a few steps. He paused and sucked in salty air. He heard nothing except the pulse in his ears to blend with the surf breaking against the rocks and sand. Was he still the hunter? Or had someone turned the tables on him, and Braden was now the hunted?

31

Cressida remained in the back seat of the county vehicle, watching from a distance, taking in the terrible images, while Deputy Riker spoke with two of the volunteer firefighters. She tugged the journal out and placed it on her lap, ran her finger over the worn leather. Was it possible the arsonist hadn't noticed the diary because the bound leather easily blended in with the desk? At least she'd gotten it, but what more had she missed in Evelyn's library? Maybe another book contained important information that Cressida missed. But it was too late now. The entire library was up in flames.

Her fingers dug into the journal as she squeezed, grief and anger washing over her. Before arriving in Hidden Bay, she had imagined it to be a quiet escape while she finished research for this one last vessel. Instead, death threats and chaos had overrun her.

But that wouldn't stop her from getting the answers she needed. She cracked the door so the interior light would come on. Then Cressida gently flipped to the last page she'd read. She still had quite a bit to read before she was done and hoped answers awaited her.

Her heart and emotions were drained, but that didn't matter. She had to finish reading this diary in case someone else got to it and stole it from her. She thumbed through to the end . . . the sight stole the oxygen from her.

What? No. No, no, no . . .

Cressida stared long and hard at the ripped pages. Just like her father's notebook. The pages were there before the fire. If they'd already been torn out of the book, she would have noticed. Why not take the entire diary?

And where was Braden? Cressida tore her gaze from the diary and stared at the manor. The window to the library was dark now rather than lit up by flames. How many volumes had been destroyed? What would Evelyn's reaction be?

Cressida needed to talk to Evelyn, but the woman had a mild heart attack already. How was she going to talk to her and get the information she needed for Diggins now that her library was destroyed, which would only add to her stress?

Deputy Riker strolled toward the vehicle, and Cressida swiped at the errant tears on her cheeks, then sat up taller. He got in and started the vehicle, as if his intent was to drive away from the manor.

"Where are we going?" she asked. "Where's Braden?"

She wanted out and opened the door to step out.

"Ms. Valentine . . . or is it Dane?"

Did she detect a bit of snark in that question? "Deputy Riker, where's Detective Sanders?"

"He radioed that he's on the beach in pursuit," Riker said.

"Are you going to help him?"

"He instructed me to take you to the Cedar Trails Lodge. I'll take your statement as well."

"But all my things—"

"Will be brought to you."

"Look, Deputy . . . I can just get them now."

"It's a crime scene. Someone set fire to Mrs. Monroe's Driftwood Manor, with you inside."

She wasn't going to win this argument, and she shut the car door.

Cressida had the feeling the fire hadn't been intended to trap them inside, but it was set to destroy whatever Cressida might learn.

Deputy Riker steered out of the estate. Cressida couldn't do anything to assist the firefighters, nor could she stay in the house now like Evelyn had wanted. She sat back in the seat and stared out the window at the black night, and Deputy Riker drove her back to the Cedar Trails Lodge.

After taking her statement, he escorted her inside, where she was met by—no surprise—Hawk and Remi, concerned expressions on both their faces.

Remi rushed forward. "What happened? We heard there was a fire."

Cressida's shoulders sagged with exhaustion and grief. "Someone set fire to the library to burn all those journals and possibly the answers I was searching for."

Remi covered her gasp, her own eyes filling with tears as she pulled Cressida into a hug. Cressida had already shed enough tears, and now she felt stone-cold numb. Except that wasn't true. A newer, stronger passion kindled inside. Whoever was trying to bury the truth didn't understand who they were dealing with. This only made Cressida more determined.

I'm going to get those answers.

She stepped from Remi's embrace.

"I'm so glad that you weren't trapped or caught in the flames," Remi said.

Who else had known that Cressida was there? Everyone here knew, including her mom's "dog" she sent to watch

Cressida. "I'm tired. I just want to go to my room—it's still available, I hope."

"Of course!" Remi gently pressed a hand on Cressida's shoulder.

Cressida glanced at the deputy. "You said you'd bring my stuff. I hope that's not going to take long."

He nodded. "I'll be right back."

Remi walked with Cressida to her room, and Hawk wasn't far behind.

"Do you think Mrs. Monroe is going to take this too hard?" Cressida asked. "She had a heart attack today. All the stress. Everything that's going on was too much. That's understandable. But the loss here is unimaginable."

"I think she'll be relieved that you and Braden are alive. That's the most important thing."

When Cressida was finally in her room alone, she collapsed on the bed. Waiting on the deputy to return with her things was going to be excruciating. In the meantime, though, she could look at Evelyn's journal and see what she had missed. But would reading without those missing pages, without the context, do any good?

But Cressida couldn't look at the book. Not yet. It was too disheartening, so she stood on the balcony in the cool night. Mingling with salty ocean air was the slight scent of smoke—from the manor fire? Burning books? No, it smelled more like a campfire. In the distance, she saw a light out on the water. Someone brave enough to be out there in the fog.

A knock came at the door. "It's Remi with your things."

She rushed to the door and opened it.

Remi handed off the belongings that she'd sent over earlier that day. "Trent brought these from the house."

"Thank you," Cressida said with as much of a smile as she could muster and closed the door. She appreciated Remi being so accommodating to her needs with this room.

Cressida really liked the woman, had clicked with her, and could see them being friends. In fact, it felt like the start of a friendship already. She emptied the duffel and realized her clothes smelled like smoke. Still, she hung up the few clothes in the closet and left the door open. Maybe the smell would dissipate, or she could wash them later. She stuck the rest in the drawers of the dresser. After retrieving her laptop, she dug inside the case for Dad's journal.

It was gone.

She let out an incredulous breath and sagged. Really? "Fine with me," she said to the walls, but in her head, she was talking to the bad guys. "I already scanned in all the pages and loaded them into the cloud."

Sure, a good hacker could eventually find the information, but at least now she had access to his notes and her notes. The main issue was that someone else also now had those notes, but she knew Dad's journal held no answers to this ridiculous mystery.

She'd come here looking for the truth behind a derelict salvage ship and what had happened to the crew, and look where that got her. Look where it got her father.

This was beginning to feel like a major cover-up of an important news story, and Cressida understood about that firsthand. Before the fire, Braden had been asking about the article she'd been working on, the one that her mother had shut down. His question had seemed innocent. Casual.

"What did you work on before you took on your father's book?" His line of questioning got her thinking—*was* there a connection between that article and what was happening to her now? Had Braden asked that question to find out if her previous job was in any way connected? He was sharp, and she wouldn't put it past him, though he'd sounded indifferent in that conversation.

She needed to look up all her notes. The environment, fishing, and underwater wrecks leaking toxins. So far in completing Dad's book she hadn't come across shipwrecks leaking toxins into the ocean.

Another knock came at the door.

"It's me," Braden said.

At the sound of the deep timbre in his voice, her heart danced a little. She pushed down the ridiculous reaction. No need to overreact in front of him, but she was more than relieved he was here. Right now, he was the only one she could trust—he and his friends, Hawk, Remi, Cole, and Jo—and she hoped and prayed she hadn't put her trust in the wrong person. The wrong people.

She opened the door, and in two steps he was in her room, gently gripping her arms like a desperate man. "Are you okay?" The question came out in a huff.

He was the one to overreact, and his concern and intensity had taken her breath away. She couldn't respond.

"Cressida?"

Shake it off. "Of course. I'm here, aren't I?"

He dropped his hands and paced the room. "You're not safe in Hidden Bay. You need to get out."

"I'm not going anywhere. But tell me what's happened." *You're scaring me.*

"I don't know how to tell you this." He didn't look at her but instead continued pacing.

"Just do it." She rubbed her arms, fearing the worst. What could have gotten him so upset?

"We believe the man who broke into Evelyn's room earlier today while we were there is Derek Harlan." He flashed Cressida an image on his cell.

"The man . . . *my stalker*? But I thought . . . I thought my mother sent him to spy on me."

"She did."

"What? What . . . are you saying?" Nausea erupted inside. "How do you know?"

"She sent him to watch over you, she says. I don't know what he's up to now, but you're in more danger than you can imagine."

Confusion erupted in her brain, with the sledgehammer hitting away at her temples. Her throat grew so tight she struggled to speak. "Wait. You talked to my *mother?*" *That doesn't just happen.*

"I'm a detective, Cressida." His brows knitted, and his voice rose, if only slightly, as if his explanation should have been obvious to her.

"You . . . you can't just call her up to talk to her. It doesn't happen like that. It's not that easy."

"I learned who the guy was. Followed the leads. Made the connections." Pursing his lips, he shook his head, then said, "I *communicated.*"

Braden let out a huff, clearly upset that he had to explain this to her, then he stepped closer and gentled his tone. "But I haven't talked to her about why the man she sent is committing crimes."

Her brain might just be shutting down. She eased into the chair next to the small table and rubbed her temples.

He grabbed the other chair and pulled it close. "Cressida, listen . . ."

"I don't want to listen. Give me a minute, okay?"

She needed space and moved away from him, stepping out on the balcony. He followed, as she knew he would. But this time she wasn't sure if she wanted him there. A cool mist coated her face, and she wished the clouds would move out so she could see the stars—metaphorically speaking, so she could see the truth. *What is happening here?*

"Cressida." He sounded nervous. "Tell me more about the article. You said your mother had shut you down and made it impossible for you to work for some venues through which you'd built your career. I can't imagine any mother would do that without a good reason. I'm saying, maybe that article has to do with what's happening here. What was it about?"

Cressida wasn't ready to respond yet. She wanted answers of her own and went back into the small room. She lifted Evelyn's journal. "Someone took pages from this journal. Didn't take the whole thing, just pages. Then when Deputy Riker returned with my things, my father's journal was gone."

With one hand on his hip, he nodded, his eyes focused on the leather-bound book she held. Then he flicked his gaze to hold hers, his eyes as intense as they'd ever been. "And *you're* still in danger."

He dropped his hand and paced the small room. "Please, can you be specific about the article?"

"Are you asking as Braden, the guy who likes me? Or as a detective?" And why did she even care? *But . . . I do care.* Because she was missing something here, and she needed to hear the truth from Braden, the man.

"Right now, I feel like that's one and the same."

"How did you talk to my mother exactly? Because you can't call her or just get through. You have to go through a layer of fifty people to get to her. I don't think you have the resources, *Detective.*"

"Just what do you think is going on here?" he asked. "I can get to her because you're her daughter, and this has everything to do with *you.* Why are you acting like I've committed some crime? I'm doing my job." He grabbed her hands and pulled her closer. "I'm worried about you, but not because it's my duty. I care about you, Cressida."

"Okay, okay. It was about environmental impacts and international waters. Fishing and sunken vessels possibly leaching contaminants and toxins."

"That's it? That doesn't sound like a reason she could have to . . ."

"To what? Braden . . . what aren't you telling me?" She pulled her hands away, and he let her. Part of her wished he hadn't. "I'm . . . I'm tired and confused. I don't know who I can trust." She rubbed her forehead. "Of course, I shouldn't have accused you." Cressida softened her voice, her heart open and raw. She didn't want to need him, but . . . *I need you.* "You're the only person that I can trust."

Cressida held his gaze, looking for reassurance. She would take that hug now, if he would give it.

Instead, at the look on his face, a fist gripped her heart and squeezed.

32

nguish rocked through him at her words. He couldn't go on like this. He couldn't keep lying. But for national security, lies were told. And for his niece—Elise—he'd committed to seeing this through.

What was the right way to go here? *God, help me! What do I do?*

But Cressida was sharp, and she'd already started questioning him tonight. It wouldn't be long before she discovered the truth, and then what?

The truth. Start with the truth. If Cressida could see the evolution of his predicament, she would understand. How could she not?

He tugged out his cell and pulled up an image. "This is my ten-year-old niece, Elise."

Her forehead wrinkled, but her eyes lit up as she looked at Elise. "Oh, she's adorable. So very cute. It looks like she's in a hospital bed. Getting an infusion of some kind?" Cressida's eyes were filled with compassion, and she looked from Elise to Braden.

God, please help me help her to understand. "Yes. She has a rare form of leukemia. My sister lost her husband in a work accident, and Elise lost her father. I've been looking out for them ever since. Lauren had a good job, but she resigned to be with her daughter. She doesn't know how long Elise will be with us."

Cressida covered her mouth, tears surged in her eyes. "Oh, Braden. I'm so, so sorry."

He saw the question in her eyes, but she didn't ask it. *Why are you telling me this now?*

"The good news is that there's an experimental treatment."

"But those are difficult to get." Her eyes widened.

"Try impossible in most cases, and that was certainly the case with Elise. A ten-year-old with acute myeloid leukemia that just so happens to have a rare genetic mutation, so it resists standard therapies. There was no treatment option left. Then we learned about this new drug that targets the specific mutation, and by the time it would be available to Elise, even if she was approved for clinical trials, it would be too late."

He stared at her long and hard, believing she would connect the dots on her own, and he hoped that once she did, she would completely understand and forgive him. But he could be asking too much here on both fronts. Cressida might not grasp on her own that her mother had offered the help Elise needed . . . for a price.

"And you were able to get this experimental drug?" Cressida's eyes filled with sincere relief—for Elise, a child she didn't even know personally.

Her understanding and compassion for others ran deep, but he feared it wouldn't run deep enough for him.

"And it's working, Cressida." His eyes surged with emotion. "It's working. God answered our prayers."

He released a sigh—almost of relief, but not quite. He wanted to bring her close and hug her because in the next few moments, he might lose her. He didn't deserve her. Never thought he would get a chance.

"Thank you for sharing, Braden." She pursed her lips and slightly shook her head.

"I know you're confused." A painful knot lodged in his throat.

"You shared something very personal," she said. "A piece of yourself. No, wait, the whole of you. That little girl has your heart. Your whole heart."

Indeed, she did. But Cressida held a piece of his heart too.

"You want to know why I told you." He said the words she refused to say.

She smiled, blinking back unshed tears. "I've cried enough. I'm not going to cry anymore tonight. Is it that you want me to share something? You think that I know something that could somehow help with this investigation? Something in my *very* personal, very private life?"

Oh, honey . . . Disappointment raked over him that Cressida hadn't connected those dots he'd willed her to connect, and it would be on him to break it to her. "I wish it was that easy."

She crossed her arms, and the frown on her face told him she was bracing for his news, and so maybe a small part of her was beginning to fully understand the big picture of his life.

"Elise couldn't get the experimental medicine without help. Without someone to pull the strings."

He expected furious tears. Or a sharp retort. He would have welcomed it. But instead, Cressida's face turned flat. No . . . cold. Stone cold.

"Octavia Dane helped you, didn't she?"

He slowly nodded, feeling the ice-cold punch to his gut. She had connected the dots, but not in the way he had hoped. Not in the way he needed.

"You're here because of her, then. You've been here this entire time, just waiting on me to get here."

"I didn't know what I was waiting on. I still don't know what this is about. Just that I need to protect you. She sent me to protect you, Cressida. She has threatened me and reminded me that for Elise to get her medication, I need to hold up my end of the deal." He lifted his hands in surrender. "If you think I've enjoyed keeping this from you, you couldn't be more wrong. This has torn me into pieces. I thought . . . I hoped that I could share the truth with you, so you could know that you can trust me. There are no secrets between us."

Without a word, she moved to the door and opened it, her gesture for him to get out. She didn't even look at him.

Should he stand here and beg? Maybe she needed space. He was hoping. Lying to himself.

As he walked by her, he knew she would never talk to him again. But he wouldn't give up.

"You do this, Cressida, you shut me out and Elise could lose her treatment. That was the price of her treatment."

He stepped out into the hall and heard the soft click of the door shutting—at least she hadn't slammed it, but remorse and grief filled him.

He walked down the hall, the lowest human on earth to allow himself to be manipulated and his niece to be used like this, but at the same time he was working to save her. This had been his only option.

But he couldn't make Cressida see that.

33

The next morning, Cressida steered her rental car down the road to a private home on the north end of Hidden Bay. Evelyn Monroe's doctor had cleared her for release that morning, and the resilient and resourceful woman was now staying at a safe house, where she'd agreed to meet Cressida.

In private.

Without the *nice* detective.

Today was Saturday, and Cressida had planned to be at the Pirates' Bash to take pictures and learn more about the *Specter's Bounty* and what the locals believed or knew. Was anyone related to any of the crew? What cargo had it been carrying, or where and what had it gone to salvage? Where did Evelyn's son, Caleb, fit into all of it? The story had been tipped over along with her world.

She better understood the term "seeing red."

Every time she thought about Braden's involvement with her mother, she couldn't see straight, and the thundering started in her head all over again. She'd taken so much aspirin, she might have given herself an ulcer.

She should have known to never again trust anyone after her ex-boyfriend had turned on her—again, because of her mother.

Evelyn's words drifted back to her. *"It isn't that he deserved my forgiveness. None of us is deserving."*

So that's it, Lord, I just have to forgive someone even if they don't deserve it? Cressida swallowed hard against the thickness in her throat.

Refusing to cry only meant that all her fury remained pent up inside. But she shoved it all away as she entered through the gate—Evelyn allowed her in via a code—and then she steered toward a very contemporary looking home that literally stuck out over the ledge. The place was the complete opposite of Driftwood Manor. Evelyn claimed it belonged to a friend, and security was top-notch.

Why didn't the woman hire protection after everything that had happened? Maybe she had, and Cressida just hadn't seen the protective detail yet. She parked and sat in her car. Took a few long breaths. She would learn everything she possibly could, and then she would call her mother and confront her, talk it through, whatever it took.

Braden Sanders.

Detective Braden Sanders.

What had he been to her mother? Cressida would guess that he'd worked for the Diplomatic Security Services and for her mother, who often utilized those agents for protection. Now that she looked back over her brief time with him, it was plain to her, and it had been staring her in the face the whole time. He'd never been *just* a detective.

Time to focus on Evelyn now and forget about Braden.

Cressida got out of the vehicle, noting the cameras at various locations. The place was only moderately safe, though, in her opinion, given that the woods closed in. Driftwood Manor had cameras too, but they had been tampered with. Cressida assumed Evelyn would be upgrading security with the repairs at Driftwood Manor.

She started toward the structure. This place might be safe, but it felt cold and lonely and creepy without all the Driftwood Manor gothic charm. As she walked to the front door, movement in her peripheral vision caught her attention. She turned to stare at the tree line.

Her heart leapt to her throat.

Diggins?

He stepped back into the shadows. He was here, watching Evelyn? Or waiting for Cressida? Who was he, really? And what did he know? What did he want? Was he . . . dangerous? She hadn't truly thought he'd been threatening her with his talk of walking a metaphorical plank of any kind. But that was Cressida's issue. She struggled to believe a nice man in his late eighties could plot such harm.

She would love to chase after him, approach and face him and get answers. Or even better, get in her car and drive away. Get on a plane and fly somewhere far away from her troubles.

The door opened before she knocked. Evelyn motioned for her to enter, then, surprising Cressida, the older woman gave her a long hug.

I should be hugging you.

She stepped back and looked her in the face, but before she could speak, Evelyn said, "Are you all right?"

"*Me?* I . . . you're the one who had a heart attack. How are you? And I'm so sorry this happened." And it felt weird, like all the walls between them—if there had been any—had suddenly come down with Evelyn's crisis.

Her gaze still contained the wisdom of ages, and Cressida hoped she would share some of that with her.

"Yes, yes, I'm fine. I'm good." She grabbed Cressida's hand and dragged her through the house and into the living room. "We don't have much time."

"Why? What's the urgency?" Cressida had her own reasons for feeling pressed for time, and she would love to hear Evelyn's.

"My dear, I'm sure you suspect the danger is closing in." She gave her a matter-of-fact look.

Sure. Okay. "Diggins is out in those woods right now, watching. Did you know that?"

"Let him watch."

"Let him watch? Aren't you concerned?"

"No one is getting into this house without my express permission."

"You said you had security."

"And I do. Now, did you bring it?"

"Yes." Cressida pulled Evelyn's diary out and handed it over. "They left it. Tore pages out and left it. Why would someone do that? They could have just taken it. I didn't get a chance to look through or read any of the other volumes. I'm so sorry. But why didn't they take it if they wanted it so badly?"

"Better for it to burn up in the fire so no one can ever read it. Those who have hold the secrets."

"But I have it now, so they made a mistake. I don't know anything, but I haven't finished reading it. I feel like the missing pages were important. Evelyn, please just tell me what I need to know."

She placed the journal back in Cressida's hands and wrapped her fingers around it. "What is it you want to know?"

"I need the truth that Diggins wants so he'll tell me what happened to my father."

"You're growing impatient and that's understandable. The truth Diggins wants, he needs to hear from me. That is between the two of us. As for your father, you don't need Diggins to tell you what happened. I can tell you." She moved to the sofa and sank into it.

"Then why didn't you just tell me before? I don't understand why you're making me work so hard to find the truth if you've known all along."

"I don't know everything. I don't have all the answers. But what I do know is this—there's a cost . . . I wanted you to fully understand the cost, but now it's too late."

Cressida stood. Those words punched the breath from her lungs. She could barely move, but she turned to look at the woman still sitting dignified on the sofa. One would never guess she'd had a heart attack and her home had burned or that danger was closing in. Maybe Evelyn Monroe had experienced this before and had practice in remaining poised at all times.

Braden was right—this woman was indomitable.

And just like that, she regretted that he'd popped into her mind. She had no idea how to get him out. But Evelyn's words . . . Cressida moved back to the plush sofa and eased onto it next to her. "Tell me everything. Please don't hold back."

"I contacted your father two years ago to look into the goings on in Hidden Bay. I'd read one of his books and thought the mysteries here could be of interest to him."

Evelyn . . . she was the reason her father had come here. "He . . . he added *Specter's Bounty* to his research list just to come here . . . for you? You're still looking for your son. To learn what happened to him." The defiant tears burned in her throat.

Evelyn slowly nodded.

"Did you get your answers?" Cressida struggled to contain her resentment, though her father's death certainly wasn't Evelyn's fault, but she had been the catalyst to bring him into danger. "Did my *father* know the cost?"

But Evelyn's cell drew her attention, and she excused herself to take a private call.

34

He'd borrowed Hawk's truck.

Yep. He'd been desperate. Couldn't take his county vehicle—too obvious. Couldn't ride his Ducati—Cressida would spot him in an instant. But maybe, just maybe, Cressida wouldn't notice him in Hawk's truck.

She'd arrived at the house where Evelyn was staying until Driftwood Manor was repaired and safe again. Braden had trailed her at a safe distance, watching as she turned into the drive. He'd driven past it long enough to avoid suspicion, then doubled back to navigate the forest road leading to the house.

He'd turned off a small side alcove and parked. The engine off, he lowered his window to listen and wait, his nerves humming too loud for him to hear anything else. He couldn't get into the house unless Evelyn let him through the gate, and he'd have to ask directly and nicely. Sneaking in wasn't an option. Evelyn was adept at shooting those she felt were a threat—that much they had learned already. Regardless, sneaking in uninvited would defeat his purpose of trying to get back into Cressida's good graces.

Like that was going to happen.

Letting out a pained sigh, he rubbed his hand over his face, his palm rasping against his stubble. That's right. He hadn't even bothered to shave. Things were ramping up into what was beginning to look like a worst-case scenario. Why was he always in the worst position when it mattered most?

Like being out of the country and unreachable when Lauren's husband died. Or like his colossal failure in Operation Horizon Shield, where he'd led a team of DSS agents working alongside Octavia Dane, providing security during a high-risk mission involving US diplomats and foreign officials and the transfer of sensitive materials through maritime channels.

Octavia had suspected something was wrong—as in, there had been a mole on his team who leaked information. But she hadn't said a word to Braden. The operation had blown up in his face. The US was accused of espionage—secretly, of course, behind the scenes. None of it made the news headlines because Octavia had that much under control. But he was blamed for the security lapse, and so he resigned.

Octavia fought to maintain her reputation. He hadn't blamed her for not doing more to protect his job, basically throwing him under the proverbial bus when she'd been the one to ignore his security protocols. He kept his mouth shut where she was concerned because that would take him nowhere good.

Plus, with his career in the rearview mirror, he'd been able to spend more time with Lauren and Elise in what perhaps were his niece's last days.

But that hadn't been the end to his relationship with Octavia Dane.

If it hadn't been for her, Elise would have no hope.

Octavia had spent years curating powerful connections

across many sectors—and she knew exactly how to leverage them. Whether through blackmail or an old favor—Braden didn't know—she'd used her influence with the CEO of a biotech firm to make available the experimental treatment his niece needed. The man's company had been held up waiting on specialized lab equipment trapped in customs at a foreign port—until Octavia stepped in. As Deputy Assistant Secretary for Maritime Affairs, she was able to make the bottleneck disappear. But Braden suspected there was more. Rumors swirled about a scandal the CEO had buried overseas, something Octavia had quietly unearthed—as was her way—to use as leverage at just the right time.

Frankly, Braden didn't care how Octavia had accomplished getting the drug. Not when it came to saving Elise's life.

After he resigned, Octavia contacted him about the experimental medicine, and he'd thought it was her olive branch. A way to apologize for what he'd gone through, and maybe to thank him for not pointing the finger at her, but no. Octavia gave nothing for free.

He thought back to his conversation with her last night when she'd finally returned his call at 2:00 a.m.

"Your man—Derek Harlan."

Her voice was sharp and edgy. "What about him?"

"He broke into Evelyn's home to search for something." His jaw clenched at the memory. "Then someone started a fire to destroy her library—probably to hide evidence or information. I suspect it was Harlan."

"What?" Octavia sounded genuinely shocked.

Braden was in no mood to let her off the hook. "You heard me."

"Are you sure he set the fire?"

Not entirely, but it fit. "Pretty sure, yes. Was he working on your orders?"

Despite his fear for Elise's treatment, he infused his tone with all the wrath that coursed through his veins.

Octavia hesitated, her silence scraping at his frayed nerves. He repeated the question, his voice taut with barely restrained fury. "Was he working on your orders? Is he here to get something from Evelyn Monroe or her house?"

"No. I don't know what's going on, Braden."

He almost believed her. Almost.

"Cressida and I were in the house." He forced his tone to stay even. "Monroe had given us access to look for answers."

"And where is Cressida now?" Octavia's voice shook.

He'd never seen or heard her composure crack, and his instincts prickled.

"Safe." As far as I know.

"Safe, as in, you're with her?"

He braced himself, preparing for her reaction. "She knows."

"What exactly does she know, Braden?"

"That I'm here for you. She was on the road to figuring it out, putting all the pieces together. I had to tell her first, to give myself a chance to make things right. If she called me out on it, then all bets were off. She would never speak to me again."

"I counted on you to keep one simple secret. So is she speaking to you now?" Her tone was livid.

"You know the answer to that question. And I plan to keep my distance, give her the space she needs—for now. But Octavia, I need to know everything." *No more pretending you don't know.*

"Let's see if you can keep *this* secret. I'm coming to Hidden Bay." Her voice was no longer shaky but cold and crisp. Octavia was back in control. "I'll be there before the end of the day."

"Why? How is your presence here going to change anything?"

But she'd already ended the call.

A gust of wind rattled the truck, and low-hanging branches scraped the windshield, startling him back to this terrible moment. Braden couldn't shake the sense of impending doom.

He rubbed a hand down his face. Octavia arriving here couldn't be a good thing. She'd have to rearrange her important schedule to fly out to what she perceived was a failure on his part. If anything, her arrival would make things worse.

He couldn't just sit in the truck all morning. Maybe Evelyn would let in the nice detective, and maybe if he pleaded his case to her and Cressida—again—Evelyn would help Cressida to see reason.

That was a good plan. His only reasonable move at the moment.

He shifted into reverse to pull back onto the road when his cell buzzed.

Lauren. His heart pinged, sharp and painful. The worst scenarios coursed through his heart and mind as he answered.

"Lauren? Everything okay?" He expected the usual chastisement that he was always expecting the worst, and couldn't she just call her brother?

"No. No, Braden, it's not." Lauren couldn't even speak for a moment, at least in a comprehensible way, her tears were so thick. "Elise's appointment for her infusion this morning was canceled."

35

Evelyn was the reason Dad had added the *Specter's Bounty* and Hidden Bay to his book. Cressida understood what Braden meant when he'd mentioned needing a crime board. She could use some assistance connecting people with current and past events to see where they all intersected. In this conversation with Evelyn, Cressida felt it deep in her bones—at last she had arrived at the intersection where all the threads would converge.

Evelyn had been gone so long that Cressida was beginning to wonder about her phone call when the woman finally returned to the living area. Considering their important conversation, Cressida couldn't imagine what call could have trumped that. But she had waited, her patience running out.

And she wanted to repeat her question—had her father known the cost before he'd taken on Evelyn's project? This whole thing had belonged to her. That news had shaken Cressida.

"My apologies, dear. I know we were in the middle—"

Cressida stood. "Did my father know the danger—the

cost—of taking on this project?" Cressida tried to stifle her frustration. She respected this woman. Admired her.

"You're upset. I understand." Evelyn sat again, calm and composed.

Cressida remained standing, shaking. Tears blurring her vision. *God, help me* . . .

"I told him everything that I knew, which wasn't much, really, and I don't think any of us knew the cost. But now perhaps we do." Evelyn closed her eyes. "I'm so sorry for your loss."

Cressida had to get her act together. She couldn't blame Evelyn if what she said was true, and she had no reason to believe otherwise. She slowly sank onto the sofa again. Drew in a calming breath.

Evelyn opened her eyes. "The vessel on which my father sent my son was meant to conduct a normal operation as far as anyone knew. But it was part of a covert operation."

"A covert operation involving what?"

"That, I'm not entirely sure. I believe your father discovered the truth. He . . . he told me as much before he left, but he didn't tell me the details. He promised to get back to me—that it was dangerous to even speak of. Then I learned he'd been killed."

"What did you think I would read or learn from looking through everything in your library? You can just tell me now since it's probably all gone. Whatever the fire didn't destroy, the water must have."

"I had hoped you would discover something that I missed. I know the answers were there, but now they're lost. Apparently, someone else believed the answers were there too."

"You said you could tell me about my father and what happened—is that all you have? A covert operation? Dangerous to speak of? That's not proof of anything nefarious happening to him."

"This is the taxi driver who struck and killed your father in the alleged accident." Evelyn thumbed through images on her cell phone and then showed a picture to Cressida.

She stared long and hard at an image of the man who'd attacked her on the beach. At the man whom Evelyn had shot and killed. What? No. That can't be. She shook her head.

"Now you see why I didn't hesitate to shoot the man in my house," Evelyn said. "I believe he was using an alias as the cab driver, and the connection wasn't made to the incident at my home."

"He was the taxi driver who struck and killed my father." Cressida struggled to wrap her mind around it. "Then his death really wasn't an accident. How did *you* make the connection?"

Evelyn lowered the cell, and her face inched closer, her expression serious. "Because I was suspicious of your father's death all along. I researched every detail I could find, and I was able to secure the picture of this man. Of course, I couldn't be sure it wasn't an accident, but with so much at stake, I couldn't dismiss that he was murdered. I apologize that I wasn't up-front with you. I . . . I was afraid for you."

Cressida wanted to curl into herself and sink deeper into this plush white sofa, but she sat taller. Had to be stronger.

"One thing I thought curious," Evelyn said, "and I didn't understand. After I shared what I knew with him and invited him to research for one of his books, he said . . ." Evelyn hesitated and stared out the window at the clouds inching forward to once again mask the bluest of skies. She turned her gaze on Cressida again. "He said that he needed to do this for his daughter."

For me? "But why? I don't understand."

"Only you can answer that. But I knew that I had to meet you. I'm glad that I did."

"I tried to meet you too, but Madeline was there. Some-one planted her, and then she was murdered. Someone wants to keep this all under wraps," Cressida said. "You're in danger too, you know."

"No one is afraid of an old lady," Evelyn said.

Cressida suspected whoever was behind this wanted Evelyn alive, or else she would already have been silenced. *Think, Cressida. Ask the right questions.*

"What were the pages ripped from your diary about?"

Evelyn picked up the diary and flipped through to find the missing pages. "What I've already mentioned—the co-vert operation. Since Harborstone Shipping already had a reputation for conducting covert operations during the Second World War, I believe it was tapped for a Cold War operation."

"The Cold War. Interesting. You hadn't mentioned that earlier. A covert mission during the Cold War. But Caleb went missing after the Cold War. I'm still at a loss to under-stand what the connection is. What was the name of the vessel Caleb was assigned to if not *Endeavor Spirit*?"

Evelyn pursed her lips. Did she know more than she was willing to share?

"Did my father go through your library to learn what-ever you missed? Where did he go to learn the truth that I haven't already been? I have to get justice for him and expose the truth. That was my job before. Writing exposés." And maybe Diggins could tell her more, after all.

Evelyn rose and moved to look at the window, then opened the door to step out onto a veranda built over the cliff face. Cressida followed and wished she hadn't. Below her, breakers pummeled the rocky beach. The wind tore at her light jacket and whipped her hair into her face.

"I don't know what it's about," Mrs. Monroe said. "Three investigators couldn't tell me. Your father, however, sent me a trinket. I got it in the mail. I wore it and never took it off, but that day that Madeline tried to kill me, I hid it under the mattress in that room. Silly, I know, but . . . I was shaken up by her assault, and I'd shot that man. I wondered who else would come for it. So I hid it well, and the day of the intruder—while you and Detective Sanders were present—I feared the worst and that it had been taken. When Deputy Riker positioned me on the floor next to the bed, I slipped my hand under the mattress to retrieve it without anyone noticing. I think Madeline was there at my house for the sole purpose of finding it."

She lifted the "trinket" from beneath the collar of her sweater.

Cressida looked at the beautiful mother-of-pearl in the shape of a whale. "Why would he send you this? What is it?"

"Look closer."

Cressida peered at the pendant. Evelyn finally took the necklace off. "This is what someone was searching for in the house. I keep my jewelry hidden away in a safe in that room where Madeline and Collins were arguing. Madeline had learned that much but never found this because I hid it under the mattress in the guest room. But I retrieved it, keeping it with me, even in the hospital."

Someone could have easily stolen it from her while she was sleeping. Cressida gently handled the necklace. "Do you mind if we go back inside?"

They returned to the living room, but Cressida remained near the window so she could look at the pendant in the light, and when she turned it at a certain angle, she could barely make it out . . . "Coordinates. These are coordinates."

"Yes. Your father found them, but I don't know what's there."

"A sunken ship—right? Surely you guessed that much.

You contacted my father. He must have understood that you were looking for your son, and he found your son."

"True, I did so he could unravel the mystery."

Which he might have done, or come close, but lost his life in the process. The pain of his death could knock her over again.

"The missing pages in his notes must detail how he learned the truth and what he found, but he ripped the pages out, realizing it was much too dangerous. The question is, what was the covert operation? What had Caleb been assigned to—meant to save his life but ultimately getting him killed?"

Evelyn winced at Cressida's words.

"You haven't shown this to anyone else, have you?"

"No, but someone must know your father found the coordinates, and they've obviously been searching. Collins, the man who murdered your father, knew. The question is, who was he working for?"

Because the hunt is still on. The danger is still present. "And this locket . . . is this the 'truth' that Diggins wants from you? He claimed that he would share what happened to my father if I got the truth from you."

"It's possible."

"But who is Diggins to know about this, even, and to want it? He could be working for the very people who killed my father."

An alert went off somewhere, and Evelyn glanced at her cell. "The *nice* detective is standing at the door."

"What? How did he get that far?"

"I gave him the code for the gate. He called to talk to me right after that initial call that interrupted us. He had quite the story. I think you should listen." Evelyn winked.

The nerve. What did Evelyn know about Braden and his relationship with Cressida's mother?

Evelyn moved to the door and opened it.

Cressida didn't feel like facing Braden—a traitor and a liar. Just how was she going to deal with this new information and the arrival of a man she didn't want to see again? Evelyn clearly liked him. Maybe she didn't fully understand that Braden was working for an enemy of a different kind.

36

Braden had no time for games. He stalked past Evelyn—he'd explained it all in a nutshell to her over the phone, including why he needed to speak with Cressida. The woman had immediately allowed him through the outer gate, though he wouldn't assume that Evelyn Monroe was by any means on his side, even though she'd initially called him the nice guy.

"I don't want to talk to you," Cressida said. "I thought I made that clear. You of all people understand that I can't trust anyone. I made the mistake of trusting you. Believing you. Even liking you, whatever that means. Whatever it meant before, it means nothing now."

"Rant all you want," he said. "Scream at me, rage at me, but your mother has ended the treatments for Elise, my niece. This is about a ten-year-old little girl. I'm here for *her*. She's my whole reason for agreeing to this assignment. I didn't know what it was when I got here. I simply worked as a detective and was told I would know. Then there you were on that beach."

"You could have told me who you were from the start

instead of taking me for a ride on your motorcycle, taking me to dinner. Making me trust you and believe in you."

"None of that matters. Do you understand the predicament I'm in? I knew that if I told you, you wouldn't talk to me anymore, and then Elise could be in danger. I don't know how your mother does it, but she pulls strings like nobody's business." He'd get down on his knees to beg if he believed that would make a difference. "Please, Cressida. Please. Work with me here."

He pulled out the image of Elise on his phone again and flashed it at her.

"You would use that to convince me? Use her like that?"

"*Use* her? I'm trying to save her life! Politicians control every aspect of our lives and the world. From the safety of their desks, they send young men and women to war. The list goes on. But in this small microcosm where Elise lives and has the chance to survive, your mother is withholding her lifeline, and I'll do what I must to save her."

Cressida's features were crestfallen. "What can I do to change that, Braden? Seems like the deal you made with her has already been broken. I know the truth now."

"You have her skills. Her talents. You're her *daughter*." Braden's voice might have cracked. "Call her now and tell her to do her thing and get those infusions going again . . . or else."

Her features softened. "I'm not sure if that was an insult or a compliment."

Evelyn stepped into view. He'd forgotten she was there. "Remember what I told you, Cressida, that I forgave my father no matter the wrong I believed he'd done. Even if someone wrongs you, you must forgive them."

"That has nothing to do with this," Cressida said.

"It has everything to do with it." Evelyn turned and walked away, disappearing into another part of the house.

"She's right, you know." He rubbed his temples. "We could argue all day. Please, just make the call."

She closed the distance and faced him, but the connection they'd shared was missing. She'd meant something to him, even before he met her, and she still did. Even if she forgave her mother, even if she forgave him, she would never choose to be with him after what she believed was a betrayal.

"For your niece, Braden, I'll make that call. For my father, I'll need your help to get him justice. To learn what happened. We work together, but when this is over, there's nothing between us personally, if there ever was. Understood?"

Ouch.

She lifted her hand to dangle a necklace. "This locket has the coordinates, longitude and latitude, embedded in the image."

"Where did you get that?"

"My father sent it to Evelyn before he died."

"But how could he have had it created in that short of time?"

"I suspect he got help from a jeweler who supplied a museum store Dad once owned." She pulled out her cell and took several photos. "I don't know if she'll let me keep it, but just in case someone steals it, then we have the images. This is what someone was after in her house."

He looked at the locket closely as she filled him in on the rest. "Let's see where this is."

Braden entered the coordinates on an app. "It's beyond the twelve-nautical-mile limit."

"I figured it would be completely out of our jurisdiction and in international waters. High seas. But the contiguous zone gives the US at least limited authority."

And why would that matter? He didn't like where this was going. "What's your plan?"

"We find out what's there."

"Cressida, I don't know if that's a good idea. Your mother wanted me to protect you."

A deep frown carved between her brows, and she blinked rapidly. "He said that he needed to do this 'for his daughter,' for me. That was his last communication to Evelyn. It doesn't make sense to me."

Unshed tears shimmered in her eyes. Her beautiful, gorgeous eyes. He shoved away the torture. This wasn't the time. Emotion would distract him from protecting her and finishing this.

"Maybe he, too, wanted to protect you. What started this? I think it could have started this entire chain of events." He still wanted to know about the article Octavia had shut down.

"Evelyn started it. She was reading one of his books and thought he could solve the mystery of what happened to her son who was sent on a covert mission."

"Okay, but your article hit a nerve. I pressed Octavia on it and she didn't have a response. Think about it."

"Mom became worried mostly when I started following the rabbit trail about shipwrecks that were leaking toxins into the ocean. I don't remember the details of my research. I'd have to go back and look at my notes."

"Shipwreck toxins," he said.

"Cold War stuff." She closed her eyes for a moment. "That was what Evelyn said."

He stepped closer and stared long and hard at her. "What comes to mind, Cressida?"

"The list is long, so I'm not sure what you're getting at."

"Does the list include radioactive materials? Did the covert mission include delivering materials to make a nuclear bomb?"

Cressida lifted her chin. "Maybe it's worse than that, Braden."

"What could be worse?"

"An actual nuclear missile could be worse," she said.

"And you think one could be just lying around on the ocean floor?"

"It's not a stretch," she said. "There have been several incidents of nuclear submarines going missing, malfunctioning, whatever, in the ocean, even recently. Again, I'd have to look at my notes."

"Your research took you that far, and then your mother shuts you down and you didn't want to listen."

"It was just research. Anyone can find the information if they look for it. And if this is what we're dealing with, then we have to see it through. The world needs to know."

Maybe Braden finally understood Cressida. Her mother was all about secrets, and Cressida had taken a completely different path in writing exposés. He might now understand why she hadn't so easily dropped the story that she now very well could have the chance to complete in a way she never imagined.

If they survived this. They needed to report this to someone in authority, but he would talk to Octavia about it first—she had known all along but hadn't been free to discuss it with him—that is, if he hadn't gotten this completely wrong. He needed to know with certainty what he was dealing with before he contacted someone in authority. He needed to know with certainty whom he could trust, if Octavia's own man she sent was now betraying her, searching for the location of a deadly secret.

He realized he'd been quiet much too long, lost in his thoughts, and Cressida was staring at him.

"Whatever it is you're thinking," she said, "we need to find Diggins first. He was in the woods when I drove up, and this locket is the truth he needs so he'll tell me what I want to know."

274

"Sounds like Evelyn has already told you."

"Diggins could know more," she said.

"You could be handing this over to the very people who killed your father."

"And this is how we'll find out." Cressida gripped the locket and moved to look out the window, then turned her attention back to him. "Let's end this once and for all. But from now on, I want the full truth from you."

"I didn't betray you, Cressida, in the sense of deliberate disloyalty." He'd wanted to be a hero for his sister, for Elise. For the two who meant the most to him, and now he was floundering. "One last thing you should know . . ." And he was betraying her mother by telling her.

She arched a brow and stepped into his space. "What's that?"

He glanced at his watch. She'd be here by late morning or early afternoon. If she took a private jet, she could be here within the hour. "Your mother is on her way to Hidden Bay."

37

On the back of his motorcycle, Cressida held on to Braden, her arms wrapped around this man who'd lied to her. Or rather, it was a lie of omission. She almost detested the feel of his taut back muscles and tight abdomen.

He'd returned Hawk's pickup and opted to take his Ducati to the Pirates' Bash for easier parking and a quicker escape if necessary.

So she held on and let the thoughts bombard her. Everything Evelyn had shared, the many possibilities of what could lie at the location, and the fact that her mother was on her way to Hidden Bay. She could already be here.

I shouldn't be surprised.

Wasn't it just like Mom to try to sabotage Cressida's efforts? Braden claimed her mother hadn't told him the reason she was coming. The woman was probably already in the state, making her way to Hidden Bay. Cressida shoved concerns of her mother behind her for now. She'd deal with her when she saw her. But thinking about something else wasn't as easy as she hoped.

She couldn't forget Evelyn's words about forgiving her father for the role he'd played in the loss of her husband and, in the end, the loss of her son. And yet, Evelyn Monroe still forgave him.

Seriously, how had she done it?

Cressida couldn't fathom forgiving her mother, but she had to admit that resentment and bitterness, the estrangement, were eating her up inside.

How, Lord, how?

How do I forgive?

Braden decelerated as they entered the packed marina parking lot. More parking was created for the bash. Time to focus on the clear and present danger. Looking for Diggins. Cressida had seen him when she'd arrived at Evelyn's safe house. Then Cressida and Braden had searched the woods near the house, but Diggins was nowhere to be found.

Supposedly, he was an important figure at the Pirates' Bash, so his presence was required. Cressida had wanted to attend anyway from the moment she'd heard about it—for research purposes, of course. Except now her reason for attending was far different. No mulling about and free-spirited exploring to learn what she could from the locals about the region and their impressions of the folklore surrounding the *Specter's Bounty.*

She hopped off the motorcycle, and Braden secured both their helmets. The sun was shining, and it was a beautiful day for the bash, but in the distance, clouds boiled up again. No matter. Washingtonians were accustomed to the rain.

She didn't even want to look at Braden, not really, but they had to work together and, in this instance, trust each other. Then when this was over, she was done with him.

Forgive.

Okay, she might forgive him because—she had to admit— he'd had a good reason to keep the information from her, but that didn't prevent her from walking away without seeing what could happen between them. She gave a quick glance his way. He was surveying the crowd, his expression as intense as she'd ever seen over the course of a few days.

He caught her looking but then quickly focused back on the crowd. "You know you should wait with Evelyn and be safe. Let *me* finish this."

"And get all the glory? This will get justice for Dad. Plus, it could get me my career back."

"Is it worth your life?"

"Is it worth *yours*?"

"I'm trained for this."

"Good, then you can protect me. You're trained to protect people, aren't you? I could tell from the start. That's how you knew my mother, isn't it? You worked as a DSS agent to protect her?" she said.

"Yes."

Cressida never dealt with the many people her mother worked with. Often her mother traveled abroad for months at a time. But Cressida had seen a few of the DSS agents. Never Braden, though. "How long did you work with her? Where were you assigned?"

"That's a story for another time."

"You mean a secret."

He didn't look at her, and that was telling.

"That's right," Cressida said. "I know she keeps secrets."

"If you know, then why do you ask?"

"Because I'd love to know. We might not get another chance for you to tell me what she is holding over you."

"You know that already."

"Tell me about your niece, Braden."

He started toward the boardwalk. "I'll tell you everything after this is over. We need to focus, Cressida. Did you notice that the *Sea Reaper* is not out in the bay?"

"Maybe it's at the marina. He brought it in for the bash."

"I don't see it, do you?" Braden led her over to the pier. "Let's confirm one way or another."

He reached for her, and she pulled away. Shoving his hands into his pockets, he picked up the pace. She had to walk faster to keep up with his long strides. People hung out on their boats, laughing and having a good time, waving at them as they passed.

"You know, it's kind of interesting people are having fun with the idea of pirates, don't you think?" she asked.

"What do you mean?"

"Well, factually speaking, they were and still are thieves. Robbers. Murderers and rapists. Look at even the modern-day pirates off the coast of Africa."

"Did you visit the region?"

"For research on one of Dad's shipwrecks for the book. It was risky, but I had a great guide and protection."

"Let's hope everyone here at the bash is only pretending," he said. "As for Diggins, I don't see the *Sea Reaper*. So he was in the woods and now he's not even in the bay. You think he knows you got the information he needed?"

"Pretty sure. I mean, why else was he waiting outside of her house? But then why did he leave?"

"Could be someone got to him. Something happened to him." Braden pushed her behind him.

"What are you doing?"

"We're looking for Diggins, but Derek Harlan is here looking for us. Or rather . . . you."

"The protector that Mom supposedly sent? Is he working for her? Or double-crossing her?"

"His prints were found in Evelyn's house, so we can't trust him." Braden glanced down at her, holding her gaze for a few breaths more than necessary.

His presence, the longing to be with him, free from all this drama, coursed through her. But he was just like everyone else—untrustworthy. She tried to free herself from his protective grip, but he was granite.

"Wait," he whispered.

Then suddenly, he quietly rushed her away, heading back toward the opposite end of the pier. "This guy shouldn't be roaming around free. I thought he would already be arrested."

"Why don't you do it, then?" she asked. "We could find out who he's working for. Oh, right, you're not really working for the county. You're working for my mother."

She needed to shut down her passive-aggressive attitude, but it was hard.

He continued ushering her away, his grip on her tight. Cressida wanted to escape. Once the pier was behind them, he slowed and released her hand, then radioed the county sheriff's dispatch, reporting their suspect had been spotted at the Pirates' Bash.

"Are you going to take him down?"

"This isn't a good place to do it. Too many people. Someone could get hurt. But once backup arrives, they'll follow him and then grab him." He released her hand and then walked along the beach toward the thickest part of the crowded Pirates' Bash.

The truth was, she *wanted* to trust him, but he hadn't given her a lot of choice. Or had he? "Listen, Braden." She stopped walking, and he paused, then looked at her. "It's just taking me time to come to terms with what's happened. I'm sorry that my mother manipulated you, roped you into this."

His steel-blue eyes softened, his stern expression brightened, if only a little. Then he gave a subtle nod. "Elise is getting her infusion today. Thank you for your help."

Cressida had sent her mother a text that Braden's niece's

medication had better be on track. She wasn't sure if her mother would respond or make things happen. In fact, she had no idea if her text had been the one to restore the treatment. Because how cruel for her mother to withhold that treatment, especially since she had the power to start it to begin with. What was she holding over the clinicians in control? Cressida didn't want to know.

"Sometimes I wonder who my mother really is. I don't like to think of it, truly. It seems to me that she's someone who holds other people's secrets and knows how to wield them to her benefit." She didn't like where the thought took her, but it was within her nature to press forward. "What secret does she hold over you?"

"You can't help yourself, can you?" he asked.

She wasn't earning brownie points with him. Together they walked deeper into the crowded Pirates' Bash. People of all ages joined in laughter and fun, many of them dressed as rough and dirty sailors or pirates—all in good fun. Sea shanties played over a tinny speaker. Cressida ducked under a string of lights that hung haphazardly between two tented booths featuring carnival food—pretzels, fried fish, and crab cakes. Funnel cakes, salted caramel apples, and "seafoam" candy.

What in the world? Cressida stopped at a booth. The line was short at the moment, so this was the perfect time. "I'm sorry but I need to try the seafoam candy."

Braden scrunched up his face. "Doesn't look good to me."

She purchased the glob of blue-green-tinted, honeycomb-textured candy and moved away so the next person in line could approach, then handed Braden a chunk of it. Cressida didn't wait on him to try it and took a bite. "Oh, it's too sweet and minty. I'm not a fan. I should have asked." She chuckled but finished off the rest.

Braden hadn't even tried his and handed it back to her,

his expression serious. What was she doing having even a little fun at a time like this? He hadn't asked the question, but she shrugged and chucked the rest in the trash.

Approaching her, a man dressed in a patched pirate coat swayed with a mug of beer, his face painted like a skull. This was supposed to be a family event, but she could see things getting out of hand.

And she was here to find Diggins. "Okay, I'm done testing the food."

Braden pressed his hand against the small of her back as he urged her forward and deeper into the crowd. "Keep your head about you."

Always.

"And let's blend in." He eyed the bandannas and eye patches at a booth.

"Are you serious? You aren't going to look like you're with the sheriff's department anymore."

"I don't look like that now."

Right, because he kept his badge in a leather case in his jacket pocket inside his black leather jacket.

He must have been getting nervous about her being at the Pirates' Bash with Harlan searching for her. Diggins had to know that she had learned the truth, and he might have shared with others.

Cressida wanted justice for Dad, but she was getting nervous as well. "Look, if we don't find Diggins soon, we should leave. Let him come to me."

"That moment is now. We're leaving. It doesn't look like he's here. I see some county deputies. Let's head to them."

A bloodcurdling scream erupted, and people scattered in every direction. Cressida was glad she'd held on to Braden's hand because he pulled her out of the way and into the shadows between two tented booths.

Two deputies rushed through the crowd, heading toward

the threat. Braden had called them to come and find Harlan, though there was other security at the bash.

"That's just what Hidden Bay needs, more drama to scare the tourists away," she said.

Or draw them in.

Keeping his grip on her arm, he said, "You'll need to come with me while I check on what's going on."

He led her forward and out into the growing crowd that had now turned into gawkers holding their cell phones up to take videos. The deputies were holding them back. Braden stepped through and dragged Cressida along with him. Deputies guarded an alley, hidden by a tent flap propped up to block their view. With Cressida in tow, Braden stepped around the deputies and behind the flap into the dark alley.

Trent stood over a body. Braden approached and Cressida remained close, though she didn't want to look at the gruesome scene. But she couldn't miss that Derek Harlan lay on the ground, his throat slashed.

She squeezed her eyes shut and backed against the tent.

The blood boiled in her ears, then rushed to her feet. The world spun at the sight.

"Wait there," Braden said.

She opened her eyes to connect with his reassuring gaze.

"Just right there," he said. "You're safe for the moment."

Because she was with law enforcement? Or because the man supposedly after her was dead?

"Give me a few moments," Braden said, "and then I'll get you out of here."

"But Diggins . . ." Nausea erupted. Dizziness persisted. "He could be dead too. Someone is killing everyone."

"Cressida, focus. I need you to keep your head about you. Trent, stay with her for a few moments, will you?"

Deputy Riker nodded and moved to stand near Cressida. His mouth remained flat, but his eyes reflected his deep concern. Cressida suspected he didn't like Braden asking him to babysit, but he also seemed relieved that he wasn't in charge of the body.

Braden took pictures of the body with his cell phone. On the other side of the flap, the two other deputies kept the crowd at bay. Cressida squeezed her eyes shut.

All I wanted was to finish Dad's book. A simple thing, really. A lovely work of history. And now she was in the middle of a horror flick featuring dead bodies and a ghost ship.

Suddenly she fell back into darkness. A hand clamped over her mouth. A familiar face appeared before putting a black bag over her head.

38

Braden ground his molars at the gruesome sight. This was their suspect. Deputies had shown up to apprehend him and now he was dead?

"Where's Thatcher?" he asked, still facing the body. "I want the sheriff here."

When he got no response from Trent, he glanced over his shoulder. The man remained standing with his back to the tent.

Braden's heart might have stopped. "Where's Cressida?"

Trent whirled around, grabbing his gun. "I don't know! She was here a second ago. Maybe she had to use the ladies' room."

He thought she understood the dangerous situation. *She wouldn't have left without letting me know, would she?*

"Stay with the body," he said to Trent, then left the shadowed alley between the tents.

"Cressida!" he called into the thick, gawking crowd. They might even believe this was a show put on for the bash. But they couldn't be more wrong.

Weaving through the mass of people, he looked for Cressida and called her name. Tried her cell but got nowhere.

Most onlookers held up their cell phones to take video. He jogged around the structures and tents, finally spotting a temporary restroom fifteen yards away. He approached and knocked on the door. "Cressida?"

"Nope!" a guy answered.

Great.

Panic set in, burning a line up his throat. Where had she gone? *Lord, help me!*

He headed toward the boardwalk and then the marina, all the slips packed with boats. Then rushed back around through the crowd to find Trent.

"Detective Sanders," one of the deputies said. "We didn't see her leave, but we were watching the crowd, trying to shut down videos. One woman got the video on her cell and showed me that no one left the alley."

No one left the alley? Then where was she? "How's that possible?"

Braden thanked the deputy, then rushed back into the alley where Trent was on his radio. He glanced at Braden. "Sheriff's on his way."

"Good. He's got to take lead in this. I need to find Cressida."

Trent lifted his shoulders and dropped them. "She was there, Braden. How was I supposed to know that she would just walk away?"

"She didn't walk away." He stared at the tent walls where he'd last seen her. Stepping forward, he pressed his hand against the canvas and it flapped inward with little pressure. He saw clearly now that someone had cut this opening. His weapon at the ready, he stepped through and found the tent empty. One look and he realized it was a weapons display tent, but it had been shut off from the public. This had to be the way she'd gone. The big question was, why had she left?

He glanced to the ground and immediately saw signs

of a struggle. She hadn't left on her own. He bent down and lifted the chain from the ground—the chain minus the locket with the coordinates to some kind of dread on the ocean floor.

She'd been taken, definitely taken. Someone—possibly whoever had killed Derek Harlan—had the information they were after.

"Diggins." He growled the name between clenched teeth. He was the one who wanted the "truth" from Evelyn Monroe.

Braden rushed out the back of the tent and eyed the boardwalk and the water. One boat headed out of the bay.

The *Mariner's Gambit*.

Braden radioed Trent as he raced to the marina shop to get his hands on a rental boat, but that was going to be tough during the Pirates' Bash. "I'm going after Cressida. I think she's been abducted and someone's taking her out to sea."

"What? Why?"

"I need backup. Get the state police. Find a marine division willing to help. Call the Coast Guard. Anyone. Everyone. I'll send you the coordinates when I have them. I believe we're going after the *Mariner's Gambit*, and I need everyone on this." It could be a matter of national security.

"But what about Derek Harlan? He was murdered."

"His troubles are over. We'll learn the truth for him. Did you get the coroner?"

"I'll take care of everything. I'll get the resources moving. Go find her!"

Braden ended the radio call and was almost at the chandlery when his cell buzzed.

Octavia. He didn't have time to mess with her, but neither could he ignore her. He answered. "Braden here. We have a problem."

"You sound breathless."

"Because I'm running. Cressida's been taken." And he couldn't be sure it was out on the water. "I've called in the resources to help me search."

"What?" Octavia continued to scream and berate him.

"I'm heading out to sea to find her."

She swore under her breath, but he still heard it. "I'll be there within the hour."

"I'm not waiting for you. I think someone's taking her to coordinates that we've found, we just don't know exactly what this is about. We have some theories, but if you know, now would be the time to tell me."

"It's about a Cold War Russian nuclear submarine, Braden. Now do you get it? Now do you understand why I shut down her article? The world was supposed to believe it was lost and never found."

"And these coordinates?" He spilled them out to her.

"Not the sub. The missing *Vanguard* that was on a CIA-funded covert mission to salvage the nukes and anything else that could be taken from that submarine—but it was all lost at sea."

"Obviously it isn't lost. Someone knows where to find it. And the *Vanguard*? What does that have to do with the *Specter's Bounty*?"

"It's complicated. Do you really want me to tell you everything now?"

"No." Braden stood at the door to the marina. "Anything else before I end this call and go find your daughter?"

"You go out there, you might not come back, Braden. You know that, right?"

He ended the call. No more time to waste. He rushed inside to find both Mavis and Kit working hard, seeing to customers. He forced his way to the front of the line. "We have an emergency. I need a boat. Cressida has been taken."

Kit paused while packaging an item, her eyes wide. "What?"

"No time to explain. I need a boat."

"I got nothing for you. Maybe see if one of the people at the bash can help."

He paced and rubbed his jaw. *God, I need your help. Cressida needs your help.*

"What about the pirates? You could get one of them to help." She gestured toward the liveaboards, who had moved their boats in for the bash. "Diggins, maybe."

Braden struggled to keep his expression neutral. Diggins was nowhere to be found. He had assumed that Diggins had taken Cressida, then he'd seen the *Mariner's Gambit*—Malloy already on his list to be questioned—leaving the bay.

At that moment, Diggins himself stepped into the chandlery, surprising Braden. "Detective." He nodded. "What's going on? I thought I would find Ms. Dane with you."

And I thought you'd found her and taken her. Clearly Braden was wrong. "I can't be sure, but I'm concerned that Malloy has her on the *Mariner's Gambit*. It's heading out of the bay. I can't know. All I know is someone took her. I've got my deputy calling in resources."

"Did he get the *Kraken* on it? The USCG cutter?"

"I hope so," Braden said. "I can't wait for resources. Cressida might not have that time."

"Let's go." Diggins led Braden out of the shop, and they rushed toward a skiff at the very end of the pier.

His old trawler, the *Sea Reaper*, was floating not too far out in the crowded bay. Either it had just arrived, or Braden and Cressida had missed it before. They hopped in without a second to waste and Diggins ramped up the motor and sped across the chop to his vessel.

They climbed aboard. Braden took in the older boat. Clearly Diggins had worked hard to repair it, but he had much work left to do. "Are you sure this is going to make it?"

"Oh, she's good for it. But a bigger question is where are we going? I don't see Malloy."

"I think I know," Braden said. "Just get us out of the bay, then I'll tell you."

Diggins was at the helm, slowly maneuvering out of the marina, and then he steered out of the bay, well away from other boaters, before picking up speed. Braden peered through binoculars, searching the horizon for the *Mariner's Gambit*.

He didn't get it. If Malloy had wanted Cressida, he had her to begin with. Then again, Cressida didn't have the information then. How did Malloy know that she finally *knew* the location? Had Derek Harlan worked that out somehow and told Malloy? Had Malloy killed Derek, or had it been someone else?

"What are you after, Diggins? You wanted the truth from Evelyn. What are you looking for? Cressida said you knew why her father was killed. Tell me everything I need to know and tell me now. Cressida got what you needed, and that got her into trouble. Into this mess. You owe her. You owe me."

Diggins handled his vessel with skill and experience as he grumbled under his breath, nodding and grimacing.

"The *Specter's Bounty*, aka *Endeavor Spirit*, went out in search of the lost *Vanguard*. The crew was a few treasure hunters."

That wasn't exactly the story told at the museum. "Treasure. What treasure were they hunting?"

"Black-market stuff."

"And you know this because you previously dealt in the same?"

"You have me all wrong, son. I wasn't there for the same reason. Regardless, everyone on board the *Specter's Bounty* is dead, except me. I was there too, looking for treasure of a different kind."

Braden stumbled back, and not because the waves knocked the hull around. "*You* were on the *Specter's Bounty*? Why did you lie about it?"

"Too dangerous. I told Ms. Dane it was all too dangerous to talk about. Her father died because of it, after all, and I knew I was done after that. I thought she deserved answers, but then I realized that I would only be putting her in danger and changed my mind. I told her not to come that night, and you both showed up."

So, sounded like Diggins had informed Alaric Dane, after all.

"What happened to the crew?"

Diggins spared him barely a glance. "Maybe if we get your girl out alive, and we both survive, I'll tell you."

"Is that why you don't need the coordinates?"

"Oh, I need them. We never made it to the *Vanguard*. I wasn't given the coordinates."

"Then how did Alaric Dane learn the coordinates? Where did he get the information?"

Wait. Braden couldn't move. This had been staring him in the face from the start.

Octavia Dane had known all along what was on the ocean floor. That's why she steered Cressida away. She'd known the coordinates of the *Vanguard* as well, and Alaric had somehow discovered the coordinates, or maybe he, too, had known all along. Perhaps even Evelyn had suspected he could learn the truth because his wife—now ex-wife—had known.

He held on to the rail.

"You getting your sea legs, buddy? You okay?" Diggins asked.

He wasn't sure he'd ever be "okay" again. Nor was he sure

that giving the location of a sunken vessel holding who knew what to someone who had allegedly sold artifacts on the black market was the best idea. But to find Cressida, he'd do it.

He showed him the coordinates on his cell via the pictures Cressida had taken.

"I can't be sure that Malloy took her. I could have it all wrong. She could be back at the Pirates' Bash, but I found evidence to suggest that she'd been taken. Tell me, what do you know about Malloy?"

"Oh, he took her, all right." Diggins dipped and bobbed his chin. "If she has the coordinates, he's the one."

"Care to shed some light on that statement?"

"Malloy has been working this angle for years. Waiting for the moment when he'd get his big payday."

Braden hated how in the dark law enforcement was on all of this. He hadn't learned anything about Malloy. But now he'd take a moment to look at the image that had finally loaded via the text he'd gotten from Thatcher just before he'd boarded with Diggins.

"Hold on. I got this before we left the chandlery. I've been waiting on the image to pop up." He looked at his cell.

The text was from Thatcher. It read, *Look closely.*

Braden expanded the image of a group of sailors posing for the camera.

He didn't know what he was looking at. All the men were young, and this appeared to be an old image.

Diggins shot Braden a squinty pirate eye. Right. Okay. But he might know something or have some input. Braden stood next to him at the wheel and showed him the image. Diggins nodded and focused back on steering.

"Do you recognize anyone?" Braden asked.

"That's Malloy. Take a closer look at the guy standing to his right."

Braden rubbed his eyes, then peered again. The man next to Malloy. Was that . . . Trent Riker? *Deputy* Trent Riker and Malloy?

Trent had been feeding Braden the information, including finding Harlan's prints—was it all a lie? Braden had been relying on him too much. He slowly looked up.

Diggins shrugged. "Been there. I've trusted the wrong people too. Your deputy? He was former CIA. He was in on the original salvage that went wrong. Don't know more than that, other than talking about it gets you killed."

Incredulous, Braden stared at this man full of surprises that he couldn't confirm as truth.

"Tell me why you wanted the coordinates from Evelyn," Braden said while he texted a special request to Thatcher and hoped he got it.

"What are you talking about?"

"You wanted the truth from her, the coordinates."

"What? No. The truth I wanted from her . . . was to know if she ever really loved her husband. She left me for dead, you know."

39

Cressida glared at Captain Malloy as though that would make any difference in her predicament. She'd been transported from his smaller trawler—the *Mariner's Gambit*—to a much bigger vessel. A state-of-the art salvage craft. He'd taken her to a spare room without a porthole and shoved her into a chair, then he bound her wrists and ankles.

"You betrayed my father. He trusted you." *I trusted you.* "And you lied to me."

She had to find a way out of this. Braden might not have a clue where she was. If he happened to see the *Mariner's Gambit* leave the bay and was following, then he was going in the wrong direction. This operation involved multiple parties, which they already suspected. Someone well-funded was backing this project—she'd suspect a rogue nation or terrorist cell.

Her ankles were bound but not to the chair. At least her wrists had been secured in front of her, but the duct tape had been put on too tight. "Can you at least untie me? My hands are getting numb and it's cold, so that makes it worse."

She wanted to point out that Malloy now had the coordinates, so why did he need her? But that seemed counterintuitive to her survival. "Please tell me what this is all about."

"You already know. It's tucked in that brain of yours."

"Know what? I don't know anything. It's a shipwreck, that's easy enough to guess." She'd landed on nuclear submarine but hoped and prayed that she was way off. *Oh, Lord, let it not be that!*

"Maybe you haven't figured it out yet, but you would have if you had kept going with your article."

"My article. How do you know about that? I hadn't published it. There's no way you could know." But her mother had known. Her boyfriend had known. And . . . Commander Elias Steel. Navy Salvage Officer—the man she had planned to interview—had known.

"That boat racing toward us on your first day when I brought you here? Those men are the enemy. They're after the same thing I'm after, only working for our enemies."

"You don't think you're a bad guy?" she asked. "You abducted me. You feel like an enemy to me."

"For all the right reasons, honey. And you're alive."

"And tied up."

"This show isn't over yet. I have work to do. Now sit still and be quiet if you want to live."

He left her alone in a room with a chair and a bed. Nothing else. Very spare quarters indeed. She heard him lock the door. Tied up inside a locked room.

She would continue to try to get out of the tape. Cressida closed her eyes, calmed her breaths, and prayed.

Lord, please let this not be about a nuclear submarine that some bad people want to recover for material to create a dirty bomb.

She didn't know much about the usability of old weapons-grade uranium or plutonium. Could it degrade underwater?

Even if it did, it would remain radioactive and could be used for a dirty bomb, couldn't it?

Weren't there easier ways to get those kinds of materials to cause trouble? She couldn't be part of this. Didn't want anything to do with it. They were not going to let her live, no matter what Malloy said. She couldn't be sure who he was really working for, and maybe he wasn't even sure—if he believed this was an operation sanctioned by the US Government. He must be a fool, or so greedy he allowed himself to be fooled.

Cressida hopped over to the door and wanted to pound on it, but where would that get her?

The thrumming of the engines went silent. The vessel was no longer moving.

Had they made it to the location? Her breathing hitched up. She did not want to be aboard this vessel messing with radioactive material. How could this happen? She had to escape this room. But how? Cressida heard footfalls. Boots. Not Malloy's cadence. She'd seen other men with guns—security?—and then others here to work the salvage equipment, navigate this vessel.

If she escaped, where would she go? How would she evade the others on the boat? Still, she wouldn't just sit here and wait for someone to come and kill her. Malloy had under-estimated her if he thought locking her in this room would keep her here.

Wrists and ankles still bound, Cressida hopped as she dragged the chair—the action much harder than she'd imagined—into place by the door where she could strike unseen. The lock clicked and the door swung open. From behind him, she brought the chair down hard at the back of a man's head.

He collapsed.

At first she didn't recognize him, and then she froze.

Deputy Riker?

Oh no! What have I done? He'd come to get her out of this. He'd gotten here so fast—he must have followed her somehow or taken a helicopter. Still, she would have expected Braden, who was with the same sheriff's department, to be the one to find her. Not Deputy Riker.

But wait . . . he wore the same black shirt and pants as the rest of the crew and wasn't dressed like a deputy, so he wasn't here on official business? Was he working with Malloy? Someone else?

She felt for a pulse and found one. At least she hadn't killed him. Just given him a grand concussion. No time to worry about him. She found a pocketknife on his body and cut off the tape from her ankles and then, after several attempts, was able to cut through the tape around her wrists. She had the slimmest chance of getting out of here.

Even if she found a skiff she could use to escape the larger vessel, if anyone spotted her leaving, they could still catch up to her and take her down. Maybe waiting in the cell was the better choice. No. Once someone decided she held no value, she'd become shark food and dumped in the ocean.

Malloy might think he wasn't going to kill her, but this secret was far too big, and to some, she wasn't worth it. They had let her live long enough to find the truth—the coordinates. And . . . she should sabotage this entire vessel to prevent them from getting what lay at the bottom of the ocean.

All this research and looking into shipwrecks for her father, and Cressida never would have imagined herself in a covert operation to retrieve fissile material in whatever form from a sunken *salvage* vessel. If she survived, she probably wouldn't even be allowed to write about it—it would be considered classified.

She looked at Deputy Riker. She couldn't just leave him

there. Cressida tugged him completely inside the room—which wasn't easy. She removed his guns and knives. His radios and communication devices. Removed his black shirt and cap and put those on. Maybe the disguise would be just the thing to save her. Then she shut the door and locked him inside. He was a bad guy until she learned otherwise. No one on this vessel could be trusted until she knew better.

Standing in the dim hall of a shiny new research-salvage vessel, she focused on what came next. Beyond sending a message to Braden regarding her location and need for assistance . . . she needed to act now. While she couldn't *wait* for help, she could hope it would come in time.

She had two choices. She could figure out how to shut down the power and permanently damage this operation before escaping on a skiff. Or she could do nothing and escape now.

Neither of those options seemed remotely possible.

Here goes nothing . . .

40

old it here." Braden stared through binoculars. "We have to figure out how to get in close enough to get on that boat without them seeing us."

He'd thought they would find the *Mariner's Gambit* at the location, but instead a large salvage vessel was anchored at the coordinates. That made much more sense. The *Mariner's Gambit* might have been able to do some salvaging, but not for the remnants of a vessel that supposedly salvaged a nuclear submarine. This incident of a foreign nuclear submarine getting this close to US soil had been kept well under wraps for far too long.

And as he looked at the sophisticated vessel, his heart sank. He should have known. Should have suspected—this was big. Who was behind it? Their government? Another government or regime? Or just a rogue group wanting to get their hands on dangerous materials left in the ocean?

Diggins stood next to him and pressed his hand on the binoculars to lower them. "Staring at that thing isn't going to get her back or make this any easier."

"Got any ideas?" Braden asked.

"A couple. We could just go in. Let them take us." Diggins's tone sounded serious.

"And get ourselves killed?" Braden looked him over. Was that head injury finally confusing him? "How does that help Cressida?"

Diggins pressed his lips into a hard line. "You don't even know if she's on the boat. You don't know if she's alive."

Not what he wanted to hear . . . or think about, though Diggins wasn't wrong. "I have to believe she is." *I can feel it.*

"I guess I could have said more early on. I'm sorry I didn't. But the day she got here and asked about me, I had a feeling that something like this was going to happen. So I've been preparing. I have tanks. We could go in that way. Maybe they won't see us."

"Scuba tanks? I didn't see them."

"They're ready. Four sets. I thought there'd be more of us. There's only two."

For now. Braden hoped he had help coming. "You dive?" Why was he asking? This news shouldn't have surprised him.

"Would I have tanks if I didn't? The bigger question is— do you?"

"I have experience, yes."

Diggins nodded. He steered his boat away.

"Hey, where are you going?"

"If we can see them, chances are they're going to see us sooner than we'd like. We'll get the tanks, get suited up, and take a skiff in closer. That'll be harder to spot."

Braden looked through the binoculars again and watched the vessel fade away on the horizon.

"Let's say we get onto that rig," he said. "Then what? How do we find her? How do we get her out of there alive?" He was usually the one explaining the plans to others. But he was always open to suggestions.

"I brought the tanks. I'll let you figure out how to save the day."

"Seriously? You trust me with your life?"

"Didn't say that. I trust you with *your* life and hers, and I won't be far behind."

Braden didn't want to put the older man in danger. Especially now that he knew Diggins's shocking relationship to Evelyn Monroe, he wanted to deliver him back safely. He wanted that anyway, but he wanted this for Evelyn as well. She'd lost enough.

And now he understood. The real treasure Diggins had been searching for aboard the *Endeavor Spirit*, or *Specter's Bounty*, hadn't been artifacts—it had been his son, Caleb. But Caleb had been long dead, lost in the depth of the Pacific Ocean by then. Maybe Diggins had hoped to discover something to bring closure to his own grief . . . and to Evelyn's. She'd spent her days by the ocean, gazing out at the horizon, watching, waiting—knowing deep down that her son would never return but unable to let go of the hope that the sea, which had claimed him, might somehow give him back.

Still, did Evelyn know that her husband was alive? Or had Diggins hidden that truth from her, waiting, watching, and protecting? They were the same—Evelyn and Diggins—in the way that mattered most. She helped those in need, giving them safe harbor, including the liveaboards in Hidden Bay, while Diggins—her long-lost husband she believed deceased—mentored those in need.

Braden prayed for a good ending to their story.

Still, he didn't understand. "Why does Evelyn keep you at a distance? Does she even know about you? That you're still alive?"

"She left me for dead to prevent her father from trying again. I don't blame her for that. She saw me once . . . in

Forestview . . . but looked the other way after reacting like she'd seen a ghost. If she believed that I was still alive, then she walked away because she doesn't want to lose me again. I know that about her. She's lost a son and her husband—twice, she thought. In my quest to find him—buried in the ocean—I had hoped to bring her closure as a gift, but I failed us both. As for the truth I asked Cressida to get from her—I simply wanted to know if she ever loved me, and if she still loves me now but she's just too afraid."

That might be the saddest love story Braden had ever heard. Too much tragedy in one lifetime.

Diggins drew in a breath and lifted his shoulders. "But today, everything changes. Today, this all ends, and if she still loves me and wants me, we'll be together." He chuckled. "I'm not sure I could get accustomed to her lifestyle, nor she mine, and maybe we'll love each other from afar like we've done for decades."

"Let's make sure you get the chance. I'd prefer it if you remained here on the *Sea Reaper* and wait for me to return with Cressida. It's too dangerous for you to go with me. I don't know what we're going to face."

"I can help you, son, and I'm going."

Braden had called in additional resources, texting to ask Thatcher to send their reserve deputies—Hawk and Cole, both skilled in military maneuvers—to meet him at the co-ordinates. He couldn't be sure if Thatcher had even received the text because he hadn't heard back. He'd tried again but his communication failed. But he certainly couldn't trust that Trent had called in the resources like he assured Braden he would.

And here he was—just him and Diggins. Hawk and Cole hadn't shown up. Though he could use their skill and knew he could trust them both, he couldn't count on them to be here if they never got the message.

"Let's do this." Braden had never been on shakier ground.

"We could wait for the *Kraken*. Didn't you say you called for the Coast Guard?"

"Cressida doesn't have the time. If they show up, that'll help, but I can't wait."

If anything happened to him today—then what would happen to his niece?

What would happen to Cressida?

He had never been more uncertain about a plan, but he was willing to go the distance and give it all to save lives, even if that meant losing his own.

He and Diggins grabbed the tanks and prepped the skiff. They'd have to wait until it was totally dark and hope and pray the vessel hadn't completed its task and moved on. He hated leaving Cressida there—if she truly was there. But he knew she was. Someone had taken her. She had the coordinates, and now here they were at those same coordinates.

The whir of an approaching vessel set off alarms in Braden's head. The skiff was attached and waiting for their mission, and they would be donning their scuba suits shortly. He looked through his binoculars and could barely make out the silhouette of a RIB—rigid inflatable boat, often used by the Coast Guard and military—carrying two men. Relief rushed through him.

"It's Hawk and Cole."

"You trust them?" Diggins asked.

"With my life."

The RIB sidled up to the *Sea Reaper*, and Braden assisted the two men onto the vessel. He gave them what little information he had.

Hawk's frown deepened as he listened, then he shook it off and managed a grin. "You're in luck. Cole here has brought everything but the kitchen sink. This'll be just like old times."

"We were never on a mission together." Cole crossed his thick arms.

"Separately, then, it'll be like old times, except I was always in the air." Hawk crossed his arms too and stared his brother down.

"All right, boys. What you got and what's the plan?" Diggins sounded impatient.

Braden was too relieved to be impatient.

"We brought scuba."

"I already got that," Diggins groused.

"Do you have waterproof comms?" Cole asked. "Handheld sonar devices? Underwater night vision?"

"No. I don't have the resources for that. You boys use your own equipment, then."

"We could use that and a plan," Braden said. As soon as he realized his friends had arrived—and now, finally, he would actually call them friends—his mind kicked into gear with a plan of his own. "Trent is running this operation. He was probably a government operative, planted years ago when Evelyn moved here, to watch and wait for news of the location. But his behavior tells me he's no longer working for the government, and this is his own private operation. Before I knew this, I tasked him with calling in resources. Thatcher's the one to discover the truth about Trent."

"He called us up and out to help," Hawk said. "I warned him that as far as additional resources, he should move with extreme caution given that his calls for assistance—the Coast Guard or the Feds—could be conveyed to Trent and warn him that we're coming. Surprise is to our advantage. No telling how big Trent's network must be to have pulled this off."

"Understood," Braden said. "Octavia Dane knows, and I'm counting on her to call in the appropriate authorities. But here and now, *we* can't know who to trust. It's just us, the Timberbrook County Sheriff's Office, working far from our jurisdiction to save Cressida Valentine Dane per her mother's request—a VIP in the US State Department. Even so, we go into this with great risk, not only to our lives but to our reputations. Our goal is to save Cressida, but we need to also prevent that salvage vessel from obtaining nuclear material."

"Whoa . . . whoa." Cole threw up his hands. "Nobody said anything about nukes."

"I don't have time to explain. Waiting for help to arrive risks Cressida's life and the lives of many other people if the wrong parties get their hands on it. Are you in or out?"

"I've been in since I got your message from Thatcher, who, by the way, told us, and I quote, 'Do what you have to do out there—we'll deal with the fallout later.' So let's hear the plan. We make a great team."

"A former DSS special agent. A former Night Stalker pilot. A former Green Beret. And an elderly artifact smuggler. I agree," Braden said. "We can do this."

Thatcher had their backs, which he hadn't doubted. Octavia would have their backs too—this was about her daughter. "Our goal is to disable the vessel and prevent it from retrieving the salvaged contents of a nuclear submarine that are allegedly on the *Vanguard*, another salvage vessel lost at sea. I'll approach underwater and take out the external surveillance. Once that's done, you three can prepare to board and secure the deck. We disable the power and communications."

"Oh, did I tell you we brought night drones?" Hawk laughed. "I've been playing around with them—"

"Focus," Cole said.

"You can use those to create distractions while we board and take control of the deck," Braden said. "Get Cressida. Take Trent and secure him while we wait for the Coast

Guard, or whoever shows up to take over. We don't know when they'll arrive. We go in as if we're on our own. Then we go public with this."

"You don't think it needs to remain a secret?"

"Secrets get out, and the wrong parties are about to get their hands on significant materials because of a secret kept too long," Braden said.

"What if this all goes south? What then? We can't let them get their hands on this stuff," Cole said.

"What's *your* plan?" Braden asked.

"I suggest explosives to completely destroy the vessel." Cole tugged scuba suits out of their gear. "Prevent the salvage and prevent the escape. Whatever it takes."

Braden didn't like that plan, but Cole was right. "Are you saying you brought explosives?"

"No," Cole said. "But I could use what they have on the vessel. Chances are they've got them."

"We stay in communication the whole time," Braden said. "I get Cressida and get her to safety, then and only then do we completely disable the vessel—that is, if things go south as you said."

"Do you know she's there?" Hawk's tone sounded heavy.

"She'd better be," Braden said. "And my guess is that she's already planning her escape."

But what he couldn't voice, the words he wouldn't put out into the air—Cressida was running out of time.

41

Cressida ducked into an alcove and pressed her back against the wall, grateful for shadows and dim lights in the hallway. The salvage boat rocked with the choppy waves.

The floor vibrated and the rhythmic clanking of chains and cables echoed into the hall. A sharp hiss startled her—the hydraulics that controlled the cranes and could already have lowered the ROV—remotely operated vehicle—to retrieve what they'd come for. A shudder crawled over her.

Cressida did not want to be on this vessel if they actually retrieved nuclear material. She assumed they had prepared shielded containers and would monitor radiation, but that was a big assumption. Plus, she needed to stop this, no matter the cost.

God, how do I make this stop?

Someone wanted the information that Cressida's father had discovered because of Evelyn's request. Cressida had to go and reach right into the heart of a hornet's nest and end up holding the prize everyone wanted . . . but now the swarm was after her. Heavy booted footsteps sounded much too close, and she stilled to listen to two men arguing, but she couldn't make out any words besides "clear" and "impasse."

They moved closer to her position. She held her breath. No one had discovered Trent yet, but as soon as he woke up, she was done for if she didn't find her way off this craft.

"I don't like this," Man One said. "We don't have all the appropriate protocols in place for a night salvage, not to mention we don't know the condition of the cargo, exactly."

"We've prepared for anything we find, but we don't have time to wait for you to get your act together." Man Two spoke, and his voice sounded familiar. "We get in and we get out before someone comes to look for her."

"And if they come for her?" Man One asked.

"Better to dump her body before they do," Man Two said. *Malloy?*

Cressida held back a gasp. How could he talk about her like that, as if she meant nothing at all, after he'd delivered her to Hidden Bay and even warned her on the pier that day, and again, to watch her back?

Yeah, watch her back for the likes of him.

The two men paused. Listening?

Lord, please help me.

A loud voice crackled, blasting over the ship's intercom system. "Team A, brace the ROV. We're lifting the package. No mistakes this time!"

The two men raced away, and Cressida allowed herself to breathe. The constant vibration and low rumble of the ship's engines and power generators filled her ears.

But the package. They're bringing the package aboard now? She couldn't allow that to happen, but how did she stop it? Trent was going to wake up soon, and they'd search for her. She had no time to waste.

I need a radio to call for help. A VHF marine radio. But they could be monitoring that. If she could get her hands on a satellite phone, she could possibly make a private call. She might find one in the captain's quarters. Whoever claimed captainship—Malloy? Trent? Malloy's son, Dax?—wouldn't be in his quarters during this most important ROV operation to bring up the package—whatever was inside the package. The thought of the contents terrified her.

Think, Cressida, think. Captain's quarters on a vessel like this would be in the superstructure, which was on the main deck. Probably near the bridge. Maybe he wouldn't be in his quarters, but those quarters weren't far from the main activity.

Oh, what are you thinking?

If only she'd found a satellite phone on Trent. But she was dressed the part, and so she would act the part. She made her way to the upper deck to find the captain's quarters or a satellite phone—some way to communicate her location and call for assistance. Even if she escaped on a skiff, she was in international waters and the chances of her survival weren't good. Might as well die trying.

Finally, above deck inside the superstructure, she stalked the narrow halls as if she had purpose and a place to be, passing a few cabins until she spotted the captain's quarters, clearly marked as such. The door stood open, confirming she was right that no one would be there during this critical moment in their operation. Inside the room, she moved right to the desk. A desktop was running but asleep, so no one had been here for a minute. Near the desk she found communication equipment—monitors and radios so the captain could communicate directly with the bridge and crew—and there she found a satellite phone. Charged and waiting . . .

Just for me.

She snatched it out of its charging station, along with a different walkie-talkie than she'd found on Trent. She eyed the radio—but again, that call out could be detected if someone monitored the frequencies. They would hear her unsanctioned transmission. Or maybe these guys weren't as professional as they wanted to believe. Whatever. It was too risky. She had the satellite phone, and that would do.

Satellite phone was her best bet for getting a message to Braden.

Now she'd have to go outside and find a quiet spot to connect the phone and make a call, then she would make her way back to the lower deck to shut down the engines and wreck anything and everything she could to stop this operation.

But who did she think she was? She was just one lone person on a vessel with a traitorous crew. She blew out a big breath.

You have to do this, girl. No other choice.

Cressida jammed the satellite phone into a pocket of the oversized black rain jacket she'd snagged from the captain's quarters to go over what she'd already taken from Trent. In the other pocket of the rain jacket, she found a stun gun. Perfect.

She walked the hall, descended the stairwell, her palms slicking around the taser in her left pocket and the satellite phone in her right. Steps pounded from above. Someone was running down the stairwell. She kept her head down, tugged the cap lower, and he passed her without a word.

Then . . .

He suddenly turned around and his eyes narrowed. "Hey, you!"

She didn't run from him.

Instead, she continued walking toward him with purpose, then when she was close enough, she hit him with the stun gun. It would only immobilize him for a few moments. Her time was shorter than she thought.

Cressida bounded through an exit, out into the rainy night—perfect—and found a corner at the far end of the massive ship where no one stood. Everyone focused on something in the sky.

Huh. A drone?

Too many shots were being fired at the drone, so clearly it wasn't part of their operation.

Then whose?

She didn't have time to think through those possibilities. Adrenaline coursed through her as she waited for the satellite phone to connect her to Braden. Then she made the call.

Come on, come on, come on . . .

The call disconnected before she could even leave a message. On the radio, she overheard their conversation. They knew she was here. The search was on. She didn't have time to keep calling people. But if she had only one more chance to do something, she had one call to make. To her mother.

God, please let my call go through. Please let me say this to her before it's too late.

Voicemail picked up.

"Mom, I forgive you," she said.

A noise drew her around, but no one had found her yet. She ended the call and tucked the phone in the jacket. She couldn't stand here on the deck waiting to be discovered, and jumping into the ocean would be suicide. She wouldn't hide and wait for no one to come.

But she could do something useful, even if this was the last thing she'd ever do. Making her way down to the engine room was problematic, given the several levels and security and other crew she'd likely run into before getting there. Dad had told her too many wartime stories for her to ignore, and she had a real chance to sabotage this endeavor. She'd studied a few schematics of research and salvage vessels. Granted, this was a new one, but she had to try.

She ducked into a stairwell, rushing with purpose to fit in with the search for the missing woman. The engine room would probably be in the lowest deck, near the stern, or rear, of the ship. She made her way down two stairwells and a set of ladders. Finally, at the lowest deck beneath the waterline, she felt sweat bead on her back and at her temples with the increase in temperature. The earlier rumble she'd heard in the upper decks was now a constant, heavy vibration through the floor. The rhythm of machinery—the engines and generators—was louder here too.

Her palms were sweating but not because of the heat.

She walked the narrow hallway until she approached a heavy bulkhead marked "Engine Room" and "Authorized Personnel Only."

Her breathing hitched up. *Can I really do this?*

The door was heavy, thick, and watertight, but she entered the engine room unheeded, finding the expected maze of turbines and generators. She breathed in hot and humid air that smelled of oil, grease, and diesel, yet the room was kept pristine.

What she needed were the control panels. The clang of tools sounded from the back—crew members working—and with the bright overhead lights, her presence would not go unnoticed. She would probably need earmuffs if she remained here because the high-pitched whirring, loud compressors, and pumps overwhelmed her ears.

Yeah, this is going to get you killed.

But she was probably already dead once they found her. *For you, Dad, I'm going to make a lot of noise going down.* Once, Dad had shared a story about shutting down fuel lines, but more than one component had to be disabled.

Whatever she did, it had to be fast. They'd search the entire rig and eventually find her here.

Fuel lines. Valves. She stared at them. She had no time

for any real plan other than to cause chaos and disrupt this operation. Simply turning off the engine wasn't good enough. She had to make this vessel inoperable for the foreseeable future.

Aha.

The engine cooling system. She turned all the valves that circulated coolant completely off. That was a start. It would overheat and seize up. But before that happened, she had time to do some other damage. Across the space, she spotted the main electrical panel and rushed over. Pulled breakers out. Toggled switches. Used a lug wrench from the toolbox to the right and tossed it into the box. Sparks flew and lights flickered. Shouts erupted.

Alarms sounded. Steam rose.

Cressida pulled the hose from the cooling system out, praying she didn't get burned or electrocuted. A main lever labeled "Emergency Stop" called to her. Cressida rushed forward and pulled it down—this was the main kill switch, but she'd disabled enough that turning the operation back on wouldn't be easily done.

The rhythm and thrum of the engines slowed . . . lights blinked on and off, and the machinery powered down.

Then the lights went out completely.

In the dark, she stood still and listened to the panicked engine room crew. Exhausted and pumped with adrenaline, she swiped the salty sweat from her stinging eyes. Flashlights came on in the engine room, including hers. She raced to the exit. And just as she almost cleared it, big, strong hands grabbed her, and she shined her light up into an angry, sweaty face.

42

Status on the comms?" Braden had made it to the main communication bay and camera-control hub to disable the cameras and onboard comms while Hawk had distracted with his drone.

Suddenly the lights went out completely, leaving him in utter darkness—above deck and below. Everything came to a stop. Chains clanked outside as even lifting the ROV had halted.

He froze and remained quiet long enough to determine he was still alone. What just happened? "Who did that?" He spoke through his ear mic. "Was that you, Cole? Because it wasn't me."

"Negative," Cole said.

They'd had a short discussion about using code names, but Diggins got confused, so they ditched that idea. But who cared? Braden had nothing to hide from these jerks.

The plan was, while Hawk used the drone to distract, Diggins would plant explosives to sink the vessel if necessary—sure enough, he'd found them—and Cole would assist Braden in shutting down the rig. Braden had wanted to go in and get Cressida first, but with the crew already extracting radioactive materials, there was no time to find her first.

"Never mind who," Hawk said. "Just go with it."

"Heard them grumbling . . . there's an unknown in the engine room," Diggins said.

Cressida? "I'm going in for her."

Flicking his headlamp on, he maneuvered out of the comms room. He'd completed his task, and even if the power came back on, the crew wouldn't be able to see them via cameras or communicate via their radios or intersystem comms.

A guard clomped toward him, his high beams blinding. Braden pressed forward and slammed his fist into the man who had looked like he planned to take Braden down first. But Braden had knocked him out cold. He tugged off the man's outerwear and donned his cap, then secured his wrists and ankles in zip ties. He relieved the man of his Glock 19 and his Heckler & Koch MP5 submachine gun—now he blended in and looked like he was part of the security. Snatching his radio, walkie-talkie, and earpiece—just in case the comms were brought back online—Braden was ready to go.

The ties would slow the man down but probably not stop him.

Braden crept forward in the hall—dimly lit by emergency power that had come on—and continued to the lower deck and engine room, where he hoped to find Cressida. She might have found her way out of the engine room by now, if she was the one to cause the issue. Braden hoped and yet struggled to believe Cressida could have shut the vessel down. Then again, her father might have shared stories with her about disabling enemy vessels. Cressida was one of the smartest people Braden had ever met.

She could do it. He might be putting too much hope in this ending well, but hope was all he had, and he wasn't letting go.

Finally on the lower deck and near the stern, Braden suspected the heavy bulkhead to the engine room would be at the end of the hall around the corner. He braced for facing off with another security guard or an engineer or any other crew members that would be present to restore power. He slowly peered around the corner.

Cressida stood over a man on the floor, who shook in pain. She held a stun gun.

Despite the danger, he couldn't help the smile spreading across his face as he stepped out from the side hall and strode toward her. Cressida Valentine Dane was amazing.

Eyes wide, she stared at him as if shocked to see him, then her eyes brightened. She raced to him. Jumped in his arms. He caught her. He hadn't expected her reaction, but he welcomed it. She eased away from him and lifted her chin, and for a moment he thought she might just kiss him—but another time. Maybe they'd get their chance on the other side of this.

"I thought you needed my help," he said.

"I do."

"I don't know," he said. "Looks like you've got everything under control."

"It was a losing gamble from the start. Where am I going to go? How am I getting off this rig? But now you're here. Can I hitch a ride?"

"That's the plan."

"You got her?" Diggins's voice sounded over his ear mic.

Oh yeah. I got her. "Yes."

He released her, rushing forward, leading with the submachine gun so he could look the part as they bounded up the steps. The exit door was at the end of the hall. He couldn't get out of here fast enough. Finally, he peeked out the porthole onto the deck, then opened the door and stepped into the cool, windy night, turning to look at his surroundings.

He motioned for her to follow him to the bow.

He stopped to peer out onto the water through his night vision binoculars.

"Look out!" she shouted.

He instinctively ducked but didn't evade the punch to his gut. At least it hadn't been a bullet. He turned to face the traitor. Though he'd known, the shock of it still rolled through him. "*Deputy* Trent Riker. Why?"

Trent aimed a handgun point-blank at Braden. He stood too close. Not a wise move. The vessel rolled with the approaching storm and the clouds unleashed a torrent. One dim light illuminated Trent's face. Braden stood between Trent and Cressida.

"Cressida, get out of here." Diggins, Hawk, or Cole should be closing in to help her escape.

"Don't act like you're a detective," Trent spat. "I know you're here for one reason. To find the location of the *Vanguard*. Now both of you, lower your guns slowly and kick them over into the ocean."

Braden and Cressida did as Trent requested, losing their weapons in the swell. Behind Trent, Braden could see spotlights out on the ocean in the distance. The Coast Guard was finally arriving, unless Trent also had reinforcements that he'd called in for assistance.

"You're weak, Trent." Braden shoved Trent's weapon up as shots went off and quickly disarmed him, but Trent slammed Braden's arm against the railing, causing him to release the gun, which slid across the deck and out of reach.

"You're not a hero, Detective Sanders. You are just a pawn." Trent lunged, aiming a punch at Braden's face.

He dodged and threw his fist into Trent's ribs. Trent hesitated for a few seconds but locked arms with Braden, trying to throw him overboard into the ocean, but that wasn't happening.

He slammed his forearm into Trent's throat and broke free, but Trent thrust his knee up into Braden's gut. He tumbled against the railing, flailing as sea spray soaked him from the growing swells. In his peripheral vision, he could see that Cressida hadn't run to escape but stayed behind to watch.

The momentary distraction had cost him. Trent came at him with a knife. Braden thrust it to the side, but it landed in Braden's arm, sending fire through him. When Trent kicked him, he toppled to the ground.

His stance wide, Trent stood over Braden.

"It's over, Trent!" Cressida pointed Trent's own handgun at him. "Toss the knife in the ocean and back away from him. Now!"

Trent did as he was told but remained too near for comfort.

Gritting his teeth, ignoring the pain, Braden slowly got to his feet.

"This location—the *Vanguard*—was never my goal," Braden said.

"You're not getting out of here alive," Trent said.

"I don't care about what you're doing here. Take what you want, just let Cressida get to safety."

He said the words knowing that law enforcement was closing in on this operation. Trent and his crew had nowhere to go, and the vessel could be inoperable, depending on what damage Cressida had inflicted in the engine room.

Cressida might be holding a gun on Trent, but his men outnumbered the team Braden had cobbled together, and he didn't want Cressida to get hurt.

"I don't know what you're talking about, Detective Sanders. You're here attacking this vessel without the proper authority, and now you're going to blow it up. You're a rogue agent—a former federal agent who's out of control. I'm a county deputy who came here to rescue Cressida, who sadly died."

Did Trent seriously think he could get away with that story? He lifted a detonator and grinned at Braden.

"No!" Braden rushed at Trent, but the man jumped overboard where a small boat waited for him below.

A concussive explosion rocked the vessel, and it tilted at a violent angle. Braden was on his back sliding down but caught the rail. He reached for Cressida, but she was too far away and screamed as she slid through the railing.

43

She caught part of the brass railing, but her wet fingers were slipping. "Braden!"

Cressida held on as fire lit up the night. Beneath her, she assumed Trent was getting away with Malloy and Dax and more of their crew.

Braden's face appeared above her, and he reached for her hand, gripped it. She thrust the other one toward him and he grabbed them both, pulling her up and back onboard, even though the vessel's integrity had been breached.

Braden held on to her as they clung to the railing. There was no gaining their footing with the angle of the slippery deck.

He pressed his finger to his ear.

"Status? Anyone?"

Braden held her gaze, then said, "Cole's alive but took shrapnel to his leg. Hawk has a broken arm."

And Braden's arm continued to bleed. He needed to put a tourniquet on it and fast.

"And Diggins?" he asked, grimacing. Another wince, then

he said, "He's in the RIB. They want us to get in the water, and Diggins will pick us up."

He sat closer to her, both of them clinging to the railing. Cressida shivered with cold and fear, for her life and for Braden's. He could bleed out.

Braden spoke again but to his small team. "We're trapped. I'm not sure we can safely enter the water from here. The Coast Guard is coming. Let them know we need help."

The deck leveled, offering relief.

He grabbed her hand. "Let's go while we can."

Together they raced toward the bow on the top level, near the superstructure. Behind them, the crane clanked and metal twisted, and then it crashed into the ocean.

He turned to her and gripped her shoulders. The look he gave her terrified her more than she had thought possible.

"I had one job. Just one," he said. "And that's to get you out alive. So here's what we're going to—"

Another explosion pulled them apart. Cressida reached for the railing again—the only thing to hold on to—as a fissure opened up in the deck. But Braden hadn't been able to grab on because he'd pushed her forward to safety. He slid toward the fissure.

"Braden!"

"Jump. Just get into the ocean. Swim to the Coast Guard cutter. Just do not fall back into Trent or Malloy's hands. You can do this."

"No, I'm not leaving you."

"Cressida, you can't help me. Don't let my effort be for nothing. Get off before it's too late."

"You're injured. I'm not leaving you." But what could she do? All her bravado to take down this operation and Trent had done it himself. She'd been prepared to give her life, but she hadn't been prepared for anyone else to die.

No, Lord, not Braden.

She blinked against the sting of tears and rain. "Don't leave me . . ."

A swell rocked the vessel, and it shifted, then Braden disappeared into the opening as flames burst around them. Cressida blinked, unable to believe her eyes.

"No, Braden, no!" *God, please . . . please don't let him die.*

This big salvage vessel was taking on water, and some floors were up in flames. With the deck tilted at such a steep angle and slick with sea spray and rain, she couldn't make her way even if she tried. She couldn't help Braden. She couldn't even help herself. Only God could help him. She regretted every moment she'd been angry with him for what she considered his betrayal. He'd only ever been protecting her.

Bright lights shone on her from the Coast Guard cutter. Above her a helicopter hovered, also shining lights. Someone slid down on a harness toward her.

If only they'd arrived mere moments before. The man reached toward her to secure her and hoist her back up. The vessel shifted abruptly, knocking her off-balance as she reached forward. She flipped over the rail and dropped toward the ocean.

Too shocked to even scream, she hit the cold, rough water. She'd be sucked under with the suction of the salvage boat as it went down if she didn't swim hard to get away. Cressida gulped air, fighting the giant waves that might be the end of her. Hands gripped her and she fought, remembering Braden's words.

"Do not fall back into Trent or Malloy's hands."

But it was a Coast Guard swimmer with a flotation device. "Ma'am, I've got you."

"There's a man. He fell into the ship. That part of the boat is underwater. Please save him. Please. You have to find him."

"We'll do our best," he shouted. "Let me assist you out of this water before you get hypothermia."

All the hope, all the energy, drained out of her, and she let the Coast Guard swimmer bring her to the cutter. The *Kraken*—the same Coast Guard cutter she'd seen on her approach to Hidden Bay. Blankets were wrapped around her. Someone tried to usher her belowdecks and out of the rain, but she refused.

"I need to see you find Braden Sanders. Is someone even looking for him?"

Dad's words rushed back to her.

"The sea never gives back what it claims."

No, Lord, please, no.

I don't accept that. The sea is going to give Braden back to me alive and well. He doesn't belong to the ocean as someone lost at sea to be remembered, or worse . . . forgotten!

"We're doing everything we can to find him." The familiar voice sent shockwaves through Cressida. Dizzy and wobbling, trembling with fear and exhaustion, Cressida turned to face the woman. "Mom?"

Octavia Dane stood before her in the rain, her hair wet, mascara smudged down her cheeks. "I got your message."

Message? What message? Oh . . . the one where she'd told her that she forgave her. Through a shaky voice and tearful sobs, Cressida spoke. "I'm sorry that I didn't listen. I'm sorry about everything."

Mom wrapped an arm around her shoulder and leaned close. "It's on me. I could have handled it much better. That's my job, after all. You're my everything, and when it comes to you, I'm not such a great liaison."

Were those tears in her mother's eyes, mingling with the rain?

Cressida hugged her, cried on her shoulder.

"Braden will be fine," Mom said in her ear. "These guys

are the best. They'll find him. Now, please, let's get you inside and out of the rain. You want to be well for him."

She pulled away. "What are you talking about?"

"I can tell in your voice he means something to you, doesn't he?"

"Yes . . ." She didn't know when it happened, but she'd gone from like to something much deeper.

"And you don't know this, but he might have fallen for you when he saw your picture on my desk. It's one reason I sent him to Hidden Bay."

Cressida tried not to let those words anger her again. Being angry was no way to live.

"Ma'am." A Coast Guard officer approached Octavia. "We have news. Detective Sanders has been retrieved by a man called Captain Diggins, and they're bringing him aboard now."

Cressida didn't like the tone in which the officer said the words. "Retrieved. What does that mean? Is he okay?"

"I'm uncertain of his condition. We have medics aboard to assist. We're bringing aboard several survivors of the sinking vessel who are in need of medical attention."

Cressida rushed from her mother and the serviceman to find Braden.

"I have to know that he's still alive!" She hurried along the side of the deck where Diggins was climbing up and spotted a man laid out on a gurney. His eyes were closed, and he looked blue and unmoving.

Braden . . .

Cressida sank to her knees next to him and pressed her mouth against his cold lips. A hand squeezed her shoulder, then cupped the back of her neck, pulling her closer.

"You're alive," she said against his lips.

"What, me? No. I couldn't die before knowing what it would be like to kiss you."

44

Braden's arm had healed, but the pain throbbed through him again now and then. He had taken a medical leave from the Timberbrook County Sheriff's Office, and considering Trent was incarcerated, that meant they were two men down. On this beautiful August day, Braden sat outside on the deck of the Cedar Trails cabin he'd rented for this special occasion. He would be picking Lauren and Elise up from the airport later this evening. The specialist had released his niece from treatment. She was in remission. Every time he thought about it, his heart almost burst with a mix of joy and relief.

Thank you, Lord.

He struggled to believe Elise was on the other side of this scare, and now the way had been paved for her to receive treatment without Octavia Dane pulling strings or manipulating clinicians, or Braden for that matter.

The woman herself stepped out onto the deck as if she'd read his thoughts, holding a glass of iced tea for him. Cressida followed her and shut the door, then took a seat next to him. Octavia sat on the other side of her. He couldn't be happier that Cressida had found a way to reach across the abyss that had separated her from her mother. But he'd prefer to spend time getting to know Cressida without Octavia hovering.

They sat in silence, taking in the smells and the sounds, and for him it was about being in this moment.

Octavia had privately briefed him regarding everything she could share, and some of it she shared even though she shouldn't. Trent Riker was a former CIA agent who had been tasked in the past with recovering the K-482 *Voron* that sank in 1980 in the Pacific Ocean, too close to the US for comfort—and some believed it was Russia's attempt to start a war between the US and China. But the Soviet nuclear submarine sank to a depth too deep for recovery until technological advancements made salvage attempts possible.

Then in 1995, the CIA's deep-sea vessel, SSV *Aegis,* had only partially recovered the submarine, unfortunately leaving behind one nuclear missile, which contained fissile material capable of being weaponized. A decade later, the CIA launched a second covert mission led by CIA officer Trent Riker on board the USS *Vanguard* to retrieve the remaining missile. Once the missile was secured on the vessel, Trent departed the *Vanguard,* believing the mission complete. But the ship never arrived at its destination. He was relieved of his position—unfairly, he believed—and determined to discover what happened to the missing vessel considered lost at sea. He quietly took up residence in Hidden Bay, biding his time, waiting for answers.

In 2010, Diggins had set out to find the *Vanguard*—his son, Caleb, had been on that doomed mission—wanting to learn the truth about what happened. But the ocean took from him again when the *Endeavor Spirit* was hijacked, and he and his crew were taken by a group of militant Russians determined to prevent them from the recovery.

He alone escaped and settled in Hidden Bay, near the mother of his child and the woman he thought he'd lost forever. She hadn't known he was alive or so close until recently.

With Evelyn Monroe's arrival, Trent Riker suspected someone knew the location of the *Vanguard*. He suspected that someone had survived the *Endeavor Spirit*'s tragedy. And with the possibility of the location of the *Vanguard* within Trent's reach, he began partnering with rogue players, offering to recover the rest and sell to the highest bidder. He used his team—which included Malloy—all while working as a local county sheriff's deputy. He'd recruited Madeline and Collins in his search for the location and redirected the investigation to point at Octavia's second set of eyes—Derek Harlan. Riker had also murdered Harlan—distracting Braden long enough to abduct Cressida right from under him. Things could have ended so differently.

As for Alaric Dane—the lost pages that he'd torn from his journal, he'd mailed ahead of his travel, fearing he would be targeted. Octavia hadn't discovered the pages he'd sent in the mail until much later, but Alaric had detailed that he'd long known the location of the downed *Vanguard* since Octavia had also known the location, and Alaric secretly kept up with her dealings. His rush to DC from Washington state was to inform her of an impending scheme by rogue players to raise the volatile contents of the lost salvage ship and that the US needed to finish what they'd started, then declassify the information.

Cressida clinked her glass against Braden's, drawing him to the moment where he had intended to be.

"You look like you're a thousand miles away."

"I don't mean to be," he said.

"It's all right. It'll take time for all of us to process everything that's happened."

"I can't wait to see Diggins and Evelyn's ceremony at Driftwood Manor tomorrow to renew their wedding vows," Cressida said. "I'm still in shock that Diggins is the husband Evelyn thought was dead, or at least who she told us had died. After I finished reading her diary, I understand why she wanted me to keep it and finish it. She talked about him a lot, only his name was Nickolas Jonas Daggerty. After his 'death,' Evelyn went back to her maiden name, Monroe—but she kept 'Mrs.' out of respect for him. People assumed she was a widow, and she let them. It was safer that way. If I had read it, finished it that night, I would have known and understood so much more. I get that he needed to remain 'dead' for multiple reasons. First, her father tried to kill him, and if he knew he had survived, Diggins would always be looking over his shoulder. And then, with the role he played in the *Specter's Bounty* and the crew, someone would try to kill him if they knew. With the threats hovering so close, Evelyn and Diggins both kept their distance and for far too long."

"Obviously Malloy suspected Diggins knew, but he was waiting for the moment when he would give up the truth," Octavia said. "And that was to your father. If Diggins hadn't . . ."

Braden kept his mouth shut. Octavia was spinning a tale now, which she must in her position. She couldn't afford for anyone to know that she was the source of the leaked classified information. Diggins had shared he hadn't known the location of the *Vanguard*, and Braden believed him because Octavia was the one person in all of this who was in a position to know those long-buried secrets. Somehow Alaric had been able to discover that information from his ex-wife, perhaps in classified documents she'd inappropriately kept in her closet before they separated, who knew? But that was the connection. Alaric had sent Evelyn the locket to give her the location of her son and provide closure while attempting to reach Octavia to declassify the information.

"You can't think like that, Mom," Cressida said. "I could blame myself for working on that article. You shut it down, and Dad must have understood something or seen a connection. He told Evelyn he was going to investigate things 'for his daughter.' He pursued this truth, I think for me—so I could finish that article despite you shutting me down. I could blame myself. There's plenty of blame to go around. So let's please not even go there."

Octavia's smile was forced. "Right. You're right." She blew out a sigh and forced an even bigger smile. "In the meantime, Braden, I couldn't be more thrilled for you that Elise is in remission. Is there anything else I can do to help?"

You've done enough. "No, thanks."

"I can have someone pick them up and deliver them, or go with you to the airport," Octavia said.

"I'm good." He wanted to see them in private. "But I'm sure Lauren will want to thank you personally. She knows the work you did behind the scenes to make this dream come true. I couldn't be more grateful."

She smiled and stirred her tea with the straw. "You're off the hook forever, Braden. No hidden strings."

Cressida flicked her eyes at her mother, then to Braden, and her cheeks turned slightly pink.

"I've already shared the news with Cressida, but you'll be the next person to know that I'm retiring."

He could only stare. Retiring for someone like Octavia didn't reduce her level of control all that much. "Congratulations. What will you do with your time?"

Please don't say what I think you're going to say.

"I've invited Cressida to travel with me. We'll see the world. Take some time."

And his heart sank, which was selfish of him. Cressida needed that opportunity to reconnect with her mother.

"Good for you."

At the look Cressida gave him, he wanted to take the words back. Octavia's cell phone rang, and she excused herself.

He couldn't help the brooding mood that hung over him.

"Let's go for a walk on the beach if you feel up to it." Cressida held out her hand.

"I'm not an invalid. My arm is fine." He took her hand, and they walked down the trail, then took the steps onto the beach where tourists flocked this time of year.

He held hands with Cressida as they strolled, listening to the soothing ocean sounds, weaving around driftwood logs and stepping over larger rocks. With all the many questions, interrogations, briefings, and Octavia hovering, he hadn't been given a lot of time alone to see where this thing he felt for Cressida might go. She'd kissed him on the *Kraken*, sure, but that had been in response to the fact she thought he might have died.

She suddenly stopped, and he turned to face her. The wind coming from the north blew her bright-red curls away from her face, and she shoved her sunglasses over her head and squinted at him, her nose crinkled.

"What are you going to do now, Braden? Are you going to stay here at the county sheriff's office?"

"I don't know. I was here for one reason and . . ." *That was you.* "I kind of like it here, though. It's beautiful. What about you?" he asked.

"I'm going to focus on finishing Dad's book. I have all the notes and a publisher waiting. That's going to take me a while. Months, probably." She bent over to look closely at a small crab that scrambled away.

"Are you going to work on it while you travel with your mother?"

Cressida stood to face him again and sucked in a breath through clenched teeth as she glanced out at the ocean. "It'll take my mother months to untangle herself from her job, and I'm not entirely sure she'll follow through."

Cressida stepped closer. Braden's heart rate kicked up. *What are you doing?*

"What I'm saying, Braden, is I want to find a place to work near you. I liked you from the start. I want to find out if I more than like you." She lifted her shoulders. "I thought we had something going there, and I want to see where it takes us. Are you on the same page?"

"Come here." He pulled her against him, and they almost tumbled back over driftwood. He kissed her eagerly and passionately and let her know the answer to her question. She wrapped her arms around him, letting him know the answer to *his* silent question—*Do you more than like me?*

Like you?

I think I love you.

A YEAR LATER

Braden and Cressida stood out on the cliff's edge overlooking Hidden Bay along with Hawk and Remi, Cole and Jo, Evelyn and Diggins, and the entire Cedar Trails Lodge gang, waiting for the moment when they might see the Coast Guard tow the *Specter's Bounty* to Hidden Bay for a restoration project via the newly established Evelyn Monroe Foundation.

Cressida held on to Braden, her fiancé, next to her new friends. Jo and Cole had gotten married three months ago, and Remi and Hawk were expecting their first baby.

Braden continued his work as a detective at the Timber-brook County Sheriff's Office. Lauren and Elise had moved to Olympia—just a couple of hours away—so Braden could see them often, but also, in Olympia, they would be closer to adequate medical facilities. Cressida had just finished the final edits on Dad's book. She had many options for working remotely as a journalist, but maybe, just maybe, she would write a romantic suspense novel set on the Washington coast. Braden had been brainstorming with her in the evenings, and they'd concocted an action-adventure story about a lost ship.

She squeezed him closer.

I love you so much.

Remi squealed next to her. "I see it. I see the *Specter's Bounty*. This is surreal. I don't know how I feel about it."

"Better it's restored if possible than having it eventually sink. It lasted a lot longer out there than it should have," Sheryl said. The museum curator had come to watch as well. "You'd wanted an end to the mystery, and you got it," she said. "The era of the ghost ship in Hidden Bay is officially over."

TWO DAYS LATER

A storm pummeled the windows of Cressida's apartment in Forestview and had kept her awake most of the night. A text disturbed her at six-thirty in the morning. Really? She groaned but might as well get up. Cressida glanced at the words from Braden.

The Specter's Bounty is once again lost at sea.

Cressida smiled.

Author's Note

Dear Reader,

Thank you for reading *Deadly Currents*! The writing process for me is often messy—I tend to unearth the story as I go. But even before I start typing the first sentence, certain pieces of the story have already been floating around in my imagination, sometimes for years. One such piece of *Deadly Currents* has been with me since I was fourteen. That's when I wrote twenty-five pages (and no more!) of my very first romance—on a typewriter, no less. I'd been devouring gothic novels by Phyllis A. Whitney, Victoria Holt, and the Brontë sisters, so it makes sense that this early story opened with a mansion perched on a cliff above a foggy, rocky beach. That image stayed with me, and decades later I finally brought it to life, first in *Storm Warning*, via the Cedar Trails Lodge, and then—because apparently I wasn't done—I created another such mansion, Driftwood Manor, in *Deadly Currents*.

But instead of a missing horse, as in that childhood tale, this time the mystery centered around a lost ship—a ghost ship. You may remember the *Specter's Bounty* from *Storm*

Warning, the first book in my Hidden Bay series. That eerie vessel was born during a brainstorming session with author friends, and by the time I reached book three, I knew I had to unravel its origin. While writing the first two books, I let that mystery simmer. And by the end of *Perilous Tides*, I realized Evelyn Monroe's story—and the fate of the *Specter's Bounty*—were tied together.

A quick word about ghost ships: They aren't just legends. All around the world, derelict vessels drift through fog and storm, abandoned, sometimes dangerous, often forgotten. Some are quietly salvaged. Others are left to decay. But each one carries its own story—of tragedy, mystery, and secrets not easily buried, and often missing crewmen never to be found.

As I searched for answers behind the *Specter's Bounty*, I finally read about the dozens of lost submarines lying on the ocean floor—some still powered by nuclear reactors. Some even rumored to be carrying intact warheads. Yes, nuclear warheads! I pored over books and articles detailing classified recovery missions and Cold War operations, and I knew I'd found the heart of my story. This was the secret behind the *Specter's Bounty*. Real-life inspiration like that always fuels my imagination and raises the stakes in the best possible way.

To liven up the world of Hidden Bay, I drew inspiration from an article about liveaboards on Puget Sound who refer to themselves as modern-day pirates—complete with a pirate king. These communities, tucked away on aging vessels in hidden corners of the bay, sparked an idea. Their quiet, unconventional existence made the perfect backdrop for this last book in my Hidden Bay series. I had so much fun creating Diggins, and I'll admit, I did wonder if my editor would let me get away with putting pirates in a contemporary romantic suspense novel!

Deadly Currents is the sum of all these pieces—submerged secrets, haunted pasts, hidden lives, and the search for truth in a world clouded by fog and shadows. I hope it stirred your imagination and reminded you that even when we can't see what lies ahead, we're never truly alone. God is with us!

Blessings,
Elizabeth Goddard

Read on for *a sneak peek* at the first book
in Elizabeth Goddard's new series,

Mercy Ridge

Available August 2026

1

Therefore whatever you have said in the dark shall be heard in the light, and what you have whispered in private rooms shall be proclaimed on the housetops.

Luke 12:3

Secrets can't stay buried forever.

The road into the North Cascades was narrow, twisting just like the path Sarah Ellison had chosen. As she navigated the two-lane highway that took her deep into the mountains, she listened to her sister-in-law, Tessa, pleading with her over the cell.

"You don't have to do this," Tessa said.

Don't I? "It's too late to back out. You and Jeremiah stay hidden, and you'll be safe. You focus on taking care of him and don't worry about me." Tessa and Jeremiah—who was only three years old—remained tucked in a safe house along the coast. "There's plenty to explore. Build sandcastles. Collect seashells. Act normal. Just . . . keep your head down."

Someone had buried the truth, and she would excavate

whatever lay hidden on the mountain that had already claimed one life. Her brother, Aaron, deserved justice. Two weeks ago, Aaron had drowned, and that left Sarah to finish what he'd started before it was too late. Since her husband had died four years ago and now her brother, that meant Tessa and Jeremy were the only family she had left.

"You could just stay here on the coast until it all blows over," Tessa said.

Sarah had no plans to simply let this go. "I know what I'm doing."

Once . . . she'd been good at her job with the federal government. She'd left that part of her life—left the secrets, the lies, and the burden of knowing too much behind. But sometimes, the past didn't let go so easily.

Silence met her over the cell. Had the call dropped? "You still there?"

"Yes." Tessa obviously had her doubts. Then she started in again, but this time only half her words came over the connection.

"Listen, you're breaking up," Sarah said. "I need to go. Call me if anything happens. Anything suspicious. Let *me* decide if it's something to worry about."

The call ended, and she turned her focus back to the winding road. Autumn leaves swirled in this place where beauty abounded and took her breath away. Considering that it was October already, she was running out of time in more than one way. The mountain would be unforgiving once the snow started falling. On that point, she could already be too late. But one thing at a time. First, she had to get to Mercy Ridge.

At times the highway edged too close for comfort to a steep drop-off, making the drive treacherous, and she imagined it foreshadowing what she could expect over the next few days.

One small veer—that's all it would take to send her over the edge. The guardrails promised safety they couldn't deliver. Life was like that too, offering comfort you couldn't count on, protection that vanished when you needed it most. One moment of looking the wrong way, one choice made in fear or desperation, and everything could change forever. One mistake could take a person farther from where they'd hoped to land than they ever imagined.

But sometimes someone else's mistake had the same effect and sent a person off the right path. She just hadn't figured out whose mistake had derailed her plans. Because just like that, here Sarah was, with a chest full of dread, on her way to a quiet Bavarian-style town in the American Alps. Perfect for tourists and skiers and outdoor adventurers. Sarah was none of those things.

Her knuckles tightened on the steering wheel as a streak of lightning split the sky, momentarily blinding her. She swerved and almost drove off the road. But corrected the vehicle. A sudden torrent pounded her windshield, exploded, and crackled across the pavement, making the road slick.

Wonderful. She didn't have time for bad weather.

But she was almost there. Almost safe. Except safety was an illusion, and she shouldn't let herself forget.

Though she'd lost her tail—that silver boxy crossover so obviously following—she wouldn't count on keeping her follower at bay forever. Sarah had known she had a shadow before she'd turned onto this road. The vehicle had been behind her, lingering just far enough back that most people wouldn't have noticed. But she wasn't most people. And she'd turned at just the right moment.

Maybe they hadn't seen her.

Maybe they had. So she couldn't risk it. She'd change up her plans. She wasn't sure how they'd found her in the first place. In this old 1999 Ford Explorer she couldn't be followed—no GPS or Bluetooth. She'd bought it off Tessa and Aaron's neighbor in Sequim. Paid him in cash. With duct tape on the side mirror and a dog leash looped around the rearview mirror, it was perfect for fitting in with the rural community and tourists in Mercy Ridge. Slowing the vehicle, she turned down an almost imperceptible forest road, then steered deep into the woods. She then turned off the road between the trees, intruding upon nature so that low-hanging branches scraped the truck.

Good enough.

She hopped out. Beneath the dense evergreens, the rain had slowed. She grabbed her backpack filled with survival and tactical gear—everything she might need in case the unexpected happened. Spare clothes and cash. Her Sig Sauer P365—though if she had to use it here, she was already doomed. She'd packed two extra mags that were wrapped and stored deep in the pack. And an encrypted laptop.

She had a locked duffel with a secondary 9mm, a tactical vest satellite communicator, and more, but that vest would have to wait until she could come back to retrieve it. She couldn't carry everything as she made her way on foot. Wasn't the first time she'd had to alter her plans.

This almost felt like old times.

Her goal was to lose her followers and disappear if they tried this road, though if they had a clue what she was after, they would already be in Mercy Ridge waiting for her. Jamming her hand into her pocket, she pulled out the cracked compass that had belonged to her grandfather. She never traveled without it because, as he claimed, it always pointed to what mattered most. Well, it was broken but inscribed with "Family is everything." She didn't need the reminder, but maybe she needed the comfort.

Once she hiked down this foothill to town, she'd blend into the Mercy Ridge community and remain off the radar.

Once there, her first task was to hire a guide to take her deep into the Cascades. These mountains held three hundred glaciers, which was more than any other US park outside of Alaska. And she shuddered at the reminders of Alaska. She didn't relish going back into any terrain that resembled her morbid experience, especially when this region was uncommonly remote.

"Yeah, and reports the highest death rate in the country," she mumbled to herself. Hikers beware.

Already talking yourself out of it, are you?

But to accomplish her mission, she needed someone who knew their way around the mountains—*these* mountains—like the back of their hand. And from what she'd read, Ryder Goodwin was the right man for the job. She'd done her research. His great-grandfather had built the town. After Ryder's stint as a Navy SEAL, he'd returned to Mercy Ridge. She'd read probably too much into his past because she knew how to get access, but regardless of what had happened, he had carved out a new life working as a guide for Good Adventures and running wilderness training exercises.

His picture wasn't on the website, but his name was listed along with several other guides. She didn't want to ruin his life by dragging him into whatever this turned into with her, but she needed his help.

Would he even be there? Could she convince him this was a good idea? Could she accomplish her self-imposed task without raising too many questions? She didn't know.

Pausing to catch her breath, Sarah looked out over the town in the valley below. She still had a hundred feet or so to go before she'd hit Five Cedars River at the bottom, flowing out of an expansive waterfall. Sarah swiped the sweat beading her forehead—even on this cool mid-sixties day—and adjusted her backpack straps.

Then she felt it.

A slight tremble beneath her boots. She frowned and scanned the ground, searching. Had she imagined it? Unease shivered over her.

The earth shifted beneath her feet, this time she had no doubt. Suddenly the ground gave way beneath her with a sickening lurch, crumbling and morphing into liquefied dirt. A scream ripped from her throat when the earth vanished from under her in a gush, racing down the slope, carrying Sarah with it. Plunging her body toward the river below, the torrent of mud whipped her side to side like she was a rag doll on a natural waterslide. Except she had no control over the landing at the bottom. The raging river and the base of the cataract waited to swallow her.

I have to stop this!

She tried to grab at branches, arms flailing and fingers clawing anything solid—a rock, a branch, roots. Anything to stop the momentum of the churning sludge, until cold, thick mud coated her, even clogging her mouth and nose. Rocks and broken branches nicked her arms and legs.

The roar of the river grew louder.

No, no, no!

If she was going under, she had to suck in a breath before she hit that frigid water.

Panic built in her chest as she struggled to spit out the mud. Then she saw him.

She must have been seeing things. Had to blink the mud out of her eyes.

A man leaned out over a thick, sturdy branch as if bracing to grab her. She didn't know how his rescue would be possible. His eyes locked on hers, willing her to understand. She barely made out his tense features.

Oh, I understand. God, please let this work!

She rushed toward his outstretched arm . . . *I have this one chance.*

Her only chance.

She reached out, stretching, her muscles screaming.

Then he clamped onto her wrist, holding her as mud poured around her. Gritting her teeth, muscles straining, she willed him to pull her up and out. But the forces of nature had other plans. She screamed as she clawed toward him.

But the mud wouldn't let go.

Acknowledgments

I always love this opportunity to thank all the many people who encouraged and informed me through the weeks and months of this creative process. I'm so grateful for my close writing friends, who are always there to encourage me when needed and available to talk things through and brainstorm when I'm stuck.

I'm especially grateful for my family: My four children and their spouses (some of whom are aspiring writers)—my daughter Rachel and her husband Patric (and my grandchildren Gabriel, Penn, and Anastasia); my son Christopher and his wife Hannah; and my sons Jonathan and Andrew. I owe a special debt of gratitude to my husband, Dan, who supported me through the many "starving artist" years as I pursued this dream of becoming a published author instead of working a regular job.

To my Revell team—I'm so thrilled to be writing for the best publisher in the Christian market. This truly is a dream come true. Thank you, Rachel McRae, for believing in my stories. I love working with you! Thanks to Karen Steele, my publicist, and Bria Conway, my marketing manager, for all the work getting my books out there and noticed in an ocean of books, and thanks to Laura Klynstra and the entire art department for creating gorgeous covers.

To my literary agent, Steve Laube. Landing you as an agent fifteen years ago was a game changer for me. I'm so grateful to have you on my team!

To my Lord and Savior, Jesus Christ—you are my all in all!

Elizabeth Goddard is the *USA Today* bestselling and Christy Award–winning author of sixty-five novels, including *Storm Warning* and *Perilous Tides*, as well as the Missing in Alaska, Rocky Mountain Courage, and Uncommon Justice series. Her books have sold more than 1.5 million copies. She is a Carol Award and Reader's Choice Award winner and a Daphne du Maurier Award and HOLT Medallion finalist. When she's not writing, she loves spending time with her family, traveling to find inspiration for her next book, and serving with her husband in ministry. Learn more at ElizabethGoddard.com.

Be the first to hear about new books from Revell!

Stay up to date with our authors and books by signing up for our newsletters at

RevellBooks.com/SignUp

FOLLOW US ON SOCIAL MEDIA

   @RevellFiction

Dear Reader,

Thank you for selecting a Revell novel! We're so happy to be part of your reading life through this work. Our mission here at Revell is to publish stories that reach the heart. Through friendship, romance, suspense, or a travel back in time, we bring stories that will entertain, inspire, and encourage you. We believe in the power of stories to change our lives and are grateful for the privilege of sharing these stories with you.

We believe in building lasting relationships with readers, and we'd love to get to know you better. If you have any feedback, questions, or just want to chat about your experience reading this book, please email us directly at publisher@revellbooks.com. Your insights are incredibly important to us, and it would be our pleasure to hear how we can better serve you.

We look forward to hearing from you and having the chance to enhance your experience with Revell Books.

The Publishing Team at Revell Books
A Division of Baker Publishing Group
publisher@revellbooks.com

Revell